I0760321

THE Corpse WITH THE Golden Nose

CATHY ACE

FOUR TAILS PUBLISHING LTD.

Second Edition

The Corpse with the Golden Nose

Date of first publication March 2013

Four Tails Publishing Ltd.
Date of first publication worldwide December 2024

ISBN: 978-1-990550-31-7 (hardcover)
ISBN: 978-1-990550-32-4 (paperback)
ISBN: 978-1-990550-30-0 (electronic book)

PRAISE FOR THE CAIT MORGAN MYSTERIES

"In the finest tradition of Agatha Christie…Ace brings us the closed-room drama, with a dollop of romantic suspense and historical intrigue." – *Library Journal*

"…touches of Christie or Marsh but with a bouquet of Kinsey Millhone." – *The Globe and Mail*

"…a sparkling, well-plotted and quite devious mystery in the cozy tradition…" – *Hamilton Spectator*

"…If all of this suggests the school of Agatha Christie, it's no doubt what Cathy Ace intended. She is, as it fortunately happens, more than adept at the Christie thing." – *Toronto Star*

"Cait unravels the…mystery using her eidetic memory and her powers of deduction, which are worthy of Hercule Poirot."
– *The Jury Box, Ellery Queen Mystery Magazine*

"This author always takes us on an adventure. She always makes us think. She always brings the setting to life. For those reasons this is one of my favorite series."
– *Escape With Dollycas Into A Good Book*

"…a testament to an author who knows how to tell a story and deliver it with great aplomb." – *Dru's Musings*

"…perfect for those that love travel, food, and/or murder (reading it, not committing it)." – *BOLO Books*

"…Ace is, well, an ace when it comes to plot and description." – *The Globe and Mail*

Other works by the same author
(Information for all works here: **www.cathyace.com**)

The Cait Morgan Mysteries
The Corpse with the Silver Tongue
The Corpse with the Golden Nose
The Corpse with the Emerald Thumb
The Corpse with the Platinum Hair
The Corpse with the Sapphire Eyes
The Corpse with the Diamond Hand
The Corpse with the Garnet Face
The Corpse with the Ruby Lips
The Corpse with the Crystal Skull
The Corpse with the Iron Will
The Corpse with the Granite Heart
The Corpse with the Turquoise Toes
The Corpse with the Opal Fingers
The Corpse with the Pearly Smile

The WISE Enquiries Agency Mysteries
The Case of the Dotty Dowager
The Case of the Missing Morris Dancer
The Case of the Curious Cook
The Case of the Unsuitable Suitor
The Case of the Disgraced Duke
The Case of the Absent Heirs
The Case of the Cursed Cottage
The Case of the Uninvited Undertaker
The Case of the Bereaved Butler
The Case of the Secretive Secretary

Standalone novels
The Wrong Boy

Short Stories/Novellas
Murder Keeps No Calendar: a collection of 12 short stories/novellas
Murder Knows No Season: a collection of four novellas
Steve's Story in "The Whole She-Bang 3"
The Trouble with the Turkey in "Cooked to Death Vol. 3: Hell for the Holidays"

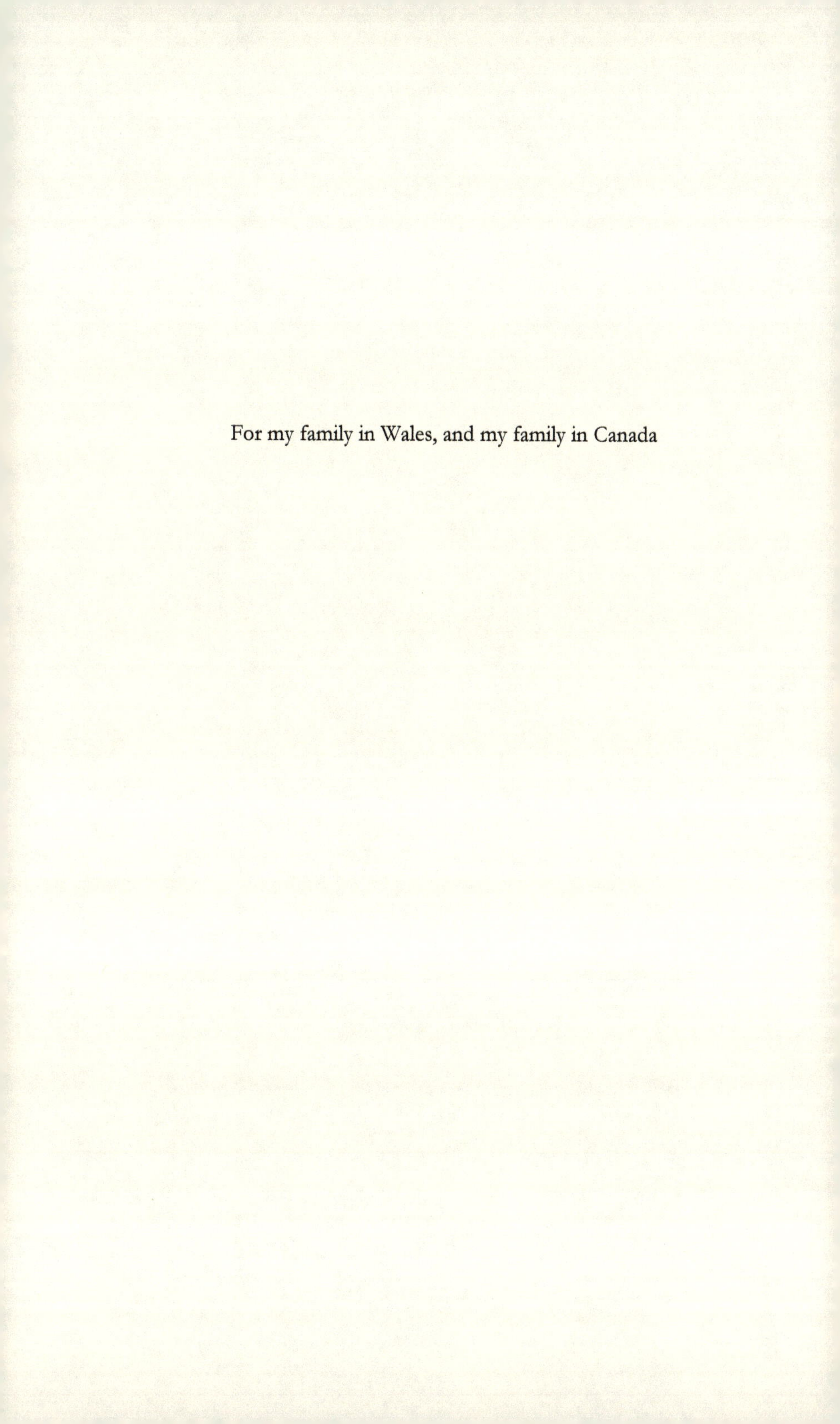

For my family in Wales, and my family in Canada

Foreword to the Second Edition

In February 2024 the original publisher of the first eight Cait Morgan Mysteries reverted the publishing rights to me, the author. Twelve years have passed since I wrote this, the second book in the series, so I suppose it's only natural that, given this opportunity, I'd want to revisit it.

Just so you know…the story hasn't changed, though the telling of it has. Think of this as you'd think of a "Director's Cut" of a movie: this second edition is the "Author's Cut".

I always strive my hardest to write the best book I can, and hope I write books that are – as far as possible – timeless, in that they're contemporary, and reflect and rely upon the aspects of humanity that do not alter.

I constantly hope to become more certain of my writing voice, and I've worked to develop my skills and my craft over time, through experience.

For those reading this tale for the first time, I truly hope you enjoy it.

If you've treated yourself to this second edition, having already read the previous one, I trust you're not disappointed that the story hasn't changed, and hope you enjoy it's re-telling, which I daren't say is "better", but it's certainly been crafted by an author who's learned (hopefully) a thing or two over the years.

Cathy Ace
December 2024

1

Champagne and Orange Juice

Bud slapped his phone, showing a photograph, onto the table in front of me as though it were a gauntlet.

"This showed up in my email a few days ago. From someone I…know. What can you read in it, Cait?"

For a man supposedly enjoying a delicious brunch with his date, he looked…too serious.

I held the phone at arm's length and squinted at the slightly blurry image. I could make out two women, both with dark, curly hair. They were smiling.

I felt my multi-purpose right eyebrow shoot up as I asked, "Is just one of them dead, or both of them?"

"How'd you guess?" Bud was grinning.

"Maybe it's something to do with me being a criminologist who specializes in victim profiling, and you being an ex-homicide detective? And the hope that if you're showing me a photo of any number of females, you have nothing more than a professional interest in them. Those facts, when taken together with my amazing powers of deduction, have helped me reach the conclusion that I'm looking at either one or two victims, or – if not victims – then at least people who are now dead."

I hurled a bright smile toward Bud and waited for him to tell me off for my cheekiness.

Bud shrugged and smiled. "You know me too well, Cait." Then his smile faded. "The taller of the two died about a year ago. The shorter one's her older sister. But that's all you get."

"No point in me asking if it was an accident, a suicide, or a homicide?"

Bud paused, refreshed our glasses, and took a sip from the champagne flute that looked almost too delicate in his hand. "I can't tell you that, because I don't know, Cait, I can only be certain it wasn't an accident. The entire local community, the cops, and the coroner, all say suicide. The sister says no way. I have no idea. There was a note, and the sister says the cops won't look into it any further as there are no grounds to suspect anyone else was involved."

Ah…you've found a damsel in distress, and you want to help her.

Immediately, I wondered why Bud felt he owed this unknown woman anything. I mentally kicked myself for allowing a pang of jealousy to clutch at my satisfyingly full tummy. I drank deeply from my glass and decided to play nice.

Bud and I had chattered happily through the delicious brunch I'd prepared in the small kitchen of my little house on Burnaby Mountain. We'd already managed to solve several global problems before I'd made the second pot of coffee.

We're good like that.

Throughout the meal of creamy scrambled eggs draped over golden, buttered toast, Marty, Bud's tubby black Lab, had waited patiently under the table, never taking his glorious amber eyes off us for a moment. Finally, his steadfastness had been rewarded, and I congratulated myself on saving at least a dozen calories by allowing him to lick my plate. It was then, when I was enjoying the memory of the food – and therefore at my most vulnerable – that Bud had produced the photograph.

I might have whined a little when I said, "You know I don't like to assess individual photographs. They're unreliable sources of insight."

Bud chuckled. "Well, you might not like to, but you're good at it. You were good at it when I hired you to consult for my homicide teams, and, though my retirement means we don't solve murders together these days, I reckon you're still good at it. So, treat this as a personal favor for me, if you must, my sweet, sweet Caitlin Morgan."

3

Oh that wicked grin of yours…do you have any idea how it makes my heart flutter and stutter?

"Just tell me what you can?" He phrased it as a question, but we both knew it was the sort of challenge I couldn't resist.

I scrabbled around under the little mound of papers I'd been grading the previous evening that I'd left on the table, hunting for my reading cheats.

Why do I seem to need them more and more these days?

I don't like wearing specs, but I reckon they at least lend me an air of imperiousness when I glower over them at any students I feel deserve a stinky look. Frankly, if they help me to intimidate anyone who needs to be brought down a peg or two, then they're worth every dollar I've spent on all ten or twelve pairs and the various cases, chains, and clips that are supposed to attach them to my body and prevent them from being lost.

Where do they all disappear to?

I looked at the picture Bud had handed me again: the frozen expressions, the way the women had been relating to each other at that point in time, and their setting.

They bore a sisterly resemblance to each other; both were casually dressed in shirts, pants, and sandals; the taller one had her arm around the other's shoulders. They were standing at the foot of a stony hill that was covered with rows of vines.

Bud petted Marty as I studied the photo. As I began to speak, he turned his attention to me.

"Okay. Sisters. The taller one – the dead one – is, or was, the more dominant. She's clearly the more confident person, and she knows how to present herself to the camera. She has a better haircut, good makeup, and she's better dressed…except that her bra's too small for her." I sighed. "She's draping her arm around the shorter sister as though to push her forward. So, one confident and supportive, one less so, but loved. I'd say the tall one has, or had, some sort of public-facing role in life, the other some sort of backroom job; that would suit the way they are presenting themselves here. They're in wine country, among vines, early in the fruiting season, but aren't wearing vacation clothes, so I suggest that's where they live, or at least spend a lot of time, and where they feel comfortable. In fact…" as I thought it through, it became clear, "the tall one looks proprietorial. Is this their land? Is this their vineyard?"

I glanced at the bottle on the table's label: MOUNT DEWDNEY FAMILY ESTATE WINERY *ANEN ANGEL SPARKLING N/V*. I wondered if I was looking at women who had some connection with the wine I was drinking; after all, Bud didn't usually bring alcohol when he came to my place for brunch.

Bud shook his head. "No more questions. Keep going."

Sometimes you can be a bit of a devil, Bud…and I love it.

I allowed my eyebrow to arch disdainfully in Bud's direction for a moment, but suspected that the hoped-for effect was lessened somewhat by the smile I couldn't hide. I returned my attention to the photograph.

"No rings on the left hand of either sister, so both probably single…though it wouldn't surprise me to find that the taller sister was divorced, or maybe even had several relationships behind her: she's comfortable, and confident, in her own skin, something that only really develops when you've been in relationships where you get to know yourself in a positive way. It's difficult to say more; I can't tell exactly where they are, geographically, though I'd suggest they're North American, given the way they're dressed, so maybe the Okanagan or Niagara? Or maybe Sonoma or Napa. Age? Close to each other, and around forty. But it's difficult to analyze a photograph more deeply than that; it captures just a tiny fraction of a second, and people usually adopt unnatural expressions in front of a camera. They're both smiling at the photographer, but that could…"

I paused, held the phone closer, and stretched the image as much as I could. I peered through my specs. I'd spotted something in their expressions.

"What is it?" asked Bud. His tone suggested urgency, which surprised me.

"I don't know who took this photograph, but I can tell you that the dead sister liked the photographer a great deal, and the shorter sister didn't like them at all. Yes, they're both smiling at the camera – and hence the photographer – but the tall one has a very positive connection with whomever is taking the picture. Her expression is soft and warm. However, the short one? Well, she's smiling too, but there's a…hardness in her face. She's almost literally gritting her teeth. And there's defiance in her eyes. She really doesn't like whomever she's seeing."

"Now that's interesting, Cait. And puzzling," observed Bud.

"Why? Who took the photograph?"

"No one. The sister who sent it to me told me they took it themselves: they're looking at a phone, set up on a rock. Odd that you should infer such emotions regarding a rock." He smiled. It wasn't an unkind smile.

I had to agree that it sounded odd, but I could see those emotions on their faces. I was in no doubt.

Bud petted Marty absentmindedly as he considered his next words. Marty didn't care that Bud was thinking about something else and reacted with licks, and vigorous tail-wagging. As Bud wiped his Marty dampened hand on his pants, he looked at me with a curious glint in his eyes.

I know that look.

As a psychologist with a master's degree in criminal psychology, who then wrote a fairly controversial PhD thesis about victim profiling, I'd been bravely retained by Bud in the past to work with his integrated homicide teams on many cases. I'd had the chance to see that same expression on the faces of various suspects he'd interviewed, as they tried to decide how to balance truth with lies before they answered their interrogator.

You're weighing how to proceed: I trust the balance will be in favor of the truth.

Bud sighed and sat back in the kitchen chair; the decision had been made. "Okay, I'll come clean. The short one, she's Ellen. I've never met her face to face, but she's been my online 'grief buddy' for a few months now. After Jan was killed, I went for counseling…"

As the words left Bud's lips, I could feel myself stiffen. I couldn't help but be surprised. This was the first I was hearing about counseling, and we were supposed to be getting to know each other as a proper couple – or so he said.

Not much chance of that happening if you keep things like counseling from me, Bud.

"Don't get cross, Cait," urged Bud, correctly interpreting the shift in my body language. "I haven't told you about it until now because I'm not truly comfortable with it. I think the best way to get over the loss of a loved one is to dust yourself off and get on with life. But my wife was killed because some low-life scumbag thought she was me, so therapy wasn't a suggestion…the high-ups insisted. I suspect it was some sort of liability thing, in case I killed myself."

Nope…not letting that comment pass.

"You told me you'd only ever thought about...you know..." I couldn't bring myself to say the words, "…for a fleeting second. That it wasn't something you'd ever seriously considered."

Do I really know you at all, Bud Anderson?

He continued; his expression was grim. "I didn't. Not…not really. But…well, I've had my dark moments. As you know. I've been told that's quite normal…by more people than just you. Especially considering the fact that Jan was killed by someone who thought they were targeting me. Anyway…the therapist I saw – the therapist I *had* to see – got me to join this online community for people who've lost a loved one through violent or unexpected circumstances. They get you to buddy up with another individual, as well as share anonymously in a group blog. None of this was what I wanted to do, Cait. All of it felt strange and unnecessary. Anyway, Ellen and I gravitated toward each other and became 'grief buddies' because she said she felt the same discomfort at doing what was asked of us. As you know, I'm not a big sharer, and I'll admit to you that I wasn't very forthcoming with personal details." He paused and chuckled. "I even used a fake name. But, despite all that, Ellen and I seemed to reach some level of quiet acceptance of each other, in writing. Online. Then, when the trial of Jan's murderer was all over the news, Ellen put two and two together and worked out who I was; that Jan was the wife I was mourning. So I opened up a bit more to her. Not emotionally. I really only talk to you…and my therapist…about my feelings."

Bud patted my hand, much as he'd been patting Marty's head.

I'll let that pass.

He continued, "As it turned out, that knowledge seemed to give Ellen the green light to write more…openly about the facts of her sister's death, and about how unhappy she was regarding the suicide verdict."

I understood: I've seen how finding out that Bud's a cop – even now that he's retired – has changed the way folks relate to him. We'd been to a few functions at the University of Vancouver, where I teach, and everyone had acted quite naturally when I'd introduced Bud as my "plus one". When they'd found out he was a retired cop, their body language had shifted completely. Trust me, I'm good at reading people, and can spot a telltale sign a mile off. For some, it meant they just watched what they said – all the jokes about drinking and driving would stop, and their micro-expressions would click into the "take care" setting – but, for others, they'd literally walk away, smiling politely…but, essentially, escaping.

Bud kept going. He knew I understood what he meant. "A few days ago, Ellen emailed me this photo and wrote in much more detail about her sister's death. Now she's invited me to visit her next weekend, over Easter, in Kelowna. I thought I'd let you use your deductive powers on the photo before I sent her a reply. I'm not sure what to do, Cait. I'm pretty certain she wants me to look into how her sister died, but I'm not comfortable with that. Besides, I've retired, I have no standing…no ability to get hold of official reports or anything of the sort. So I thought I'd turn to my old 'secret consulting weapon' and see what you have to say about the whole thing."

"You don't often call me that, these days," I commented.

Bud tilted his head and whispered to Marty, "Now I get to call her other…much more personal…things, don't I, eh, boy?"

Bud smiled, then looked more thoughtful as he took his phone from me, and put it back into his pocket, all the while stroking Marty's comforting, velvety head.

I suspected that I, too, looked thoughtful as I studied Bud: his strong jaw; his salt and pepper hair; the threads of silver in his eyebrows above those brilliant blue eyes of his…and that slightly snubbed nose, and weathered complexion.

Out of the corner of his eye he probably caught me looking at him but, if he did, he didn't seem to mind. I sipped my champagne, grateful that this wonderful man wanted anything to do with overweight, over-indulgent, insecure, bossy me.

At least I know some of my shortcomings.

I admitted to myself that I did feel a little hurt that this was the first I was hearing about Bud participating in grief counselling, though I was glad he was doing it. Of course I listen whenever he wants to talk about Jan, but there's only so much support one person can give.

9

I'd met Jan Anderson on many occasions, but – truth be told – I hadn't known her well…only in the way you come to know the wife of a colleague. I'd heard all about her interests and habits, but Bud had filtered her being, and had presented it to me in conversation. He spoke of her frequently, and always with warmth and admiration. Every time Jan and I spent time together, we got along well. However, we couldn't have been more different; Jan was very much into group activities, and hobbies. Me? I'm a bit of a loner, I suppose. At least, that's how I've heard folks describe me. Jan reveled in mixing, and Bud enjoyed hearing about what she'd been up to while he'd been chasing down villains. They had a well-balanced relationship, and Bud had always referred to her as his "soulmate", which made me wince, at the time. However, he'd meant it – so when Jan was shot and killed…the shooter believing he was targeting Bud himself…it came as no surprise to anyone that Bud's life, and even the way he looked at life, changed completely.

I'd seen how hard it had been for him to try to carry on in his then-role heading up a gang-busting task force with a local focus and an international reach, but it still shocked me when he told me he'd decided to retire. He'd said that he'd felt he was endangering his colleagues because he'd lost focus, so – of course – I was supportive of his decision. He'd taken early retirement from the service to which he'd given his entire professional life, with a hefty pension, and unwanted – but huge – insurance, and compensation, payouts.

"To reassess my life," was what he'd said.

A part of that "reassessment" had been to take himself off on a vacation to Egypt – one that he and Jan had planned before her murder. When he came back, he told me he'd made another decision…that he and I should get married.

You didn't expect that reaction of mine to your clumsy proposal, did you, Bud? I'm glad we've been able to laugh about it since.

As a psychologist, most folks believe that I'm possessed of an intimate understanding of why people do what they do. However, it seems that sometimes I don't; not when those people are close to me, in any case. Bud and I had worked together off and on for a year or so before Jan had been killed, and I'm prepared to admit to myself that I'd had strong feelings of respect and admiration for him even before her death…in the way a person can about someone with whom they work and who is totally, blissfully, happily married. To their soulmate, no less. It's safe to admire, and respect, and come to rely upon the advice of someone like that because they're completely involved, emotionally, with the person they're meant to be with.

But when Jan was killed, all that changed.

For you, Bud…and for me.

Yes, it was bonkers of him to ask me to be his wife just months after Jan's death, but to him it made some sort of sense. Of course I'd turned him down: he certainly wasn't in any fit state, emotionally, to make such a big decision at that time, and I wasn't at all prepared for such an about-face in our relationship. However, I'd told him he could ask me again in a year's time – if he still wanted to – and that we could spend that time working on getting to know each other…differently.

He'd agreed, and that's where we are now…six-ish months down that road. If we weren't the age we are, you'd probably say that we're dating. "We're dating." "He's my boyfriend." There needs to be a new vocabulary invented for all those of us over forty-five – or, in Bud's case, over fifty – who are beginning new relationships. It's not as though there aren't a lot of us, after all, and it can't be just me who feels uncomfortable about the available terminology.

Bud was still petting Marty…who was loving it.

"So, considering this conversation, will you go to Kelowna to help this woman?" I asked.

11

Bud didn't look me in the eye. "Would you come with me? You won't be teaching over Easter, right? You could come." He spoke softly.

"Exactly what has this Ellen said by way of an invitation?" I wondered if Bud had told his grief buddy about me.

"She's invited me to stay at her bed and breakfast place, which is housed in her dead sister's old home..."

"Sounds cheery."

Bud tutted. "It's the old family home that's she's turned into a B & B to save herself from having to sell it. And she wants me to join her on something called a 'Moving Feast' or some-such. No idea what that's all about."

No! Really? He can't mean it…dare I hope?

"Do you mean the 'Moveable Feast'?" I hadn't meant to snap, but did.

"Yes," replied Bud, suddenly wary. "That's what she said. Does it mean something to you?"

I could feel the excitement grip my tummy. "I should say so. But the Moveable Feast is notoriously private. It's a completely closed event. Or, rather, a set of events. It happens every Easter, hence the borrowing of the religious term 'moveable feast'. At least, I expect that's the reason for the name, because it doesn't really seem to work in relation to the Hemingway diaries…"

"Hemingway?"

I decided to get back to the point I meant to make in the first place. "It's one of the most talked about gourmet happenings in British Columbia each year. But it's all rumors and whispers, because you can't simply show up, or even buy your way in, so no one knows exactly what it's like. You have to be invited to host an event, and only then do you get to attend all the other events. It's really only something that's accessible to great chefs and vintners, and those with the money to put on an amazing spread. Bud – you should go. You must go. And, yes, if I can come, then of course I will. It would be the culinary experience of a lifetime. Tell me all about it. Precisely what did Ellen say? Word for word. Come on, spill."

Calm down, Cait.

Bud looked rather taken aback, but he rallied and explained coolly that Ellen had invited him and an "accompanying other" as her guests for the weekend, "to stay at her B & B, where she'll be hosting some of the meals, to accompany her to the other events, and to meet some folks who played a big part in her sister's life, and still do in hers."

"So, to be clear," I reined in my horses as best I could, "Ellen thinks her sister was murdered, and she's invited you to one of the most exclusive foodie events in the region to introduce you to the people she presumably sees as suspects. Is that right?"

"Hmm…I guess you could put it that way, though I hadn't thought of it like that before," replied Bud, looking slightly alarmed. He raked his hand through his hair, as he does when he's bothered about something. "You know, Cait, I don't think I should go. I don't want to get dragged into something I don't understand. I'm not a cop anymore."

You're sounding less Bud-like by the minute.

I began to panic, seeing my chance to indulge in some of the finest food and wines in the province receding into the distance. "Oh come on Bud, nothing ventured…" I allowed the sentence to hang above the table between us.

Bud's expression told me he'd made a decision. "I can't. It's not right. Like I said, I'm not a cop anymore. I know how much I'd have hated it if an ex-officer had turned up on my patch and started nosing about. Besides, from what Ellen's told me, I think it probably was a suicide. I suspect she's just grappling with guilt and grief. We both know how those left behind when someone takes their own life can find it tough to come to terms with what's happened: the guilt is tremendous."

"Okay, so tell me…why do you believe that's what happened? What were the exact circumstances of the dead sister's demise? What's her name, by the way? The dead one, I mean."

"Annette. Annette Newman. Annette and Ellen. Hence, Anen Wines – their parents named the wines after their daughters – Annette Newman and Ellen Newman, A.N.E.N. Anen Wines. Sweet, eh?"

I felt my eyes roll. "If you say so. Sweet."

Oh, Bud…you can be a sentimental old thing, sometimes.

He continued, "When Annette and Ellen Newman's parents died, the sisters inherited fifty percent of the winery each, and decided to make a go of it, rather than sell up. Ellen ran the business, putting her background in accounting to good use, and Annette was the 'nose' – the vintner – and she was good at it too. Won gold medals pretty much everywhere for her tasting skills, and the blends she created. Gained a worldwide reputation for herself, the vineyard, and their wines. I gather it was pretty tough at first; they lost their mother and father in a road traffic accident when Ellen was twenty-five and Annette was only twenty. Sorry Cait, I know you understand how that feels." He patted my hand.

It's been more than a decade since my parents died in a tragic car crash, but the passing of time hasn't made the loss any easier to bear. Their ashes are still sitting on my mantelpiece in two matching urns which I know – as a psychologist – speaks volumes about how well I've come to terms with their deaths.

I was determined to not get lost in sad memories. "Got it. So… let's talk about Annette; tell me how she died, exactly. And why you believe she took her own life."

Bud's tone was grave. "You know as well as I do that the statistics for female suicides show certain trends – pills, not guns, for example; they tend to use passive methods, not violent ones.

Annette Newman's case? Classic scenario: she was found in the cab of a truck – her sister's truck – with a hose leading from the exhaust, and the windows sealed with duct tape. There was an empty bottle of wine on the seat beside her, along with a note that made her intentions pretty clear. Of course I haven't seen the note, but Ellen told me that it kicked off with 'I can't do it any longer. I can't go on'. It sounds to me like an open and shut case."

"And that's how the local cops treated it? And how the coroner ruled? A suicide?"

Bud nodded. "If it were my case, that's how I'd see it."

Interesting…

I had just a few more questions. "And why does Ellen insist it was murder?"

Bud sighed. "She says there's no way that Annette would have taken her own life. *No way.* She said that Annette was in fine form on the day she died, and that they'd have talked about any problems she might have had. They got along well."

"So she believes it's murder, not suicide – though I can tell you think she's a bit wobbly on why that might be the case. Has she said who she thinks killed her sister?"

Bud shrugged. "That's another reason why I think it's just Ellen trying to manage her guilt; she claims no one had a bad word to say about her sister, but still maintains that someone had it in for her…which makes no sense. Also, she hasn't the faintest idea of who *could* have done it. She at least admits that."

I gave what he'd said some thought, and downed the last drops of my champagne.

Bud tutted. "By the way, are you ever going to drink that glass of orange juice I poured for you?" His tone was quite caustic. "I get it that you might not want to mix the two, but you should probably drink some of it. I've finished mine. Go on, spoil yourself with some vitamin C, why don't you?"

Sometimes you can be a bit of a nag...in a caring way.

I drank the whole glass of juice in one go, then wiped my lips with the back of my hand, which Marty kindly licked clean.

I said, "Well, that's it then, Bud Anderson, we'll both be going to the Moveable Feast as Ms. Newman's guests next weekend, and we'll be doing our best sleuthing too. Whatever you – and the cops and medics in Kelowna – might think, I agree with Ellen: I believe her sister was murdered."

Bud looked taken aback. "But the facts don't support that theory at all. It was clearly a suicide."

"Bud, you've told me that a woman blessed with an incredibly acute, and presumably highly trained, sense of smell – a sense of smell and taste that made her a gold award winner in her field – chose to kill herself by inhaling noxious fumes. It makes no sense, psychologically speaking. The level of self-loathing it would have taken to have killed herself that way couldn't have gone unnoticed by a close and loving sibling. And yes – before you say it – I know that carbon monoxide is odorless. But the exhaust fumes in which it would have been present certainly aren't. I suppose I can't say with certainty that she wasn't considering taking her own life; she could have hidden such feelings and thoughts from those who loved her. People do, sadly, all the time. I just don't believe she'd have killed herself *that* way. We'd better go to Kelowna and find out what really happened. Let's hope you still have some contacts in that neck of the woods, because I think we might need them."

"Oh good grief," sighed Bud, "I've created a monster. Or is that the Welsh in you coming out?" He smiled, a little apprehensively.

"I don't know what you mean, Bud." I sounded as wounded as possible at the cultural slight. "Yes, I'm Welsh through and through...though what that's got to do with anything I don't know. You're the one who retained me as a consultant on victim profiling – you knew I was good at it, and you know how many cases I helped with. In fact, I'm not sure what you mean by throwing my Welshness out as some sort of insult."

Bud rolled his eyes and smiled. Rather feebly, I thought.

I wasn't going to let him persuade me to stop that way. "I don't know Ellen or Annette Newman from a pair of holes in the ground, but if a killer has – so far – got away with taking a life, shouldn't someone do something about it? Shouldn't we find out the truth? You've spent your whole career upholding the law, and bringing those who break it to justice. You might have retired, but you haven't stopped being a person who knows the difference between right and wrong. Nor, in my opinion, will you ever be one who's not prepared to do something about it. You know we should step up. Right?"

Bud held up his hands in mock surrender. He looked sheepish. "I didn't mean to use your Welshness against you…"

"Good start…"

"…and I do see the sense in what you're saying about doing the right thing. But I'm honestly convinced that Ellen doesn't want to see things the way the authorities do. And you do have to admit that the Welsh can go rushing into things with hot heads sometimes. You've only got to see them on the rugby field to know that. Don't forget, I've had several Welsh colleagues, other than you, in my time, so I know how your lot can get."

I play-thumped him. "Oh, come off it, Bud. *My lot?* That's like me saying that you can be a miserable so-and-so at times simply because your parents are Swedish. I get it that not all Swedes walk around glumly contemplating the grim mysteries of life – in the same way, we Welsh aren't all short-tempered bulls constantly pawing the ground and snorting in close proximity to china shops."

Bud chuckled. "Singing or swinging, Cait. That's what one of my old colleagues used to tell me about the Welsh: when they're backed into a corner, it's always fifty–fifty whether they'll burst into song or come out fighting. I've never had any reason to doubt that he knew exactly what he was talking about; he was Welsh himself. And I know it's something you've said yourself, more than once. So there you are – hoist by your own petard…and thanks for giving me an excuse to use that phrase, because I don't get to do that nearly often enough."

"Bud," I gave him my sternest possible look, "I've been a Canadian for a decade now…well, becoming a Canadian at least, though, of course, I'll always be Welsh. Anyway, the Canadian Cait says let's go and help this woman; let's try to sort it all out. Okay? Or it's four choruses of my favorite Welsh hymn for you. Don't take this lightly, Bud: I'm not. Hopefully – since this poor woman died a year ago – a cold case like this should be safe for us to look into, even though you've retired. It sounds like something of an academic exercise…the sort of case I'm used to considering, now that we're no longer actively working together. So, yes, I think we should go, and, yes, I think we should look into it. Right?"

Bud's eyes crinkled into a smile as he reached out and ruffled Marty's head. "Yup, we'll do our best to help poor Ellen to…umm…understand the circumstances of her sister's death."

I felt relieved that Bud was back to being Bud-like again, and knew I had nothing to worry about with him in charge.

As I cleared the dishes, and allowed Marty to lick the bowl I'd used to scramble the eggs, I thought about what clothes I owned that could both stand up to an entire weekend of enjoying some of the best food and wine that British Columbia had to offer – *so, stretchy* – while still being smart enough for the occasion. There's only so many times you can wear bouncy, drapey black outfits and still make an impression. I sensed some panic-shopping in my very near future.

18

Coffee with Cream

I'm not a heartless person, but, if I'm honest, the unfortunate death of Annette Newman was not uppermost in my mind as Bud collected me in his shiny new truck to drive to Kelowna the next weekend. Given the rain that pelted us sideways for two hours, and the massive trucks that were laboring up the long hills at no more than a crawling pace, the journey went surprisingly smoothly. The Vintage Vinyl radio station we'd agreed on cut out a few times, but it didn't stop us singing at the tops of our voices for long periods. Even though some of Bud's memories of the music inevitably included Jan, we talked it through, and overall, it was great fun.

All very important in a burgeoning relationship.

It was almost eleven o'clock, and I knew there'd be no stopping again until we reached our destination, so I suggested a "nature break". Understanding well enough what that meant, Bud pulled off the main road, and we swept down toward Merritt where we stopped at the first coffee shop we spotted. Within moments, I'd happily used the facilities and was nibbling on a delicious lemon and cranberry scone, while managing to slurp gingerly from a steaming vat of coffee with as much cream in it as I could fit into the paper cup.

"Road trips make you hungry?" asked Bud, chuckling.

I didn't stop nibbling or slurping to answer. By way of an acid retort, I simply looked in his direction and put my multi-purpose eyebrow to good use.

Eventually, I mumbled at him through cakey crumbs, "I haven't eaten since breakfast, and that was four hours ago."

"I seem to remember you polishing off that packet of cookies not too long after we'd dropped Marty at Jack White's acreage in Hatzic," he replied, not unkindly.

"Blood sugar was low," I muttered.

It's a phrase that allows for a fair few snacks each day.

Bud smiled broadly as we ambled back to the truck, then, while I brushed crumbs off my "ample bosom", as we large-chested women like to refer to our boobs – *well, I do, anyway* – he wiped off the worst of the insects that had splattered themselves across his shiny new fender.

"Well and truly christened," he observed wryly. I think he was a bit sad that the brand new-ness was now marred.

With another coffee in hand for the next leg of the journey, Bud hauled himself back into the truck, then passed me a blue cardboard folder that he'd pulled from behind his seat.

"Here you go, some reading for you," he said, smiling wickedly. "You can interpret it for me."

I leafed through the contents of the folder; sheets and sheets of notes spread across my lap.

I was puzzled. "And this is…?"

"It seems that Ellen Newman thought we'd like some background on our fellow attendees at the Moveable Feast. That's what she emailed to me. I printed it out before I left the apartment this morning," replied Bud as we drove up the incline toward the highway.

"She's very thorough," I observed dryly. "But then, she's an accountant, so maybe she's one of those 'all detail and no perspective' people."

"Don't be so judgmental, Cait. You're always doing that."

"Doing what?"

Bud was at least smiling when he replied, "Reaching snap decisions about folks two seconds after you've been introduced, or – worse still – before you've even met them."

I supposed he was right, but I've never been any different, and I just can't help being myself. "You've told me a fair bit about her…and what people do for a living, and where they live their lives are significant indicators of personality type, as well as beliefs and desires. But, on this occasion, you have a point: I was judging Ellen Newman on a pile of papers I haven't even read yet, and that probably isn't fair. I'll withhold any more opinions until I've seen what she has to say, and maybe even until I've met her."

Bud chuckled. "Excellent plan. So…radio on, or off?"

"Off, thanks, it'll make the job quicker."

"Right then. Get on with it," he quipped.

I pulled my big old handbag from between my feet, scrabbled about for my reading glasses, pushed them onto my nose…took them off again, cleaned them, poked them back into place…and began to read. There must have been about thirty pages in all, so it took about five minutes.

When I'd finished, I gave what I'd read some thought for a moment or two, then pronounced, "Okay, I'm ready. What do you want to know?"

Even from his profile I could tell that Bud was surprised, and amused. "It still freaks me out a bit that you can read and digest so much information so quickly. I wish I could do it; over the years, I bet I could have saved months of my life that way. You're lucky."

"Lucky, and…well, you know how hard I work at it, Bud," I retorted with a dramatic – and totally unnecessary – throat-clearing.

Having what some call an "eidetic memory", and what others call "a quick eye and a fast brain" – because they don't believe that true photographic memory exists in reality – means that I can see, understand, interpret, and encode information into my memory banks at great speed. It's been a phenomenal help to me in my academic life, but it also means that I carry with me images and sensations I'd really prefer to forget. Sometimes they haunt my dreams, as vivid as when I first experienced them, because I don't just hold on to words on pages, I do it with everything that surrounds me. Insofar as I've been able to encode it accurately in the first place, of course. And that's another problem with my "ability"; I sometimes encode things wrongly, overlaying them with my own, sometimes erroneous, interpretations. I color them with my attitudes and biases, based upon my own incomplete knowledge; it's something that's landed me in trouble in the past.

"So shall I tell you what I think about the writer before I tell you about what she's written?" I asked, a little glibly.

"Sure. Even though you just said you wouldn't do that. But, go ahead…I'll take it all in, as best I can with my poor, feeble, non-superhuman brain."

I had to stop myself from giving Bud a friendly slap on the arm…*don't smack someone when they're driving.*

"Okay," I began, "Ellen Newman has written up a list of the people we're going to meet throughout the weekend, with some background on each person. It looks like a thorough list – unless she's left some people out. She's obviously given it all a great deal of thought, and of course, she knows the people she's writing about. So, what does this tell me about Ellen?"

Pause, for effect.

Bud didn't respond…then he cracked. "Okay, okay…come on, just get on with it."

"Ellen likes to organize. Here she's organized her thoughts, but I suspect she likes to organize everything around her, including people. Don't get me wrong, Bud, I wish I could be a bit more like her in my own life; you know how I am with the piles of papers, textbooks, and reports I have to read and grade – I like to use the 'strata method' of filing, where the oldest things are at the bottom of the pile. It doesn't matter so much for me, because I can recall when I put something, so can usually find it right away. But Ellen? I suspect her sock drawer has those little divider things in it, and she probably fills her kitchen cupboards with items in height order. You know the type."

"You mean she's tidy?"

"More than tidy," I replied thoughtfully. "Highly ordered, I'd say. Who knows, maybe she's bordering on being clinically compulsive about order, or maybe not. As you know, I'm not a psychiatrist so don't diagnose such issues…but I do study behavior, and this behavior of hers – as demonstrated in these papers – probably manifests itself in most parts of her life."

Bud nodded and gave me an, "Uh-huh," which I took as a sign to continue.

"Moving on then, let's consider the cast of characters she's detailed. Well, they're an interesting group, with a variety of origins and some fascinating stories behind them. I think the best way to help you understand is to explain the context in which we're going to meet them first."

Bud bobbed his head again.

You're beginning to look like one of those nodding dogs.

I pressed on. "So...by way of overall background, the Moveable Feast takes place every Easter and is attended only by those who are hosting meals and their invited guests – of which they are allowed two, maximum. Which is where we come in – we're Ellen's guests. Each host is responsible for providing food and drink, as appropriate to the meal they're hosting. There are no budget limits. No sponsors are allowed, but – otherwise – there are no rules, as such. There is, however, a timetable: this evening we'll attend a 'cocktails and canapés soirée', which differs from the rest of the weekend in that every host will have contributed something to tonight's event, and it'll take place at a venue they've hired. No one person is responsible for tonight."

"A *soirée*? Fancy."

I chose to ignore Bud's quip, and continued, "Tomorrow and Sunday, we have a breakfast, a lunch, and a dinner each day, and there's a final breakfast, again un-hosted but contributed to by everyone, on Monday morning. After that – if we can still move at all – we're free to leave."

"Good grief," said Bud, looking a bit taken aback. "I don't even eat three times a day, let alone three special, probably very rich, heavy meals. I'm glad I packed the antacids."

"I packed mine too." I chuckled, reflecting happily on how, for all our differences, we're really very similar in some respects.

Bud resettled himself behind the wheel as I went on. "Other than lining our arteries and broadening our beams this weekend, it seems that the other thing we'll be doing is mixing with some pretty well-heeled folks." As I spoke, I began to worry that my wardrobe wouldn't stand up to the scrutiny of the people with whom we'd be mixing.

"Go on then, I can take it," urged Bud. "Tell me all about them. But bear in mind I'm going to need the potted version."

I dared a gentle pat on the arm for him, and he didn't even swerve, so that was good. "First, then, I'll tell you about where we're staying. The Anen House Bed & Breakfast is the old Newman homestead, as you knew. The late Annette lived there after the death of the Newman parents, but, since her death, Ellen has set it up as a B & B with two double rooms and a restaurant that, obviously – due to the second 'B' in that title – supplies breakfasts…but not just for residents, it seems. Apparently, it's *the* place to go for breakfast in the whole area; you even have to book a table, it's so popular. The chef there, one Pat Corrigan, makes award-winning sausages."

"Sausages?"

"Delightful, right? It seems that while the late Annette Newman might have had a lock on all the gold medals when it came to wines, your Ellen has found herself a chef with the same sort of stranglehold on the world's sausage-making circuit. I didn't even know there was such a thing, though I must say that

I like the sound of it. I suppose that's why breakfast will be served there on both Saturday and Sunday mornings, which makes life a little easier for us at the start of those days."

"True," replied Bud, "and I guess they must be very good sausages." He sounded quite excited about the food – for Bud.

"Anyway," I pressed on, "there's a married couple who live-in at Anen House. They've been there since the place opened as a B & B about eight months ago. Pat Corrigan is, as I said, the chef, and his wife, Lauren, is the housekeeper. Ellen brought them over to work for her from a restaurant near Dublin, after that place closed down. Due to the death of the owner, who was ninety-five – she notes that here. From the way she's written about them I can tell that she likes Pat, the chef, but merely tolerates his wife, whose cleaning standards are not quite the same as Ellen's own it seems…which is a bit alarming, since we're staying there. Mind you, it's unlikely we'd either of us notice the odd cobweb, right?"

"True," Bud replied, with a chuckle. "I've got the excuse of having a muck-loving dog living in the apartment with me. And I'm not sure you feel the need to have an excuse for not owning a long-handled feather duster, right?"

"Oh, I own one," I countered. "I'm just not sure I remember where I left it…"

I grinned at him, though Bud didn't see me because, very sensibly, he kept his eyes on the greasy road ahead.

"And there's me thinking you remember everything." Bud smiled, winked, and clucked at me.

Oh Bud, your smile can be very distracting.

"Possible cleanliness issues aside," I continued, "Ellen seems content that she has the right people running the B & B, but, from our point of view, as murder suspects—"

"Hey, they're your suspects, Cait, not mine. I'm still not convinced this was a murder. *Remember*?"

"Hardy-har-har. Okay, from *my* point of view," I conceded, "as murder suspects, the Corrigans – who I'm assuming are not just from Ireland but are in fact Irish – can't be considered to be in the frame at all: they weren't even in Canada when Annette died."

Bud looked a little disgruntled, even though I'd given in to his point.

"Onwards and upwards," I said, as our route did exactly that. "Now there's a whole collection of people listed as 'suspects' – and that's Ellen's word, not mine, before you get on your high horse again, Bud Anderson. After tonight's cocktails and canapés, and the chance to try those sausages for breakfast just yards away, Saturday lunch will be hosted by the MacMillan family at their home, Lakeview Lodge – which I'm going to go out on a limb and guess overlooks the lake. Rob MacMillan is something big in oil in Calgary, and Sheri Macmillan lives in Kelowna, in fine style by the sound of it. Ellen seems to think that Sheri spends all her time wandering from day spa to day spa, sitting on committees, shopping, lunching, and spending her husband's money. She refers to her as 'vapid and fussy, but harmless'. Apparently, Rob MacMillan himself only shows his face in Kelowna from time to time and basically spends the year in Alberta, where the family has another house. Ellen admits to not knowing him very well. The couple has a seventeen-year-old son, Colin, who lives with his mother and attends high school in Kelowna. Ellen describes him as 'annoying and weird': she says he lacks any social skills, and is known for cycling around the area too fast. All three MacMillans were in town at the time of Annette's death, though Rob left on an early flight to Calgary the morning Ellen discovered her sister's body. Ellen doesn't give any reasons for why any of these people might want Annette dead, so don't hold your breath waiting for motives to emerge," I added.

"I wasn't expecting any motives to be forthcoming," Bud replied calmly. "Ellen's told me on several occasions that Annette was universally loved and respected."

"Hmm...well, that's not true about anyone," I replied. "Except you, of course," I added in my sweetest voice.

"Oh Cait – you know that's not the case…" Bud sounded grim, and I realized that I'd just said something stupid, thoughtless, and painful. The guy who'd shot Jan Anderson had meant to kill Bud himself.

"I'm so sorry…" At that moment I was terribly aware that Jan would always be with us, in some way.

"It's okay, Cait. It can't be helped," replied Bud, still sounding bleak.

"Yes it can. I should be more thoughtful about what I say." I was cross with myself, not Bud, but it didn't sound that way.

"Alright then, if it makes you feel better, go ahead and beat yourself up about it. But I won't do it for you, Cait. Blame. Guilt. 'Would-have. Could-have. Should-have'. None of it gets a person anywhere. Trust me on this…I should know…I've given it all enough of my time that I've developed a certain level of expertise in the field."

I didn't say anything for at least two minutes, which, for me, is a very long time indeed.

I watched the road wind far ahead of us as I reasoned that I couldn't walk on eggshells forever, and that I still had to think about…so many aspects of our relationship. I allowed the millions of trees covering the rolling mountains surrounding us to become a soothing blur.

Finally, Bud said, "Come on, Cait, I'm fine, really. Now, are you going to tell me about these people, or what? We're almost at the summit, so not much longer now. You'd better get a move on. I know you're bursting with it." He smiled a warm smile that dissipated the tension and freed me to continue.

Thank you, Bud.

"Right. Next up are the fabulous Sammy and Suzie Soul," I announced, rallying.

"*The* Sammy Soul?"

"Yep, *the* Sammy Soul who famously took every drug, drank every drink, and bonked every groupie available to him throughout the '60s and '70s."

Bud looked confused. "Bonked?"

"Yes, you know, 'had biblical knowledge of'. Though I can't imagine there was any sort of ecclesiastical element involved."

Bud nodded. "Is 'bonked' a Welsh-ism?"

"No, but I suppose it's a British-ism. Bonk means hit: you can bonk someone on the head, or cyclists bonk when they're tired, because they've hit a metaphorical wall...and we Brits use it to mean 'hit' in the sexual sense. But not like when North Americans say 'he hit on someone' – that just means chatting them up, not actually having sex with them..."

Bud laughed heartily. "Ah, the joys of being separated by a common language."

He often says that when I lapse into Brit-speak, as he calls it, or – even more confusingly for Bud – when I chatter to myself in Wenglish. To be fair, that's a sort of middle ground that exists between Welsh and English, which is really only spoken around Swansea, and the Swansea Valleys area, where I'm from...so it's hardly surprising he can't make head nor tail of it.

I pressed on. "As I said, yes, *the* Sammy Soul who was well known for hell raising and womanizing when he headed up his band, the Soul Rockers. I have to admit, I thought he'd be dead by now. He probably should be. Anyway, it appears that he bought a winery in the Okanagan, now called SoulVine Wines, and he's been there for about twenty years. Who knew?"

"Not me, for one," said Bud.

"And not me, for two," I added, grinning.

I like the fact we've reached the point in our relationship where we have little "us" things.

Feeling warm inside, I added, "He lives there with his wife, Suzie. She must be quite a strong character to have put up with him for the almost forty years that Ellen says they've been married. They have a daughter, Serendipity. Poor thing. Imagine growing up with that as a name."

"Seems to fit the bill for the child of a rock star. Weird names were quite the fashion, once upon a time, right?"

I agreed. "It could have been much worse for her, I suppose." My mind wandered to all those bizarre names that are carted about by the children of the hip and wealthy. I mentally thanked my parents for being so traditional in their choice for me. "Ellen writes that Serendipity Soul has turned out to be quite a star in the kitchen. Apparently, she trained in France, has an excellent reputation as a chef, and now runs the restaurant at her parents' vineyard. It's called SoulVineFineDine, which seems to be quite a mouthful for the name of a restaurant…but maybe that's the point. Anyway, it's where we'll be having dinner on Saturday evening, so we'll have a chance to see if Serendipity is all she's cracked up to be. Ellen only has good things to say about her, but she calls Sammy Soul 'drug-addled' and 'lacking a moral compass', and she refers to his wife as 'a man-eating whore'."

"Good grief." Bud sounded shocked. "I had no idea Ellen could be that…well…'unkind' is the best word, right?"

"I'd agree that her characterizations of Sammy and Suzie are quite scathing. But, of course, I'm trying to not be too judgmental."

"Okay, touché. I guess I can be a bit judgmental, too, under certain circumstances."

"Hmm, right. Well, we'll both have a chance to assess Ellen's judgment tonight, when we meet these folks at the cocktail party, but, in the meantime, on to the next hosts. After another breakfast at our own domicile on Sunday morning, we'll be heading off to something called the Faceting for Life Restaurant on Pandosy Street in downtown Kelowna. There, the owners, Grant and Lizzie Jackson, will be our hosts, and one Ray Murciano is the resident chef. Ellen says that Lizzie Jackson is an 'alarming' woman originally from Phoenix, who met Grant Jackson at a 'Faceting Camp' – whatever that might be – about five years ago. It's his second marriage, but Lizzie's first. He's originally from Vancouver. It seems that the Jacksons are into that whole sustainability and organic movement, as well as this Faceting thing, which Ellen reckons is the 'crack-pot scheme of some flaky so-called guru in Sedona' – her words."

Bud raised an eyebrow-in-training.

I chose to ignore him.

I pressed on. "Lizzie Jackson is a 'healer'. Ellen says she 'plays around with' hypnotherapy and aura alignment, and that she's 'forever carting about a load of crystals', which is all bound up with the Faceting dogma, apparently." I added a quiet, "Sounds interesting," while I pulled a face that Bud couldn't see.

His eyes were locked on the road ahead...a very good thing, I reckoned, because we were at the Pennask Summit, which was swathed in icy fog. The highway was slick and challenging, the winter's snow piled so high at the sides of the road that it towered over the huge trucks we passed as they crawled along. I inwardly praised Bud's insistence upon packing a shovel, warm blankets, a thermos, and lots of snacks, because there are often times when an accident on the road shuts it down for hours, so you're just stuck there.

However, we got through the worst of it, and I knew that at least from the summit onwards the journey was, quite literally, all downhill and it wouldn't be long until the landscape would open up ahead of us and show us the Okanagan Valley and the beauties it held. But there was a good way to go yet, so I carried on with my assigned task.

"In summary – in terms of our hosts – we have the Irish Corrigans who live at the B & B; the all-Canadian MacMillans who live in Lakeview Lodge, farther along Lakeshore Drive than Anen Close; the all-American Soul family, at SoulVine Wines in West Kelowna, the opposite bank of the lake; the Canadian and American Jacksons who live at Anen Close, located immediately below the B & B, and who run a Faceting shop and restaurant in Kelowna itself."

"Got it. I feel full just thinking about all that food…all those meals."

I chuckled. "Then there's the du Bois family – parents Marcel and Annie, and their two daughters, Gabi and Poppy. They own and operate *C'est la Vie*, the French restaurant where we'll be dining on Sunday night. It seems that the parents had a background together in the food business in Montreal before they arrived in Kelowna, when they bought a rundown hole-in-the-wall and upgraded it to become a well-respected brasserie-type restaurant, with a traditional menu and a reputation for fine ingredients and good cooking. He runs front of house, she's the chef, and the two girls are servers. I must say, that's probably the meal I'm looking forward to the most; there's just something about French food…I can't get enough of it."

"That's not what you said when you got back from France last year," quipped Bud, still concentrating.

"True…but those were extraordinary circumstances, you have to admit. And, in any case, I'm over all that now. Other residents we'll meet are Gordy and Marlene Wiser, who also live in Anen Close below the B & B, opposite the Jacksons, and have been there for about four years. Both the Jacksons and the Wisers have lived in the two houses that comprise Anen Close since they were first built on part of the land that used to belong to the Newman homestead. Ellen says that the Wisers are very nice people – old, reliable, and trustworthy – but that he's a real nosey parker, and she's fixated on her garden. Take that as you want."

Bud smiled. "No judgement from me."

I tutted. "Our final group are those Ellen describes as 'latecomers and others'. By 'latecomers', I gather she means those who have been in the area for less than five years or so. I suppose that having grown up there she thinks of everyone who's been a neighbor for less than a lifetime as a latecomer, but this is her term, so I'll use it. However, as far as her use of the word 'others' is concerned...well, it seems to me that she's discounting these people as suspects. First there's a bloke called Vince Chen, who's the new vintner at SoulVine Wines. He's been in town for less than a year, so wasn't around when Annette died; he was brought in by Sammy Soul from a winery in Niagara, though he's originally from Vancouver. It seems that Sammy Soul's last vintner had to leave, because...get this...Ellen's sister Annette left him her half of the family wine business in her will."

"You're kidding," Bud responded sharply. "Ellen never mentioned that to me."

"Well, she's mentioned it in her notes. She says that a Raj Pinder was the vintner at SoulVine Wines for about three years, then, when Annette's will was read, it came as a great surprise to everyone that she had left her half of the family business to this relative stranger. Interestingly, Ellen writes that she's very pleased her sister did that, because he's the best vintner in the business, now that her sister's no longer around."

"That's...weird."

"Yep, definitely odd. Especially since Ellen's put him into the non-suspects category. I think I need to poke around that a bit when I meet everyone."

"Poke away, Cait. Poke away," was Bud's rather patronising reply.

Don't rise to the bait.

I left it at that, because we'd finally rolled into West Kelowna. The picturesque part of the journey was behind us, and endless strip malls now hedged both sides of the road. The highway had been busy with an unexpected number of trucks, given that it was Good Friday, and now the local roads were laden with folks hurrying from A to B, presumably stocking up for the Easter weekend's family get-togethers.

"How much longer before we're there?" I asked.

"I guess about half an hour or so, depending on the bridge. It might be busy because it's lunchtime, or maybe not, because it's a holiday. It'll be what it'll be. Ellen's expecting us when we get there. I didn't say we'd be there at a certain time, just some time after lunch, which I guess it is, now."

I wondered if Bud assumed that a few cookies and a scone would hold me until dinner time – which was only going to be nibbles – but I thought it best not to say anything. We were, after all, about to jump headlong into a whole gourmet weekend. Besides, it was clear from Bud's expression that the carefree road trip had now become a journey to a specific destination. I imagined he wasn't looking forward to meeting his "grief buddy".

I'm not, but I don't really know why.

As we wound down through West Kelowna and approached the Bill Bennett Bridge, the sun finally poked through the clouds, glinting off the ribbon of vehicles below us. On the opposite side of the vast lake, the rapidly growing city of Kelowna nestled beneath the hillsides, which were yellow with wintry grasses and still showing patches of snow on the ground. Here and there were copses of evergreens that had survived the terrible forest fires – which seem to get worse, and last longer every year.

"Gonna keep an eye out for Ogopogo as we cross the lake?" quipped Bud.

"Sure," I replied, smiling, "but give me a minute while I get my phone out; just one photo of the Loch Ness Monster's Canadian cousin, and we'd be worth a fortune."

I love monster myths; the human distrust of deep bodies of water allows us to populate them with all sorts of terrifying creatures. Okanagan Lake, at almost eighty-five miles long, and with water as deep as seven hundred and seventy feet, is prime monster-story territory. I always remind myself that no one knew that the giant squid was a reality until the early twenty-first century, so – who knows – maybe out there somewhere, in one of the world's deepest and oldest lakes, there might actually lurk a creature descended more directly from the dinosaurs than even our feathered raptor friends. But…then there'd always have to be a breeding pair available to keep the species going, so there'd always be more than one of them…unless they'd evolved to be able to reproduce asexually, like Komodo dragons.

The world's a fascinating place.

We zipped across Okanagan Lake into Kelowna and negotiated the knots of traffic that jammed each of the city's crossroads, finally heading south along the edge of the lake. We passed undulating hillsides planted with neat rows of bare vines, but I could glimpse the white fuzz of blossom in apple orchards in the distance. The clouds had broken, and it promised to be a golden afternoon.

"Okay, keep your eyes peeled," said Bud.

The voice of the truck's GPS told us that we'd reached our destination, but it was clear to both of us that we'd done no such thing, because we were on a bit of road that gave us a wonderful view of the lake but not much else. We pulled over.

"There," said Bud with surprising certainty, given the narrowness of the track he was indicating.

He swung the truck sharply away from the lake and the track soon presented a wider vista. To our right was a large, single-storey traditionally designed house with a wrap-around porch; to our left was its mirror image. The only discernable difference between the two homes was that one was cream with blue trim, and the other cream with red trim. Each house was set on about an acre of its own land and, between them, the track widened to a road that wound in hairpins up to a small, two-storey older-looking home, which sat atop the weird, knobbly hill facing us. It looked rather like those houses that children draw, even to the white, picket fence that surrounded it.

A large sign at the foot of the winding road announced ANEN HOUSE B & B, with an arrow pointing up. As Bud changed gear to take the steep road ahead, I saw the curtains in the front window of the house to the right of us twitch. Anyone living there would have a great vantage point for keeping an eye on all the comings and goings in Anen Close, and at the B & B.

"So, there it is, then," I said solemnly as we wound upwards.

"Yes, and here we are," Bud replied.

"From now on, almost everyone we meet might be a possible murder suspect," I added.

"If Annette was murdered," he replied, pointedly.

A sign directed us to RESIDENTS' PARKING – an open structure built to offer housing for two large vehicles, set to one side of the house. Soon, Bud was carrying his bag, and I was wheeling my slightly battered suitcase, along the narrow path that led through the picket fence toward the front of the house. Before we reached it, the jolly red door flew open and a long-faced, lean woman of about thirty came toward us; she had a sallow complexion, and dark hair piled high on her head.

"You must be Bud and Cait," she said in a sharply accusatory tone. She wiped her hands on her apron, then scooped my suitcase from me as she limply shook Bud's free hand.

We both smiled. She didn't.

In flat tones she said, "Ellen told me you'd be here after lunch some time. I'm happy you had a safe journey." She sounded nothing of the sort. "Let me get you settled, then I'll call and tell her you're here." She held open the front door and impatiently waved us in.

"Thanks," replied Bud hesitantly. I decided to let him take the lead…after all, I wasn't the real guest, he was. I was just his "accompanying other".

Surprisingly, immediately I stepped inside the house, I fell in love with it: a symmetrical layout, sunshine-hued walls, vases of flowers dotted about. It felt like a home, not a temporary residence for nomadic tourists. The smell that filled the air made my tastebuds ache. *Some sort of beef dish?* I was instantly ravenous, and couldn't help but wonder if the food might be for us.

As if she were telepathic, the woman announced, "Pat, my husband, made soup. He thought you might be hungry." She said it as though it were a very stupid idea.

Thank you Pat, I like you already.

"I'm Lauren. Lauren Corrigan. Chief dogsbody." The woman thrust her arm toward me, having balanced my suitcase in the entryway.

I shook her small hand and felt it crumple in my own. Closer to her now, I could see a network of fine lines on her face that suggested she was more used to frowning than smiling. She smelled of plain soap, and seemed haggard for her age. Not a happy woman, I suspected. Her body language backed me up…every movement was filled with anger. She wrenched my bag back onto its little wheels and nodded toward the staircase that headed from the front door to the upper level.

"I'll take your bags up. You have something to eat. Unless you want to freshen up, of course." Her tone suggested this would be a poor decision on our part.

"Thanks, some food would be great," said Bud.

Lauren shouted, "Pat, they're here," making both Bud and me flinch.

As Lauren began to clatter and bump up the stairs, huffing and puffing as she went, a short, red-headed man, wearing full chef whites, appeared from what I assumed was the kitchen. He grinned broadly…almost wickedly.

"Ah-ha, our esteemed weekend guests. You must be Bud," he shook Bud's hand firmly, "and you must be Cait." He took my hand in both of his and shook it warmly. "I've been looking forward to meeting you. Ellen has spoken very highly of you, and with good reason, I'm sure." His lilt was even more pronounced than his wife's. Certainly a southern Irish accent, but not Dublin…although Ellen had written that that was where she'd found him.

Maybe from Cork?

"You'll be wanting something to eat, I'm sure," said Pat Corrigan, as though nothing could be more natural, nor make him happier. "I've made a lovely soup for you, hearty but not too heavy, just right to get you through to this evening's event. You'll be glad, later on, that you've had it now, given all the drinking you'll be doing with your food tonight."

Definitely Cork. Lovely accent.

Bud and I happily allowed the beaming chef to seat us at one of the several tables in what was clearly the breakfasting area. We greedily tucked into the steaming, aromatic beef, barley, and veggie soup that he served us, accompanied by large chunks of fresh, homemade soda bread, and curls of yellow, salty butter. It took us a while. Neither of us spoke, except to make little noises that showed how delectable we thought the meal was.

I love the way that "Mmm…" can communicate volumes.

When we'd finished, we both pushed back a little from the table and looked equally satisfied. Almost immediately Pat reappeared and asked if everything was alright. Bud and I nodded, and showered his abilities in the kitchen with praise.

As Pat collected our dishes, Bud asked, "Do you know what the exact plan of action for the rest of the day might be, Pat? Ellen's very kindly sent us an outline of what the weekend will hold for us, but she left us a bit in the dark about where to be, and when, for this evening."

"Now that's not at all like our Ellen," remarked Pat with an impish grin. "I reckon she'll be here before too long to tell you for herself. Lauren texted her, and she said she'd be right over. Her office is at the vineyard, which is only about ten minutes along the road. In fact, you'll have passed it on your way here. I do happen to know that Ellen's booked a taxi from her place to here, to collect you at six, and take all three of you to the cocktail party at the Arts Centre downtown, which kicks off at six thirty. And it's formal dress. Although it's only canapés, you'll sure have plenty to eat there; I've sent down enough tiny sausage rolls meself to choke a horse. The car'll bring you back here afterwards. Knowing that lot, I think midnight'd be about right. There's breakfast here at eight tomorrow morning, so we can't come tonight. It'll be a busy night for me, and a busy morning for me and Lauren both. It'll be grand, though. It's my first time, you know, for the Moveable Feast. First time. Truth is, I'm a bit nervous about it all. Used to some fancy fare, all those posh folks, so they are. But Ellen agreed we should keep it simple, and plain. So it's a traditional Irish breakfast you'll be getting tomorrow morning, and an Irishman's version of a 'North American' start to the day on Sunday. Think on that when you're noshing it up tonight, and save some room for my famous, award-winning bangers."

I said, "I'm looking forward to breakfast already in that case, Pat. But, tell me, how formal will the event be tonight? When you say 'posh' folks, how 'posh' do you mean?"

"Compared with the old country, nothing seems very formal around these parts at all," replied Pat, smiling. "Even if it's a wedding, the men all seem to make do with open-necked shirts, and even trousers for the ladies. But tonight? Well, maybe you'd better ask Ellen. She'd know better than me."

As though on cue, Ellen Newman walked quietly through what had been her childhood home's front door into what had, more lately, been her dead sister's home…and was now a place for fee-paying guests. I thought it odd that she looked around as though she was uncertain if it was acceptable for her to enter. I knew from her notes that she'd chosen to move to an apartment closer to the downtown core about five years after her parents' deaths; maybe that accounted for her manner…this hadn't been her actual home for decades.

Pat disappeared into the kitchen bearing our bread-mopped bowls, a smile on his face.

Bud stood and moved to greet Ellen. Of course we both recognized her from the photograph she'd sent, but I saw a woman who appeared to have aged at least five years since that shot had been snapped. I knew from her notes that it had been taken just about a year earlier, a few days before her sister's death. Now, her once bouncy dark hair was lank, with yellowish-gray strands popping up like little wires; there were dark circles under her once-bright eyes; her mouth was set in a thin, grim line. Her general size and shape didn't differ too much from the photograph, but she seemed to stoop, and looked frail. A couple of inches taller than me, so about five-five, she might have been five-six or -seven if she'd straightened her back.

Bereavement can take its toll physically as well as emotionally.

"Ellen. It's good to meet you at last," said Bud with feeling.

He strode across the hardwood floor to gather her in his arms in a warm embrace. She hugged him back, a little awkwardly.

Then Bud turned toward me and announced, "This is Cait. The woman I love. I've spoken to you about her, I know."

Good grief.

Bud's told me he loves me, and I've told him that I love him too, and not just as friends…we reached that point in our relationship about three months in. But to hear him proclaim it?

Tingles are running up and down my back.

Ellen replied, "Thanks for coming. I know it's going to be alright now. I trust you, Bud. You'll find out what happened to my sister."

And there it was: the real reason for us being there. Not the food, the scenic drive, nor the carefree weekend together knowing that Marty was happily visiting doggie friends on acreage. No, we'd come to help Ellen.

Bud and I locked eyes for a moment, exchanged a slight smile, then he said, "Right, Ellen. We'll do what we can. So where do you want to start?"

40

Listerine

"Come with me," said Ellen as she started up the staircase.

Bud and I nodded, and dutifully followed Ellen. At the top of the stairs, I took her cue to walk into the room that led off the righthand side of the landing. It was tastefully decorated: paisley fabrics, good landscape prints, substantial old, dark-wood furniture, and walls the color of clotted cream. Cozy.

Once Bud and I were inside, Ellen closed the door, then gestured toward the sofa nestled in front of the floor-to-ceiling window, where we sat, overlooking the hairpin road we'd ascended and the glinting expanse of the lake beyond. She pulled a slipper chair from the corner and sat between us and the window, becoming not much more than a silhouette. It lent her a conspiratorial air, and put me at a disadvantage because it became difficult for me to read the finer points of her facial expressions. I tried shifting to get a better angle, but failed.

Ellen hunched toward us. "Tonight you'll get to meet everyone," she said excitedly. "I know how confusing it can be to meet a lot of people at once, and to have to remember them all, so that's why I prepared those notes for you. Did you read them? If you're going to work out who wanted to hurt Annette, you'll need to hit the ground running."

Bud raked his hand through his hair, a sure sign he was feeling stressed, but he didn't say anything.

I said, "Bud let me have a look at your notes – I hope you don't mind?"

Ellen pounced, "Oh no, not at all. Anything either of you can do – really, anything – would be helpful. Thank you." She was almost bouncing off the chair.

I dared, "Well, I do have a couple of questions for you, but if now's not a good time…"

"Oh no, now's fine. Just fine." She was almost panting with excitement.

Just like Marty, when he thinks we're about to take him for a walk.

I plumped for a challenging opening gambit. "Okay then. On the third page of your notes, you've referred to Sammy Soul of SoulVine Wines as a 'drug-addled, ageing hippie with no moral compass'. Do you know for a fact that he still does drugs, or are you talking about all the acid he famously dropped in the '60s and '70s, when he was making his lead guitar bleed and scream as the frontman for the Soul Rockers?"

Ellen snapped, "No one ever sees him taking drugs, but he can't possibly be the way he is without them. Besides, he keeps going on about how it should be legal for anyone to grow as much cannabis as they want, and then to be able make wine with it, without the government always poking about in your business. In fact, I'm pretty sure he's doing it already because he's absolutely dead set against following any rules."

That seemed to settle it for Ellen, and it helped me to build another layer of her psychological profile. I know Bud reckons I'm sometimes alarmingly judgmental, but I reckoned that Ellen Newman might be even more judgmental than me.

"Have you lived here all your life?" I enquired, tactfully trying to change the subject to one that might infuriate her less.

"Why would I leave?" Her tone spoke volumes; her answer implied she'd be just as unhappy anywhere.

As I dwelt momentarily on Ellen's response, Bud asked, "You went to university in Vancouver, right?"

"I did," replied Ellen coolly, "but I didn't like it there. The people were unfriendly. Hard. Always trying to get on. And the city was dirty and noisy."

My eyes had adjusted enough to the conditions for me to be able to see that the straight line of her mouth had become thinner, and more firmly fixed.

I suspected that Ellen had left her home to go to a city she'd been determined to dislike, and she'd done just that. People always seem to forget that they pack their own emotional baggage and lug it about with them everywhere they go.

Changing tack, Bud asked, "Ellen, who have you told these folks I am? How will you introduce me?"

Good question, Bud.

Ellen didn't hesitate. "I've thought about that and I'm going to say that you are who you are – Bud Anderson, my 'grief buddy'. They'll understand. They all know about my online stuff."

I feared that Bud might draw blood, he was scratching through his hair so hard. "That's all supposed to be private, Ellen. We've blogged a great deal about how it's the anonymity that allows us all to share as much as we do. You've written that yourself. More than once." He sounded…*frustrated.*

Ellen replied airily, "Yes, but it's different now. We know each other. We can be open about it all. Besides, I've already told Pat and Lauren Corrigan who you are, and they were okay with it."

I hope she hasn't told them what I do for a living, was what I thought; "And what have you said about me?" was what I said.

"I've just told them you're his girlfriend. Bud hasn't even told me what you do. It never came up. What do you do? Is it interesting?"

I gave it a split-second's thought and blurted out, "Marketing professor. At the University of Vancouver. Business school."

Stop looking at me as though I'm having a stroke, Bud.

I added calmly, "I love it. Been there ten years."

"Nice," Ellen replied, smiling. "That's where I studied. Is Professor Colling still there?"

I had no idea who Professor Colling was, nor whether she, or he, might still be at the university.

Luckily for me, Ellen answered herself by adding, "Oh, but that's a silly question, of course she won't be. She was ancient when I was there. She's probably dead by now. And good riddance."

That was a close call, was what I thought; "Indeed," was what I said, glad to have escaped a self-laid trap.

"Well, back to the matter at hand," I added, hoping to elude any more challenges. "I know that you're due to collect us here in a cab at six o'clock this evening and that dress is formal tonight, so I'm assuming a long dress will be okay for that?" I raised my eyebrow in query, and Ellen nodded. "Right, well, that means I'm going to have quite a bit of getting ready to do. I'd like to clean up a bit, and so forth. Would it be okay if we meet you downstairs at five thirty, in case we have any more questions before we leave? Could you arrive early, and the cab wait?"

I thought that my rapid exit strategy might be a bit abrupt, but Bud was raking his hair with frustration, looking worried, and seemed keen to get away from Ellen, too.

"Oh, absolutely," agreed Ellen with enthusiasm, and she bounced up out of her chair, put it back in its place and started toward the door. "This'll be your room, Bud, and Cait's across the hall. Unless you'd rather be the other way around. You'll have the place to yourselves, of course…well, except for Lauren and Pat. They live in, as I said in my notes. They're out back, in a double-wide. But that was in my notes, too, right? Yes. They won't be a bother; they'll be busy getting things ready for tomorrow's breakfast. Let's get tonight behind us first. See you at five thirty, and we can clear up anything you need to know before we leave."

And she was gone.

Having risen to accept Ellen's parting words, I watched from my vantage point until I could see her walking out of the front door, then turned to Bud and said, "Having promised in the truck to hold off with my opinions until I'd met the woman, I have now met her, and she's…a nut job, Bud."

"And that's your professional psychologist's opinion?"

"Sometimes, Bud, I revert to the vernacular so that non-psychologists like you can understand what I'm talking about. So, the full two barrels of assessment are: she's judgmental, closed-minded, and unused to male attention. She might have had a boyfriend or two when young, but nothing serious – not for them, anyway…though maybe for her. She's controlling, passive-aggressive, and repressed – in every way. Do you want me to go on?"

Bud asked pointedly, "How about the fact that she's grieving her dead sister and maybe can't see the wood for the trees?"

I deflated. "You're right. Sorry. I'm being too harsh. Too…judgmental." I smiled guiltily at him. "She's operating under duress, and her sense of perspective is likely to be way off. This might be unusual behavior for her…but, then again, it might not. That's part of the problem; everything's coming at us from her point of view, and we don't know how accurate, or wide of the mark, that is."

Bud finally stopped rubbing his head. "Talking about wide of the mark – what was all that about you being a marketing professor? You could have given me the heads-up on that one."

I shrugged. "I made a split-second decision, Bud. It might be too late for you to be anonymous here, and – given what you've done for a living – I dare say it was always likely that wouldn't have worked anyway." Bud nodded his agreement. "But there's no reason for folks to know that I'm a criminal psychologist. That's not the sort of person a murderer usually opens up to, is it? At least folks might be less on their guard with a marketing professor than they are with a retired cop."

Bud grinned. "When she asked about that old professor of hers? She nearly caught you there, eh?"

Again, I shrugged. "I never thought of that. I'll be better prepared when I meet the other suspects; I'll just claim to be bad with names. Also, I'll draw on my time back in London when I worked for that advertising agency, and waffle on about return on investment and brand building…if I have to talk about anything to do with marketing at all. After all, it's unlikely, right? I mean, we're both going to be trying to direct our conversations towards possible motives, opportunities, and all that. Right?"

Bud shifted uncomfortably.

"Come on, Bud. That's why we're here. Well…there's the food, too, of course."

"Diet on the backburner this weekend?"

I patted my tummy. "I'll start again on Tuesday."

"Good luck with that." He smiled indulgently.

I dragged my thoughts away from the long days filled with little more than Greek yogurt and cauliflower soup that I'd have to endure to make up for my forthcoming indulgences, and refocused on our current situation.

"Listen, Bud, about Ellen's notes: the physical descriptions and the factual backgrounds – you know, who does what and lives where – might be useful, but I don't think we should rely on any of the character assessments she's written. Or maybe I should just call them what they are – character assassinations. People might not have had a bad word to say about her dead sister, but she certainly has a lot of dreadful things to say about everyone we're about to meet. Something I didn't have a chance to comment upon before we got here was that she said nothing at all about Annette in the notes, other than, as I just mentioned, that no one ever had a bad word to say about her. Now, if, as you say, she also told you that everyone loved Annette, I don't quite know what she expects us – sorry, *you* – to do. If she's telling the truth, then why would anyone want Annette dead? Well, other than this Raj Pinder, the bloke who inherited half of

Ellen's family business, which sounds like a possible motive…if he knew about the bequest, of course."

I suspected that Bud was desperate to gloat, but he didn't.

I continued, "Yes, okay, I admit it's not looking too fruitful on the motive front, but it's early days. Maybe we'll meet someone with clear homicidal tendencies at the party tonight. But…I really do want to clean up, and I'll need to take my time getting ready; I'm sure that marketing professors are well aware of the importance of making a good first impression."

But stretched. "Yep, me too. I could do with a long, hot shower to ease the stiffness in my legs and back a bit. In my own shower, of course. In my very own bathroom." He smiled. Wickedly. "You got all that, eh? The separate rooms?"

"Yes, Bud. Hence my assessment that she's 'repressed'."

The question of rooms, and sharing, hadn't even crossed my mind until Ellen had mentioned it; I'd been thinking that the delights of the weekend would be food, drink, and an investigation into a probable murder, in that order.

I added, "I'm fine with separate rooms. Then I can take as much time in *my* bathroom as I like. Okay with you?"

Bud nodded, still grinning. "You'd better come across the corridor and get your bag, if that's where it is. Then I can jump in the shower and get ready for this thing we're going to tonight."

After Bud eventually carried my bag into my room, I brushed my teeth, twice, and gargled with Listerine until my eyes watered. It was the only alternative to having a cigarette, which wasn't an option.

Why did I promise Bud I wouldn't smoke all weekend?

With my fussing and primping completed – which seemed to take forever, largely due to my inability to patiently apply mascara – Bud knocked on my door at five-twenty-five, with a warm smile on his face, and his arms open wide.

"You look great, and you smell good, too," he said, reaching out to hug me. "Give me a sniff of that Cait Juice."

I love it that you call my Coco Chanel perfume "Cait Juice".

"You brush up exceptionally well, too," I replied, as I tried to avoid getting my lipstick on his jacket.

He looked so handsome in his dark navy suit and crisp white shirt.

In an effort to be a bit dressier than usual I'd decided to keep my hair down, rather than tied back, which is my normal thing. I'd done my best with curling tongs, half a container of mousse – which was supposed to give volume to fine hair – and enough hairspray to jeopardize the entire ozone layer. But I wasn't happy with the outcome. Something which Bud quickly deduced.

He smiled. "Your hair looks great when it's down like that, Cait. And you look lovely in that gown. It's very flattering."

"It's plain black, with this over thingy to hide my arms, and you've seen it before," I replied.

Bud pulled up my chin and looked into my eyes. "Caitlin Morgan. You're gorgeous. I love you. And you need to learn how to accept a compliment."

I smiled back up at him. "I love you too. And that you think I'm gorgeous means the world to me." All of which was true. "But you have to bear in mind that I'm still getting used to receiving compliments. You know I've been on my own since Angus's days, and he was a master at stripping away any confidence I might have had in my appearance. So…I'll try to be more gracious." We kissed. Gently.

"Are you two coming down?" Ellen Newman called to us from the bottom of the stairs. She sounded much cheerier than before.

"We're on our way," I replied jovially.

Downstairs, Bud and I followed Ellen into the lounge area that was the mirror image of the breakfasting room where we'd enjoyed our soup. Now, the earlier beefy aroma had been replaced by something more oniony, herby, and porky, yet still pleasant…and my tummy rumbled.

We settled into comfy chairs, and I opened with, "Thanks for taking the time to write all those notes – they've been most helpful. I don't think there's anything else we need to know right now except, maybe, one or two things."

Bud was on the edge of his seat, probably worried about what I was going to say.

"Ask anything," replied Ellen, who seemed to think that a short, forest-green velvet skirt, with a too-vivid orange silk blouse, comprised formal wear.

I could tell by the way she was eyeing us that she felt uncomfortable about something, so I thought it best to follow my instincts. "Is something wrong?" I asked.

Ellen wriggled in her seat. "Not really," she replied, clearly not meaning it.

Bud quickly followed my lead. "Are you sure?"

Ellen sighed. "It's just that I thought that you'd be the one helping me, Bud. Not that I wouldn't want your help, too, Cait…but Bud's the one with the policing background – it's his experience that counts here. That's why I asked him to come. When I was here earlier, you were the one asking all the questions, Cait. And now, with all due respect and all that, it seems like you're going to do the same thing again." She all but glared at me.

Ex-cop versus a marketing professor? Fair point, Ellen.

Bud used what I recognised as his "calming voice" when he replied, "I know what you mean, Ellen, and I also understand that it's my opinion you're really interested in. But I told Cait she could be involved, and she's often discussed other cases with me. Besides, she was a real help, reading your notes aloud to me as we drove here, so she's as up on the facts as I am. Possibly more so, because I was concentrating on the road. In any case, two brains are always better than one, right? You see, while you value my professional input, I know the value of Cait's amateur approach. It helps me see things from a different point of view."

Ellen nodded grudgingly, and I suspected that Bud was beginning to enjoy painting me as a complete outsider in the world of crime detection.

"So," continued Bud, immediately comfortable in his role as head-of-investigation, "would it be possible to see the coroner's report, your sister's will, and at least a copy of her suicide note?"

The words hung heavily in the air. The clock on the wall tocked away five seconds.

Stop counting them, Cait.

I wondered if Ellen had counted too, because she spoke exactly on the sixth beat. "I have all that at home, not with me. But, of course, I remember her note word for word. Do you want me to recite it?"

Both Bud and I nodded.

Ellen cleared her throat and began. "It said, 'Ellen, It's no use, I can't do it anymore. I can't go on. It just won't work. I can't do my job anymore. And if I can't do my job perfectly, then there's no point to any of it. I'm sorry. I know you'll miss me. But that's it. I'm done. Love, always, Annette'. And then were three x's. You know, kisses. That's it." She looked at both of us as though seeking our approval.

"Good job, Ellen," said Bud, smiling sadly. "That can't have been easy for you. Those words must hurt."

Ellen's downcast eyes suggested Bud was right.

He added gently, "Were you…are you sure it was Annette's handwriting?"

Ellen looked up, seemingly surprised. "Oh she didn't write it. Annette never wrote anything. Her handwriting had always been dreadful, so she always typed everything."

Bud urged, "But she signed it, at least?"

"Oh yes, she'd signed it," replied Ellen calmly. "Of course she signed it."

Bud and I exchanged a glance.

"So are you sure it was Annette's signature?" It was out of my mouth before I could stop myself.

"Well I was at first…but then I wasn't," was Ellen's less than illuminating response.

"So you mean...?" I didn't dare continue.

Ellen seemed to sense my confusion, adding, "At first I thought it was Annette's signature, but then I realized later on that of course it couldn't have been, because there's no way she'd have killed herself, so there's no reason why she'd have signed a suicide note. So it can't be Annette's signature, you see?"

Count to ten, Cait.

"So it looked like her signature, but now you're sure it wasn't?" I pressed.

"Yes. No. It can't be." Ellen seemed to be done.

I can feel the will to live deserting me.

"Okay, so, one more thing then," added Bud, "could you dig out an example of your sister's signature that you know is definitely hers? Then we can compare them when you show us the actual note."

Ellen nodded.

I managed to give Bud a quick kick. Luckily, he worked out what it meant and said, "We do have a few more questions, but I promised Cait she could ask them. You don't mind, do you?"

I took Ellen's shrug to mean that she was now more relaxed with the idea that I would have an involvement in the case too, so I pounced, smiling sweetly as I spoke. "Your notes say that Raj Pinder has been the vintner at your winery since shortly after your sister's death almost a year ago – but he was previously the vintner at SoulVine Wines, right?" Ellen nodded. "And I understand that Raj now owns half your vineyard because Annette willed her half of the business to him, and that, furthermore, you're pleased she did that. Is that also correct?" Again, Ellen nodded. "So, my question is this: did you know about Annette's will before she died? Had you discussed her intention to bequeath her half of the vineyard to Raj at all?"

Ellen smiled, "Oh silly me, I guess I didn't put that in the notes. I'm sorry, it's just that everyone here knows what happened. A week before Annette died, she changed her will, but we only all found out about that when the will was read, and that was weeks later. So, no, I wasn't expecting it. No one was."

Ellen sounded unnaturally calm as she announced that she'd been robbed of what I'd have imagined she must have always assumed was her birthright.

Bud couldn't hide his surprise at Ellen's delivery of this explanation; I could see his hand begin to move towards his now perfectly combed hair. I shook my head and rolled my eyes at him. He sat on his hand.

"I'm sorry, Ellen," he said, sympathetically. "That must have come as a shock for you. I guess you expected that the whole business would be yours?"

Ellen shifted her shoulders. "Well, of course I did. Mom and Poppa built it from nothing. They imported the vines, they prepared the ground and planted it, and then it was me and Annette who got the real benefits of the crops. And we were able to make wonderful wines because of Annette's special gift…that nose of hers. So, yes, I did think it would all be mine. But Raj is a good and kind man, and he's an excellent vintner. He hasn't got as good a nose as Annette had, but he took silver behind her golds for the three years he was with SoulVine Wines, so he's not only the best in the area, but he's just about the best in North America. I'm glad to have him. Without him joining the business, I'd have had to find a vintner from overseas, or use someone from Canada or the USA who isn't as good as Raj. I'm so lucky that Annette thought of it. When Raj found out about what her will said, he left SoulVine Wines immediately. He couldn't work for anyone other than the company in which he's a fifty percent owner, of course. And we get along really well. He has a wonderful vision for the business. I think that Mount Dewdney has a fabulous future ahead of it, and Raj and I will work toward it, together."

I could see Bud shifting in his chair, and recognized his tone when he spoke. It was as though he was breaking bad news…the worst possible news…to someone. Sadly, I'd heard him use the same tone several times before, when I'd been at his side during murder cases we'd worked on together.

He said, "Ellen, do you think that Annette might have planned the whole thing? That she was feeling depressed…had made the decision to end her life…then set things up for you in a way that would be good for the business after she'd gone?"

Ellen stood, her fists clenched. "No! Annette wouldn't have killed herself. I thought you believed me, Bud."

I used my own interpretation of Bud's calming voice when I said, "Bud's just playing devil's advocate, right?"

"Yes…Cait's right," he lied. "I had to be sure…before I go digging about. And, obviously, you're quite certain. So that's good. Well…not good. You know what I mean."

Then he, too, stood and announced, "I'm sorry. I hope you don't think we're rude, Ellen, but Cait hasn't quite kicked the smoking habit yet, and I know she'll be hoping to have a quick puff before we leave for the event. We'll just head to the smoking porch for a few minutes, if that's alright?"

What?

Never one to turn down the chance to have a smoke without Bud nagging me to stub out, I was out of my seat as quickly as possible, and slapped a guilty smile on my face by way of cover.

"You should speak to Lizzie Jackson about that smoking, Cait," called Ellen as I headed toward the front door. "She's helping Serendipity Soul to give up, and she got Marcel du Bois to stop, which, given who he is and how attached he was to his cigarettes – and I mean that literally – is quite something. So maybe she has some redeeming qualities, after all."

"Thanks, I'll bear that in mind," I replied, while pulling open the front door before heading off to the smoking porch as fast as my feet could take me, leaving Bud trailing behind.

Even before I got there I was lighting up.

Evening purses should always be big enough to carry emergency smokes.

"So," I inhaled as I spoke, "interesting, right? An amended will, and a typed suicide note…with a possible fake signature. It all points to murder."

"No, Cait, it's a real suicide note, signed by Annette, but read by a sister who can't forgive herself for not recognizing her own sibling's anguish. As I just said to Ellen, if Annette had been planning to kill herself, she might well have had the foresight to make sure that the next best vintner for the job would be bound to take it because he'd be part-owner of the winery. Besides," he added somewhat grumpily, "look…there's no way anyone could get up to this garage we're standing beside – where Ellen found her sister – without those nosey neighbors at the bottom of the hill seeing them approach. It's definitely a suicide, I'm even more certain now that I can see exactly where it happened."

"And I'm even more certain that it was murder," I replied, cockily puffing toward Bud.

"Why?" he sounded completely mystified. "What are you hearing or seeing that I'm not?"

"Who stood to gain by Annette's death, Bud? Ask yourself that. Not Ellen, she's lost control of the family business. But this Raj character does. In Ellen's notes, he's almost the only one about whom she didn't write a bad word. I reckon he's trying to worm his way into her affections, and that he's succeeding. It sounds like he's as good as running things now – it's all about 'his vision'. I don't get the impression Ellen would argue against him if he said black was white. It's a pretty good motive, Bud, you have to admit it. He sounds dodgy to me."

Bud was tapping his foot. "Dodgy, eh? Is that another of your 'technical terms'?" He sighed. "Finished that thing yet?"

I chided playfully, "Hang on there – you're the one who used my addiction to give us a chance to vent in private about Ellen. Don't you go venting at me instead."

Bud tutted, and shrugged in submission. "Sorry."

"Me too," I said, puffing hard.

The chemicals are making me feel quite light-headed.

Ellen emerged from the house and made her way to the waiting taxi. I ground the remains of my cigarette into the sparklingly clean ashtray that stood on the plastic table tucked beneath the roof of the porch.

"Time to go?" I asked, knowing the answer.

"Time to go," replied Bud. "You'd better be sharp tonight, Cait; you know how much I value your skills, and we'll need them all. You can read people when you meet them and compare your impressions with the notes that Ellen gave us. And you can use your wonderful photographic memory to conjure up the events of the evening for us to discuss at leisure afterwards. Oh…and let's not forget…you can make me proud to be the man who's bringing the best-looking woman in the world to the party."

"Thanks, Bud. That's kind of you."

"No, it's not 'kind' of me, I really mean it."

"Oh, but my hair…"

"Oh, good grief, it looks great."

"Sorry. Like I said, I haven't had a lot of experience at receiving compliments."

"Well, get used to it, or I'll stop doling them out."

I sighed. "Okay. Thanks for the hair thing. Let's just hope it stays where I've put it."

Bud tutted loudly and began to walk away.

I cantered after him. "I'll be good. Promise." I added, "Let's try and have a nice time, eh? Even though we're sort of working. I'm looking forward to the food. Is that bad of me?"

Bud didn't answer as he opened the taxi's door.

Gamay Noir

The "Cocktails and Canapés Soirée" launch event for the Moveable Feast wasn't quite what I'd expected. For some reason, I'd imagined an elegantly attired gathering bubbling along wittily, in something akin to the great hall of an historic English manor house. What I got was a small, almost rag-tag group of people rattling around under the beautiful but yawning wood-beamed glass atrium of a very modern building in downtown Kelowna.

To be fair, the organizers had installed massive voile curtains to contain about half the room, and had provided dim lighting instead of overhead fluorescents, but our voices floated up to the glass that arced above us, then bounced back. Most people tried to talk in hushed tones, as though in a cathedral.

I declined a cocktail in favor of a glass of fruity *gamay noir* – one of Ellen's; she'd provided all the wine for the function. It had a good body, but wasn't too heavy to drink for an entire evening. And the canapés were exquisite: tiny little martini glasses filled with cold, savory soups – the strawberry and basil was particularly wonderful; tender local meats, marinated in tongue-tingling herbs or rubbed with nose-tickling spices, presented on elaborate bamboo skewers; little pastry packages full of flavor that burst in my mouth with cheesy, meaty, fishy, or mushroomy delights. *Heavenly.*

Having taken the edge off my appetite, and having managed to grab a second glass of wine, I knew that Sammy Soul was high on the list of people I wanted to meet…but for personal reasons rather than murderous ones. He'd supplied parts of the soundtrack to my teen years; his wailing guitar riffs had sounded wonderfully raw and dangerous to a young girl listening to her transistor radio under the sheets long after bedtime, in Swansea.

I'd have recognized him even without Ellen's notes, because he hadn't changed a bit – except that he was now in his seventies, was almost bald above his trademark ponytail, had filled out somewhat, and his complexion was ruddier than it had been. Otherwise, it seemed that Sammy Soul had decided to completely ignore the ageing process; he was dressed in tight snakeskin jeans, with a magenta silk shirt – straining at its buttons – and more earrings than you would think it's possible for the human ear to carry. The earring thing was helped by the fact that, as with most older men, his lobes had lengthened; it seemed he'd taken this as a sign to add even more gold hoops. My heart sank a little when I saw him; my youthful idol had become a pastiche of himself.

After Ellen had introduced us, I reached out to shake his hand. When he replied with a peace sign and drawled, "Yeah, man," in a slightly nasal voice – higher-pitched than I'd imagined – my heart sank even further. Then he slapped Bud on the arm and added, "Ex-cop. Wow, man. Lost your wife? Downer."

Never meet your heroes. Indeed.

Could this sad, pathetic figure, clinging to past glories, have wanted to kill Annette Newman? First, I'd have to find a motive, and I didn't hold out much hope on that front.

"Hey, meet the missus," said Sammy Soul as he waved in the general direction of a woman's back. "Hey guys, this is Suzie, my Soul-Mate…ha, ha."

I saw the back of a short, slim but curvaceous, beautifully coiffed blonde, wearing an immaculately cut, bronzy pantsuit, and towering, leopard-print Louboutin heels. Effortlessly holding a martini glass, her perfectly manicured left hand was bedecked with umpteen carats of bling and sported long, curving nails encrusted with diamanté.

When Suzie Soul turned, what I saw shocked me; the woman had to be well into her sixties – her neck was a dead giveaway –

with the cat-like features that scream bad plastic surgery. She was caked in layers of carefully applied but woefully obvious makeup, and, as if to add insult to injury, her lips had been plumped to alarming proportions and were the color of dried blood. I tried to hide my alarm as she flashed a perfect porcelain smile at me and extended her decorated hand in my direction. As she allowed me to shake her fingertips, she was looking at Bud.

Eating Bud alive, with her eyes?

I bristled.

Bud beamed.

"Hi, always happy to meet friends of Ellen's," she purred in gravelly tones. "I didn't catch y'rrrr name." She drawled provocatively, and directly at Bud.

"That's 'cos I didn't throw it, Babe," replied Sammy Soul, laughing too loudly at his own joke. "He's an ex-cop, would you believe, Babe? Doesn't look like any cop I know. And, jeez, there've been a few over the years."

"So pleased to meet you, uh…?" As she waited for Bud to respond with his name, Suzie Soul actually ran her tongue along the edge of her upper teeth.

Down Suzie.

Bud, ever polite, took her extended hand and said, "Bud. Bud Anderson."

Are you blushing? Good grief – so un-Bud-like.

"And what brings you to these parts, Bu-ud?" Suzie Soul was in full-on-flirt mode, tilting her head and fluttering her false eyelashes so hard they were almost creating a breeze.

Grit your teeth and smile, Cait.

She cooed, coquettishly, "Have you come to arrest Sammy for making his oh-so delicious cannabis wine? Oh, please don't, Bu-ud. It's lovely wine, whatever that nasty sister of hers, Annette, might have said about it."

Interesting.

So no one ever had ever had a bad word to say about Annette, eh? Well, here was one woman who did. Suzie had uttered Annette's name with true hatred...and it sounded as though her husband was, in fact, already making cannabis wine.

Very interesting.

"No," replied Bud, "All my arresting days are behind me."

Sammy said, "His wife got shot, Babe. Shot dead. That's how he met Ellen. They're, like, 'death buddies' or something."

I judged that Suzie Soul was more disappointed that Bud had relinquished his grasp on her talons than that he'd lost his wife.

She proved me right with a throaty, "So...you're single?"

I pounced. "No, he's not. He's with me."

Bud's head snapped around in my direction.

Sammy Soul shrugged and said, "Oh yeah, Babe, he's with her." It sounded as though this thought was occurring to him for the first time.

The ageing rocker's ageing groupie wife looked me up and down, slowly and unkindly. Then she tried to curl one of her unnaturally full lips, and said coolly, "Oh really? I wonder why."

She turned on her thousand-dollar heels and walked away purring, "See you boys later – especially you, Bu-ud."

Sammy Soul was grinning like a fool when he observed, "Hasn't changed a bit in nearly forty years, my Suzie. That's how long we've been together."

He was clearly besotted, though how he'd put up with her for that long, I didn't know. He became even more pathetic in my eyes, for letting himself be walked all over by that...

"I'm sure she hasn't," remarked Bud cryptically, cutting across my less than charitable thoughts. "And that's a fantastic marriage to have had...especially in your business, I guess."

"Sure is," Sammy replied, still beaming. "Met her when she was in her twenties, then married her just before we had

Serendipity, our beautiful, magical girl. But, hey, you know man, she's not just the mother of my child, she's a forgiving woman. And I'm a forgiving man." Sammy's eyes gazed into the nothingness ahead of him. "Forgiveness is important, right, man? You gotta forgive to be forgiven, you know? Gotta forgive. I'd forgive that woman anything."

"And I bet you often have," I said. Aloud, as it turned out.

Bud glared at me.

Sammy just nodded. He looked resigned. "Sure have, man, sure have. Man – I'd even forgive her icing someone, if it was, like, to save my hide, or something." He seemed to be in his own little world, then it was as though he snapped back to our shared reality. "Not that she would, cop-guy, not that she would. Ha, ha! Hey, gotta go. Gotta see my man Grant Jackson over there." He waved at no one in particular, then ambled off in the direction of a short, incredibly thin man wearing a burgundy-colored Nehru jacket.

I wanted to take my chance to have a few private words with Bud, but he was quicker off the mark than me.

"What do you think?" he whispered.

I dared, "She should have spent more money on a better plastic surgeon?"

Bud shoved me and looked shocked, "Oh stop it, you devil. Be serious." Then he broke into a smile. "Oh, Cait – you do make me laugh." And he did.

Your laughter is the most wonderful sound, Bud.

He leaned toward me as though to plant a kiss on my cheek, but Ellen's imminent return meant I pulled away and hissed "Stop it," then giggled like a naughty schoolgirl.

Ellen was beaming – *maybe a little too brightly?* – when she rejoined us.

"They're a real couple of characters, eh?" she whispered, nodding her head in the general direction of the Souls. "Do you think one of them did it?" Her eyes gleamed conspiratorially in the dim lights.

I thought about the way that Ellen had described Sammy and Suzie Soul in her notes: she'd been spot-on with her physical descriptions – though rather kind about Suzie, I thought – and I was beginning to wonder if she wasn't far off the mark when it came to her assessments of their characters, too.

"They could have done it together, you know," she continued, her intensity unabated. "Annette said she didn't trust Sammy when he was negotiating for *marechal foch* grapes from us. Said he was manipulative, and bossy."

Sammy Soul manipulative? Bossy? Really?

I asked, "You sell grapes to SoulVine Wines?"

"Oh yes," replied Ellen, as though it were the most natural thing in the world. "Mom and Poppa started by only growing grapes to sell to other people, which is why we have some of the more unusual varieties, like the *foch.* We have *malbec* and *zweigelt* too. It took them some time to start to make our own Anen Wines…they were more interested in the crops, than in winemaking. Even now, there are some years when we have more grapes than we need of several varieties, so we'll sell them off to other wineries for them to use in their own products. Of course, we keep everything we want for ourselves first, though some people would like us to be actively growing on their part… like SoulVine Wines, for example. Sammy argued that we could apportion part of our crop to him each year before we even knew what the yield and quality were going to be. Annette said no…that Anen would always come first. That's why he's playing around with all these crazy ideas like cannabis wine, and wine in guitar-shaped bottles. It's all just marketing stuff. You know, the sort of thing you do."

Ellen made it sound as though it were my fault that Sammy Soul was jeopardizing the purity of winemaking. It seemed that choosing the fake role of a marketing professor was going to bring me in for some hearty criticism.

Who knew?

Ellen was pulling at my wrist. "I know Raj can't have had anything to do with Annette's death, but I do so want you to meet him." She turned and looked across the room. "Oh no, that stupid Serendipity is talking to him now. Oh well, let's butt in – he won't mind." And we were off, with Bud following meekly behind, and me trying to not spill my drink.

"Raj, this is Bud and his partner, Cait. Bud, Cait – Raj Pinder…*my* partner," she grinned.

We all shook hands.

As if an afterthought, Ellen added, "And this is Serendipity Soul – you just met her parents, Sammy and Suzie."

We continued with the polite greetings.

Both Raj Pinder and Serendipity Soul were slim and well formed, and both towered over me…which immediately made me feel short, and very wide. They made a handsome couple; and couple they were, I was immediately certain about that. Their body language, the way they related to each other, literally screamed "lovers" at me, but, from what I'd gathered from Ellen's notes, they weren't known to be an item.

At least…Ellen doesn't believe them to be so.

Raj Pinder had finely chiseled features, latte-colored, even-toned skin, and well-styled ink-black hair, with a few strands of pure white threaded through it here and there, as befitted a man approaching forty. He wore his expensive suit and snowy open-necked shirt very well indeed. And – surprising me – he spoke with the flat tones you only develop if you've grown up in the north of England.

"Hello Bud and Cait," he said, his voice strong, yet soft. "Pleased to meet you. As Ellen said" – he nodded first at Ellen, then Serendipity – "this is Serendipity Soul, a very talented chef and someone I enjoyed working with for several years. In fact," here he patted his annoyingly flat midriff, the way slim people do when they think they've gained an ounce, "I'm only just now losing all them pounds she made me gain, feeding me at her restaurant every day." They smiled at each other.

Can't Ellen see that these two are a couple?

Serendipity couldn't have differed more from her parents, both physically and, it seemed, in terms of personality: she was tall – maybe five-ten – had long, flowing, lustrous black hair, dark eyes, and a pale complexion that suited her perfectly. A rose-tinted lip-stain and a hint of mascara were all she needed to look stunning, yet fresh. She was clearly a woman who felt totally comfortable in her own body and her surroundings, and had a calm, unflappable demeanor that I suspected would stand her in good stead in the heat and noise of a busy kitchen.

"A pleasure." She shook my hand with hers – short nails, perfectly clean, a strong grip, quite a low voice. Nice.

I said, "Hello, lovely to meet you."

"Is that a Welsh accent I detect there, Cait?" asked Raj Pinder affably.

"Yes, it is," I replied, smiling. "Swansea. And you?"

"Aye, well, there's no hiding mine, is there? Bradford."

"Do you miss England…or Bradford?" I asked.

People always ask me if I miss Wales, so I'll get in first.

Raj smiled broadly, his teeth white and even. "No, to be honest, I don't. But then, how could you compare this place with Bradford, or even anywhere else in England? I mean, don't get me wrong, Bradford's not a bad place, in fact, it's got a lot going for it, but it's not like the Okanagan. It's like a little bit of heaven here. When I first came to Canada to visit me mum's cousin and help out with his blueberry harvest in the Lower Mainland, I couldn't get over how big and open, and far apart, everything were. Same for you, were it?"

Raj...you're quite engaging.

I smiled, thinking back to my arrival in Vancouver. "Yes, you're right. I still grapple with it. The cities here are like tiny dots on the map...and isn't it amazing how even some suburban streets just end in wilderness? The emptiness is magnificent. But then, the UK has almost twice the population of Canada, with less than three percent of the land mass, so I suppose we're bound to feel differently in our new home...there really is that much more space. I love it."

"Aye, me too. It's grand." He looked wistfully into the distance.

"Do you get back to the UK much?" I asked.

That's the other question people always ask me.

Raj shrugged. "I try to get there a couple of times a year. You know, family and all that. Don't want to miss the little 'uns growing up. And you?"

"No family there, these days, but Wales will always be my 'home', even if no one's keeping the actual home fires burning for me. Blood is blood, after all."

"Aye, that it is," Raj grinned.

I was disappointed. Having come to the soirée thinking that Raj Pinder was the one man with a strong motive to kill Annette, I found myself warming to him almost immediately. Surely this pleasant, urbane, and apparently talented, man couldn't have murdered Annette Newman. I pulled myself together: some of the most murderous people in history have looked innocent...you really cannot judge a person by their outward appearance, nor by how they present and project themselves. You have to observe them, know and understand what you're seeing, analyze it, and then dig beneath their skin, or their costume. I decided to do just that.

Raj had a good reason to kill Annette – to get his hands on half of the Mount Dewdney Family Estate Winery – and I needed to follow up on my initial instincts, however pleasant he might seem.

"So how's it working out for you, Raj, suddenly owning half a winery?" I asked. Quite out of the blue it seemed, judging by everyone's expression; I'd been thinking, not listening to the small talk they were all exchanging.

Raj seemed to not know what to say, so Ellen answered for him. "He's loving it, aren't you, Raj. We have such fun, don't we." Her comments weren't questions, they were statements.

"We certainly do, Ellen, we certainly do," he replied.

Reminds me of Laurel and Hardy.

"Raj is in even earlier than I am," Ellen added brightly, "then he scoots off to the gym to keep himself in shape in the afternoon, don't you? That's what he says – 'I'm scooting off to the gym now, Ellen'." She giggled.

"I certainly do, Ellen. I certainly do."

Definitely Laurel and Hardy.

I tried again. "Was it a surprise to hear about your inheritance, Raj?"

"That it were, Cait, aye. Maybe Ellen has told you how it all happened?" Both Bud and I nodded, with appropriate expressions on our faces. "Very sad," he added. "Annette were a wonderful woman. Full of life. Extremely talented, and worked hard at it too. I admired her effort, and envied her skills. She beat me at every competition, you know?"

"Except once," interrupted Serendipity. "That tasting competition in Sonoma, just a month or so before she…" The poor young woman realized she'd talked herself into an awkward corner.

"Aye, but just that once." Raj jumped in and rescued her. "But, other than that? Well – she had one of the best noses in the business. Such a loss. Her death came as a shock to all of us, of course." He smiled sympathetically toward Ellen, who dropped her eyes. "And then there were the will. No messing, you could have knocked me down with a feather. And that's the truth. I told Ellen at the time she should contest it. I mean, Annette's balance of mind, and all that? Not that I'm not grateful for the chance, of course, because it's not often that a vintner gets to part-own an 'estate vineyard', where the winery owns all the vineyards that grow all its grapes."

Ellen's gazing at him...star-struck.

Raj didn't notice Ellen's interest, and chattered on happily. "Ellen and Annette's parents were true visionaries. They bought just the right pieces of land, in all the right places, to be able to grow the very best of the different types of grapes that give us...well, just about the widest choice in the area. It's an honor. A great chance to do something...meaningful." I judged that he'd chosen his word carefully; he gave it a reverent emphasis. "I owe it to Annette's memory, and the memory of her parents who started the vineyard and the winemaking, to make sure that I do the very best I can."

Raj's comments made me think again about how devastated Ellen must have been upon hearing her sister's wishes; it would have been bad enough to lose her sister, but then to lose half the family business too? Now it wasn't Ellen's family business anymore. Annette had handed something that should have rightfully passed to her sister, to a stranger – an outsider...a relative newcomer to the area. After all, what's three years or so in a place? Not much.

True, Raj had almost as good a nose as Annette's...and maybe she'd honestly thought that the business wouldn't have survived as well without him. But it was a bold, and potentially hurtful, move to make. I realized I'd have to try to get to understand Annette a lot better than I did, or I'd never know why she'd changed her will...and I was certain that changing it had something to do with her death.

"Of course you'll do your best," Ellen gushed at Raj. "I know you will. You're a good, and talented, man, Raj Pinder. And I know, now, that Annette did the right thing." She began to address the whole group. "At the time, it puzzled me a great deal, but Annette knew that Raj would be good for the business, and so he is. The best possible person for the job. But it really was a shock, coming right after her death…which is a silly thing to say, because that's when wills are read, but you know what I mean. I don't think I handled the meeting at the lawyers' offices too well, and I'll always be sorry for that, Raj," she added.

What does she mean?

"What do you mean?" I asked, sensibly enough.

Bud glared at me.

"Oh, it were all very understandable," said Raj gently. "Of course, Ellen hadn't come to terms with Annette's death, and then she had to face this other shock, so soon afterwards. You lost it a bit for a while there, didn't you Ellen?" Ellen nodded and sipped her drink. "But it were all summat and nowt. Right? Storm in a teacup, luv," he said, his accent thickening by the second. "And, when you calmed down, you were just a darlin'. Worried about how I'd manage to tell Sammy that I'd have to resign, weren't you?" Ellen nodded, now staring into an empty glass. "And she comes right back to SoulVine Wines with me and tells him herself, didn't you? Said Sammy would have to understand that I couldn't be working for him for a moment longer, and that she were there to help me gather up me bits and pieces and get me out of there that very minute. Well, that took the wind out of his sails, right enough. And there I were, at Ellen's place, before the day were out."

"We were sorry to see you go," said Serendipity quietly.

I bet you were.

She added quickly, "But it's great to see you already achieving so much."

"What's that?" I asked.

Once again Ellen answered on Raj's behalf. "Raj was with us for the last winter season and we both think...no, we both *know*...that Raj has created a winning new wine for us. Obviously, we won't be truly certain for some time, because it won't go into competition for years yet, but the signs are excellent. Excellent."

"Thanks," Raj said, smiling. "I've called the wine 'Annette'. It's a pinot noir ice wine, and it's going to be fabulous. Dark berries, honey, caramel...it'll be a great hit, I'm sure. One hundred cases of magic, in honor of Annette."

Ellen said, "And at a hundred dollars a bottle, it'll be a good way to raise funds for the scholarship I've set up in her name at VORC. Oh Cait, I forgot, that's where you teach, right?"

I shook my head and shrugged, puzzled. "I'm sorry, do you mean the University of Vancouver?"

"Yes," she replied, "VORC, at UVan. My *alma mater*." She grinned.

Bud asked, "What's 'VORC', Ellen?"

Thank you, Bud.

"It's the Viticulture and Oenology Research Centre. Surely you've heard of it, Cait? I know they do a lot of work on brand building with your business school there."

Here we go again...

"Maybe I've heard something about it, Ellen," I lied, "but there's a good number of us teaching at the school and we don't all get involved with each of the inter-departmental programs that exist. Probably my colleagues who specialize in consumer branding are involved. I'm more business-to-business, myself."

"Oh, really?" Serendipity sounded excited. "Could I maybe pick your brains at some point? I'm developing a range of peanut-free sauces for catering companies – not selling direct to the consumer you know? I don't really know what I'm looking for in terms of advice and so forth. A general chat through the whole field would be really useful, if you could spare the time?" She smiled a warm, hopeful smile.

"Of course," I said cheerily. "But not at one of the events. It would spoil the food." I forced a chuckle.

Oh good grief, how deep is this hole I'm digging for myself?

Bud looked alarmed, and chivalrously threw himself in front of the train that was hurtling toward me. "Oh, come on now guys, let's leave all this shoptalk and enjoy the food, eh? That's what we're here for after all, right?" His eyes scanned for a server bearing canapés somewhere in the vicinity. He spotted one. "Hey, over here," he called, rather too loudly. "I wonder if we could have some of those..." he peered at the tray, "...those...things. They look great."

He took a black porcelain Chinese rice spoon, laden with a mound of tiny white pearls, topped with a delicate grating of something red, and a sliver of something green. He poked it straight into his mouth.

The young server looked rather taken aback by Bud's actions, then calmly announced, "It's snail caviar, marinated in fresh, local herbs. It's often referred to as 'pearls of Aphrodite' because of its aphrodisiac powers – you know, like oysters." She failed to hide a smile as Bud tried not to show his disgust and embarrassment. "It's supposed to taste quite mushroomy," she said, almost giggling. She bent her head closer to our group. "It didn't taste like that to me when I tried it earlier on, though...it tasted like dirt. Enjoy."

She took the tray to her next victims, and the three of us who'd taken a spoon, but hadn't yet eaten, looked at Bud for guidance. Serendipity had declined a spoon.

I wonder why.

"She's right," said Bud, when he could. "Dirt. But not bad dirt. It's not gritty. It's just not – well, it didn't taste of mushrooms. But you should try it. Especially you, Cait. I know how you love this gourmet food, right? And I'm guessing that snail eggs are real expensive, so this might be your only chance."

Oh Bud, I'm surprised you didn't just shout, "Dare you."

Despite the fact that my last close encounter with snails had involved the sudden death of an old boss of mine, I popped the spoon into my mouth, and let the eggs slip onto my tongue, where I squished them, like "ordinary" caviar. They were lovely: soft and yielding, each tiny little globe popped with a burst of woodland…not quite truffle and not quite mushroom…flavor. I also noted hints of basil, tarragon, and cilantro. I knew what Bud and the server meant by "dirt", but I quite liked it. It was certainly an experience I'd never had before…though one serving was probably enough.

"It's delicious – go ahead," I said, aware that all eyes were on me. Ellen and Raj popped their spoons into their mouths, and I watched their expressions.

Ellen pulled a face. "Yuk – not nice."

Raj took a little more time and, when his mouth was empty said, "Sorry," to Serendipity, "not my cup of tea. But I'm sure lots of folk'll like it."

Bud and I exchanged puzzled glances.

"It's one of the three canapés I contributed tonight," explained Serendipity. "Sorry it wasn't to everyone's taste. I thought I'd try something new and different. But maybe snail caviar is a bit too different, even for this foodie crowd."

"Oh, I'm not a foodie, Serendipity," said Bud quickly, trying to get himself out of a tricky spot, "so please don't concern yourself about my proletarian palate. Cait liked it, and Cait knows her food. You should listen to her."

Serendipity smiled. "Please don't panic, Bud. We chefs have to be able to take criticism, you know, otherwise we'll never grow and learn. Good chefs don't force food on people that they really don't like. I need to know how far I can go without pushing people over the edge. But if you're not a foodie, this weekend may not be quite the place for you…though I know that Ellen's planning traditional breakfasts at her place in the mornings, and I think that's just super. Pat will do a great job, and I have no doubt he'll be using all the best, freshest local ingredients he can find. But quite a few of us – me, and the Jacksons for sure – will be pushing the boundaries a fair bit." She looked a little concerned, and turned to Ellen. "I thought Bud was one of your foodie friends?"

Ellen's reply to Serendipity's relatively innocent question came at exactly the point in the evening when all the chatter seemed to die at once, so only her voice could be heard echoing around the entire atrium: "Bud's here to find out who killed Annette, right, Bud? And I'm quite sure the killer's here tonight."

I scanned the entire room, hoping for another glass of wine, but there wasn't a server in sight.

Typical.

Eau-de-Vie

In the silence that followed Ellen Newman's blunt accusation, you could almost hear people's heads swivel to look at her. A collection of open mouths and shocked expressions greeted my darting eyes, as I realized that spotting a fresh glass of wine had to take second place to watching everyone's response to her statement.

Immediately, I wished that the lighting hadn't been subdued to such a low level by the party's organizers; many people were just too dimly lit for me to be able to read their expressions. I knew it was vital to observe everything I possibly could because – if Ellen was right, and Annette's killer was in the room – the murderer might give themselves away.

Abruptly, it seemed as though everyone in the room exhaled at the same time, and an embarrassed hub-bub of "Oh my God," and "What does she mean?" and "Let's get another drink," rolled around our little gathering.

Raj Pinder shut his mouth, then opened it again and said, "What do you mean, Ellen? Annette wasn't murdered…she killed herself. I miss her, of course, and no one can understand why she did it – but she did do it. You know what the coroner said. What the police said. It couldn't have been clearer. You found her yourself, in the truck. With that note. Ellen, you…you don't know what you're saying."

People were shaking their heads, glancing our way, and whispering. Ellen threw back her shoulders and lifted her chin.

Wow…you've just grown by two inches.

"Raj, I know exactly what I'm saying. My sister wouldn't have killed herself. If she'd been that unhappy, I'd have known. You can't work with someone every day – especially a sibling – and not know how they're feeling, even if they don't want to talk about it. You can sense that something's wrong. And there wasn't anything at all wrong with Annette."

"Come on now Ellen…" It was Serendipity's turn to speak; she looked quite cross. "That's not true. Everyone knew she'd been acting oddly for weeks before she…died."

This is the first I'm hearing about it.

"No, she hadn't," snapped Ellen.

"Okay then," responded Serendipity sharply, "so why did she pull out of four tasting events? Events she'd committed to months earlier, including a really big one at my restaurant? Why did she miss the all the Moveable Feast functions last year? Why did she change her blessed will and force Raj to leave SoulVine Wines? Eh? Answer me that, Ellen. And why, if she was acting so normally before she killed herself, did she start haunting the thrift stores downtown, buying up loads of stinky old clothes? None of that was normal, Ellen, not for Annette."

"Garbage. All garbage," was Ellen's indignant reply.

"You have to admit, Ellen," said Raj in a more sympathetic tone than Serendipity's, "Annette weren't her usual self those last few weeks. She seemed very short-tempered with everyone, and she kept wandering off, missing meetings at the local vintners' association, and, like Serendipity said, she pulled out of several events. People were depending on her; she were a big draw at tastings. I know for a fact that I didn't value my wins as much because she weren't in the competitions. I mean, it's grand to come first, of course, but not when you only win because your main competitor in't there."

"Raj is right. Poor Annette was acting irrationally in those last, tragic days. I tried to help her, but she wouldn't talk to me. She wouldn't connect. I failed her."

The voice came from behind me: preacher-like intonation, Canadian accent, scent of lemon and sandalwood. I turned, and found myself eye to eye with the almost emaciated man wearing a Nehru jacket that Sammy Soul had referred to as "Grant Jackson". From Ellen's notes I knew him to be the owner of the downtown Kelowna Faceting for Life store and restaurant, a devotee of the Sedona-originated dogma, and a man who – according to Ellen – was too pious for his own good.

His wire-rimmed spectacles, soul patch – *oh dear* – shaved head, and burgundy, high-collared brocade jacket all told me he was keen to portray an image of spiritual studiousness. I wondered what the man himself was like.

Ellen's response to Grant's words was openly angry. "Shut up, Grant. You hardly knew Annette. She avoided you like the plague. All that Faceting stuff you're always pushing? She couldn't stand it, and neither can I."

Ellen was clearly determined that everyone should hear her, and she wasn't pulling any punches; I was beginning to wonder just how much she'd had to drink. I also noticed that Bud was suddenly more alert, ready to employ his professional tension-defusing techniques at a moment's notice, I hoped.

Grant Jackson looked shocked…or, to be more accurate, he'd adopted the appearance of shock – that's how I read him.

That's not a natural facial expression – you've rehearsed that one.

"Hey, Ellen, let's not say things we all might regret later on, eh?" Bud was using his calming voice.

Grant chimed in with, "Come now, Ellen. You're blocking me. Connect. Facet and Face It."

Catchy mantra.

"Now might not be the time, Grant." Another voice entered the fray from behind me. Calming tones, musky scent.

"It's always the time, Lizzie," Grant replied firmly. "Faceting for Life can help us when we're up, or down. We should all seek to connect every day. Facet and Face It."

Bud and I managed a quick eyeroll in each other's direction, and he added a quick wink…which assured me he was on top of the whole situation…so I mentally referenced a page from Ellen's notes: "Lizzie Jackson, Grant's second wife, five years his senior; a transplant from Phoenix, less pious than her husband, but a Faceting person too. She's a hypnotherapist, waves crystals about the place when she says she's 'healing' people and looks like she's wearing clothes she's patched herself. They met at Faceting camp about five years ago, in Sedona."

I looked at the woman Ellen had described. She was taller than her husband, and had a good deal more meat on her bones…which wasn't really hard to achieve. She wasn't wearing the best put-together outfit I'd ever seen – lots of royal blue crushed velvet, with a yellow scarf, and several crystal necklaces – but, there again, Ellen's get-up wasn't much to write home about either.

I could see that Lizzie Jackson's long white hair was trying to break free from some type of bun arrangement at the back of her head, and she stared at us all through heavily horn-rimmed, totally round spectacles that gave her the air of a constantly surprised owl.

Highly theatrical.

Lizzie cooed at her husband, "Grant, Ellen's clearly not well. I can sense it. Her *chi* is not flowing properly. Let her alone. Here, Ellen, take this, it'll help you communicate more effectively." She pushed a turquoise stone into Ellen's hand.

"Oh, she's communicating just fine," slurred Suzie Soul as she tottered on her massive heels toward our growing group. "She let her sister fight all her battles for her when she was alive, and now she's gone and got herself her very own personal pet cop, Bu-ud, to back her up, right Ellen?"

She's drowned her earlier coquettishness in a vat of alcohol.

Suzie ranted on, "You're a lush, Ellen Newman. Put your glass down and go home to your sorry, pathetic little life. And take your goddam cop with you."

Bud had stepped forward, ready to keep the peace and prevent the situation from escalating, when Raj Pinder surprisingly took matters into his hands.

"I think we should all calm down," he suggested firmly. "There's nowt here to be getting hot under the collar about. Come on." He was almost pleading. "We're here to start a weekend of celebrating all that's good about the area: its food, its wine – and its people. We're all old friends here. If we can't get along, who can?"

Suzie spat, "And what would you know about us all being old friends, Raj? Didn't wanna be no friend of mine when you had the chance, didya?"

I sensed a slippery slope, with Suzie already halfway down. Bud looked alarmed, but clearly decided to give ground to the woman's husband.

"Suzie, Babe, you gotta let it go." Sammy Soul had followed his unsteady wife across the room.

It appeared that everyone was drifting toward our immediate circle – which was handy for me, because it meant I could see them much better.

A hostile situation can reveal significant truths about people.

"Let it go?" Suzie squawked toward her husband.

"Yes, Babe. Let it go. Raj didn't wanna be your lover, and that's that. I don't get it, but that's that." He'd reached his wife's side and put his arm around her shoulders.

Bud watched them intently.

The folks who'd started to move toward our group did so with more purpose; clearly it was where all the action was.

It was pretty obvious that Sammy's comments had surprised and shocked everyone as much as Ellen's had. I suspected that anyone with two brain cells had pegged Suzie as a man-eater, but it didn't look as though they'd considered that Sammy knew as much as he did about her habits.

"Yeah…well…" Suzie's anger seemed to subside as Sammy rubbed her back. Rallying, she shot back at Raj, "Just as well your replacement's up to the job, right, Vince?"

All eyes turned toward the man I quickly identified as Vince Chen, the new vintner at SoulVine Wines and, apparently, its owner's lover. He looked horrified, as did most of the other people in the room.

Except you, Sammy Soul.

"Babe, don't embarrass the poor guy. Let him be."

I was beginning to get a clearer understanding of what Sammy had meant earlier on when he'd said he would forgive Suzie anything; it seemed he did mean literally anything.

The atmosphere was electric. In Raj Pinder's home county, Yorkshire, they have a saying I like, and often quote: "There's nowt so queer as folk." It's true. Nothing, absolutely nothing, is as strange or unpredictable – nor as fascinating – as human behavior. As a psychologist, I've studied human beings for years, trying to understand why they do what they do. I've narrowed that field by focusing on why criminals do what they do, and, if I've learned one thing in all that time, it's that we don't have a clue why some people do some of the things they do. I wondered what would happen next.

"Desserts and *eau-de-vie*!"

The dramatic cry came from the far side of the room. Everyone turned. Two of the servers had pulled back curtains which had been hiding a table laden with platters of sweet morsels. A barman was showily pouring clear liquid from a frosted bottle into the top of a long chute made of ice that was bedecked with glimmering lights. It was quite the moment, and it produced a gasp, which the barman assumed was for him.

"Come on, Babe, you've had enough, we're going home," muttered Sammy Soul as he steered his wife toward the exit. She was playing with her hair and giggling as they left.

"Oh doesn't it look wonderful," exclaimed Ellen, surprising me with her reaction, and she dragged Raj Pinder toward the display.

It seemed that the evening's dramas had been successfully defused.

As everyone else headed to the table, I grabbed Bud's sleeve; we hung back.

"It's turning out to be quite an evening," whispered Bud.

"You're not kidding," I replied quietly. "I could see you were on full alert."

Bud smiled. "Years of trying to de-escalate arguments before they turn into fights, I guess. At least all my training wasn't really needed tonight."

I nodded. "Lots of motives emerging. Suzie clearly hated Annette, and Annette might have messed with Sammy's access to grapes he wanted, to be able to build a better business for himself…and that's just for starters."

"Okay, I'll give you that." Bud smiled. "But we've also discovered that Annette was acting oddly for weeks before she died, which you might expect if she were to go on to kill herself. I'm not hearing anything that makes me more likely to think she was murdered, and I haven't met anyone I can figure as a killer. However odd they might be."

"Odd, yes, but acting within the normal parameters of their personalities, I'd say…except maybe Vince Chen, who's pretty stressed right now, and probably feeling more than a bit guilty."

Bud followed my gaze toward the subject of Suzie's affections, who was hovering between the door and the dessert table looking more than a little awkward.

"And what about those two?" Bud nodded in the direction of a couple to whom we hadn't yet been introduced. "They both look pretty nervous. Angry, even. What's up with them?"

"Let's find out," I said.

I left Bud's side and casually moved myself to within earshot of a couple who were hissing at each other. Words were pouring out of them angrily and rapidly.

"You said we were okay to stay until ten," stage-whispered the man, clenching his martini glass a little too tightly.

"If you'd listened, you'd have known that I said I wanted to be home by nine," the woman replied angrily, pushing a silk wrap roughly off her shoulder. "I don't like him being in the house on his own at night."

"For God's sake, Sheri, he's seventeen. He's going to be leaving home to go to university next year. He's just fine in the house on his own. I mean, it's not like he's going to throw a wild party or anything. He doesn't even have any friends."

"Don't worry about that…it's him not having a father that you should be concerned about. You need to visit more often, Rob. A boy needs his father. He never sees you. You haven't been here since February, and even then you only managed a couple of days' skiing with him."

They must be Rob and Sheri MacMillan, talking about their son.

"Skiing?" The man sounded incensed. "He didn't ski, Sheri. He just sulked around the chalet, playing those video games of his. The only skiing he does is on a flat-screen TV. He wouldn't know a free-ride board from a free-style one if they were right in front of him, and that's not normal for a teenager in these parts…on the doorstep of Big White. You're not letting him grow up, Sheri. You treat him as though he's still a child."

"He is a child, Rob. My child. Ours. If you were here more often, you'd know how vulnerable he is…" The woman stopped as she realized we were drawing close.

"Oh hello," she beamed – *too brightly.* With the confidence of an experienced mixer, she held out a small, perfectly manicured hand, damp with sweat. She was red in the face, and perspiration gleamed on her forehead. I suspected she was having "a moment or two of her own personal summer", as my mother used to say whenever she'd suffered a hot flash.

She bubbled, "I'm Sheri, Sheri MacMillan, and this is Rob, my husband. Pleased to meet you. Lovely evening, eh?"

We all smiled, and hands were shaken.

"Hi. I'm Bud Anderson, and this is Cait Morgan. We're Ellen's weekend guests, up from the Lower Mainland," replied Bud with almost alarming joviality. "It's turned out to be quite the party," he added, combining under-statement and keen observation in one phrase.

"Yes, I suppose it has," replied Sheri MacMillan hesitantly. She nervously smoothed her too-tight cardinal red gown.

"Sure has," was her husband's blustering reaction. His expensive suit didn't quite cover his spreading midriff. "For a small place, it's all really going on here: murder, intrigue, illicit affairs, open marriages. We think we've got it made in a sprawling city like Calgary, but you've got to come to a place like this to realize it's all happening right under your nose."

"Oh Rob," Sheri cooed, clearly using a tone reserved for company, "don't say it like that, dear. I'm sure if you only got to know everyone, you'd see that it's really a lovely place." As an aside to Bud and myself, she added, "Rob has such a lot of responsibilities at his job in Calgary, he can't be here as much as he'd like. Isn't that right, Rob?"

"Sure," replied her husband, taking a large swig from the glass he was clenching. It was quite clear to me, from his tone and body language, that not only did he not see himself spending more time in Kelowna, but he wasn't even too keen on being in the company of his wife at that very moment.

"It's all about the life-work balance," said Bud, which was about as un-Bud-like a sentiment as I'd ever heard him express. Bud had always been, to my knowledge, a classic workaholic, though – to be fair to him – murder investigations don't wait for anyone, and you really have to be all in, from the get-go: balance doesn't come into it at all.

As I tried to keep my face rigid to hide my shock at meeting this "new" Bud, I found that my top lip had stuck to my teeth, so I took a sip from my almost empty glass.

Rob offered, "Can I get you another? I'm getting one for myself." He was clearly pleased to have found an excuse to head to the bar.

His wife looked livid as she said, in fake-calm tones, "I thought we were going to hit the road, Rob.".

It was too late: Rob was merrily heading for the bar, and Sheri was obviously going to have to wait.

Ever the master of managing the awkward moment, I asked, "Have you lived here long?"

It seemed an innocuous question, the sort that any visitor might ask of any resident. Unfortunately, it had an effect on Sheri I hadn't seen coming – she burst into tears and started scrabbling around in her evening purse, sobbing.

It looked as though she were actually talking to her purse, not me, when she said, "Oh please don't ask how long I've been here. I've been here too long, that's how long. I want to leave…to live in Calgary with him. But I can't because of Colin; he's doing so well at school now, I don't want to move him. It hasn't been easy for him, you know, because he never seems to fit in with people very well. But now – oh, he's finally getting good grades. I can't do that to him, can I? It's not fair. We've moved so many times over the years because of Rob's work. I can't move him again…but, if I stay here, I'm going to lose Rob. And I do love him, you know. So very much." She finally found a hanky.

What an extraordinary evening, and what a weird bunch of people.

Judging by Bud's expression, he was thinking much the same sort of thing as me.

What on earth had led this woman to speak to someone she'd met mere moments earlier in such an open and intimate manner? It was very odd.

I know odd when I see it.

Sheri wiped her eyes and nose – just in time for her husband's arrival with a much-needed fresh glass of wine for me, which I took and half-downed with one gulp.

"There, that's better," Sheri said, as she tucked the tissue back into her purse and looked around, seemingly refreshed. "Facet and Face It. Thank you for allowing me to connect with you as I polish my love for another – my son, for whom no sacrifice is too great."

"More of that gush, Sheri?" Rob glared at his wife. "These poor folks have only been in town two minutes, and already you're trying to shove that rubbish down their throats. You're weird. As is that idiot Jackson. And his ridiculous wife. Mind you, maybe they're not as stupid as all that – at least they're building a business on the back of it all...you're just spending my money on it. Packets of tea, special water, stupid crystals everywhere..."

It sounded as though Rob MacMillan could have gone on for some time about the ways in which his wife was spending his money on her discipleship of Faceting for Life. It seemed equally clear that Sheri's moment of connecting with Bud and me had passed, and that she and her husband were about to launch into another round of backbiting.

The fight or flight instinct is well named: as adrenalin increases with stress and pumps through our veins, we humans revert to base-animal instincts and apply all our decision-making abilities to making the best possible choice for survival – do I stay and fight it out, or do I run away and live to fight another day? It seemed that both Rob and Sheri were going to stay and fight – a decision I suspected they'd both made many, many times before, but one which Rob generally avoided having to make by not visiting Kelowna very often. In him the flight instinct was stronger; in her it was fight…largely, as she'd revealed, because she felt she was fighting for both herself and her son.

I could sense that Bud's instinct was to leave them to it. I was leaning in that direction myself too, but I wondered how we could make a polite exit, since it was difficult to get a word in edgeways.

"Come and try this plum *eau-de-vie* – it's exceptionally good," were the words that saved us.

Ellen Newman had returned to rescue us, and not a moment too soon. She added, speaking to Rob and Sheri, "Hey, you two lovebirds, I'm taking my guests away."

The MacMillans had been stopped in their tracks by Ellen's innocent, if completely inaccurate, comment…which allowed us the chance to escape.

Still totally oblivious to how wide of the mark she'd been with her interpretation of why the husband and wife were just inches apart and staring into each others' eyes, Ellen steered Bud toward the ice sculpture that was the current center of attention.

It was an impressive structure: a swooping funnel made of ice delivered the liquid, poured into its top by the flamboyant barman, to a large bowl at its base, where a female server was scooping the now-chilled fluid into small glasses, with a silver ladle.

"Is that still the plum?" asked Ellen.

The barman didn't take his eyes off his task, but nodded his head. "Yes, I've almost finished the bottle though, and then it'll be apricot."

I grasped my remaining *gamay noir* tightly; I'm not one for sweet liqueurs, as a rule, and the thought of either plum- or apricot-flavored alcohol set my teeth on edge.

"Oh quick," exclaimed Ellen, "you must try the plum, it's delicious, especially when paired with the salted chocolate squares at the end of the table."

Dark chocolate, embedded with crystals of sea salt? Excellent.

Ellen was quite right; my tastebuds thanked her for encouraging me to try something I really hadn't thought would taste good.

Live and learn, Cait.

As I sipped and chewed, Bud joined me, grimacing. "Way too sweet for me," he whispered, trying to smile.

"Oh, but it's wonderful," enthused Ellen.

I had to agree with her, "Absolutely. And those folks seem to be loving it too," I commented. This was my chance to get Ellen to introduce us to the man and woman I guessed, through a process of elimination, must be the Wisers of Anen Close.

Ellen turned and looked in the direction I was indicating. She smiled a half smile. "Oh, he's probably criticizing the fruit flavors. That's Gordy Wiser and his wife Marlene. He was a fruit farmer for his whole life, then, about five years ago, he managed to drag his property out of the Agricultural Land Reserve and sold it to a developer. He couldn't cope any more, and none of his kids wanted to replant the orchards after the wildfires had swept through them, so they sold up and bought one of the houses Annette and I had built on our old family property. There he and Marlene will probably stay until – well, until they can't cope with that longer, I guess. They're both into their eighties now, and neither shows any sign of slowing down. Six children they raised, you know. Six. And all of them adopted."

As the couple approached, Ellen bubbled, "Come and meet Bud and Cait."

"So you're the folks with that shiny new silver truck?" Gordy Wiser asked.

Ah-ha – the Curtain-Twitcher of Anen Close.

Bud was immediately engaged. "She's mine alright, and this is her first Big Trip. Took a bit of a beating from the bugs, though."

"Yep, that'll happen on the Coquihalla Highway," replied Gordy Wiser sagely. "What was the road like? Bad?" Gordy struck me as a "glass half empty" type.

"No, not too bad. Lots of ploughings at the summit, but almost nothing as we swung down into the valley," replied Bud, back to being Bud-like.

"Yep, snow's all but gone here, except the mounds in the parking lots," observed Gordy. "Doesn't mean there won't be more, though."

Bud nodded. "Hopefully not before we get over the top, around lunchtime on Monday. They said it would hold off until at least then."

"Don't trust those forecasters." The old man shook his head. "They don't know their arses from their elbows," he observed dryly.

"Language, Gordy," chastised Marlene Wiser. She uttered the phrase with such ease that it was evident she was used to encouraging her husband to watch what he said. I suspected she'd honed her skills on her brood of children.

"Well, it's true," the man added, with a cheeky wink.

"Gordy always thinks he knows best," said Marlene, with such an indulgent tone that I wouldn't have been surprised if she'd patted him on the head.

She looked by far the older of the two, who were a spare and short couple. Her face was incised with those incredibly deep wrinkles that some people develop as the result of a largely outdoor existence; I suspected a life well and truly lived not as a spectator, but as an enthusiastic participant. Her body was small and slim, and gave the appearance of litheness, despite her age. Her hair was like white candyfloss. Her husband was more bowed than she, but less wrinkled, with a narrow horseshoe of white hair around a bald pate. Despite his apparent negative attitude toward most things, he had a twinkle in his eye whenever he looked at his wife.

"That's because I do, actually, know best," replied Gordy. "Like I know that the apricots they used for this drink came from that orchard down on the Naramata Bench where I wouldn't have planted them in a month of Sundays. They're facing north too much. He should have planted them full-on facing east. They'd get the sun on 'em first thing in the morning that way."

"You used to grow apricots, Gordy?" asked Bud.

"Sure did. And better than these. Apples too. Best in the whole valley. See, if I still had my land…"

Marlene seemed a little testy when she snapped, "Well, you don't Gordy Wiser, and we all know why. So let's not go there, dear. These nice people are here to enjoy themselves, not to listen to you talking about how it was all so much better back in the day."

The couple rolled eyes at each other, then grinned.

She turned to Bud and me. "You *are* here to enjoy yourselves, right? Not to solve a murder that didn't happen." She turned to Ellen. "You know very well that your sister killed herself, Ellen, and that's an end to it. A sad end, to be sure, but that's what she did." She turned to us again. "We loved Annette dearly, you know, Cait. With all the children gone, and her just up the hill there, we saw a great deal of her, didn't we, dear?"

Gordy nodded. "Annette was a good girl. Always had time for us. Even had time for me, and I know I'm not an easy man to be with."

"Exactly," replied Marlene enigmatically. "She'd pop in with all sorts of treats for us. She rarely just drove up to her house without stopping by, right? She'd hop out of her little car to collect her mail from the mailbox at the foot of the hill, then she'd come inside to visit with us."

Again, Gordy nodded, sadly. "Except for those last few weeks. Seemed to be distant. Didn't bring me my bonbons then, did she, eh? Didn't even bother to collect her mail every day."

Marlene nodded. "True. She did seem to avoid us for a while there, toward the end. But listen, Ellen," Marlene turned her attention to our weekend hostess who was, by now, swaying more than a little, "I, for one, know that no one else was involved. No one could have got up to her house without passing ours, and nobody did. Nobody. No people, no vehicles. You know very well, Ellen, that one of us is bound to look out of the window if we hear anything – anything at all – and neither of us did. Not all that evening. Not once. Well, not after Annette herself drove up to the house, that is. And then you, the next morning. Nobody between the two of you. I'm not a good sleeper, and I'd have been woken by anyone driving, or even walking, past our place…whatever the time. It can't have been murder. I'm sorry, dear, but you're just going to have to work harder at coming to terms with it. She might have been your sister, but you two were always as different as chalk and cheese, so she obviously hid something from you – something that made her so deeply unhappy that she chose to take her own life. People hide things. People lie. Often, they think they're doing it for the good of those they love. So you'd better get used to it, dear – your sister lied to you. She killed herself." Marlene used a very matter-of-fact tone, which seemed to subdue Ellen so much that her swaying became quite pronounced.

Marlene wasn't finished. She turned to Bud, patted him on the arm, and said, "You know, young man, I think your time here would be much better spent enjoying the glories of the meals we're all about to enjoy, rather than trying to help this poor woman find a murderer who doesn't exist. Tell her to stop being silly and to face facts. No one came up that hill between the two of you sisters. Oh…dear me…"

Bud was lucky to catch Ellen before she fell. As it was, only his glass, and hers, hit the floor, rather than Ellen herself.

"Oops. Sorry." Ellen looked embarrassed as she pulled herself together. "I'm fine, I'm fine…" she rambled, as servers approached to pick up the shards of glass, mop up the spilled drinks, and wipe down Ellen's badly stained shirt and skirt.

Bud made eye contact with me as he himself was patted dry, and he nodded his head toward the exit. I nodded back.

"I think maybe we should be going," I said as firmly as possible to the flapping Ellen.

"Would you like us to drop Ellen at her apartment?" asked a suddenly close Grant Jackson. "I haven't been drinking, because I'm driving," he added sanctimoniously.

Ellen shouted, "I'm fine. Just everybody leave me alone. I can manage by myself. I'm quite used to it – managing by myself. However wonderful you all might think Annette was, and however perfect you all might think she was for the business, it was always me who ran it. Me who balanced the books, me who knew what we could and couldn't afford. Me who had to do all the dirty work, making sure all the machinery and equipment was fixed, and that everything worked out in the fields when we couldn't afford mechanics or engineers. Me who had to make sure we both had a roof over our heads for years before we were a success. I looked after her, not the other way around. And now she's gone, I've got no one to look after. No one to make successful…"

Raj Pinder approached, looking worried and confused. He murmured to Bud, "Bit too much to drink?" Bud nodded. "Leave it to me," he added, then, to Ellen, he said, "Right-o, Ellen, me dear. I'm going to get you into a taxi and home to that apartment of yours before you know it. Just pop your arm around me shoulder…oh, right-o then, me waist…oh, that's a bit tight…and off we go."

Ellen looked pathetic as she tottered toward the exit, supported by Raj, but she managed a weak smile and a quiet, "See you in the morning," as she left.

"Time for us to go too, I think," said Bud.

"Look forward to seeing you at breakfast," I said to the Wisers. A thought suddenly occurred to me. "Would you two like to share a cab with us? We'll be going right past your door, as you know."

They both smiled. "What, and miss all the fun of talking about Ellen, and the Souls, and you two of course, when you've gone? You must be kidding." Marlene chuckled wickedly.

I felt my eyebrow shoot upwards; such honesty was unusual.

The woman smiled and patted my arm. "Oh, go ahead, don't panic, there's nothing very interesting to say about you two…but the others? Just you go on, and we'll be fine. There was a rumor earlier on that they've got a rhubarb *eau de vie* next, and Gordy and I know our rhubarb, don't we dear?"

Gordy nodded. "I grew a lot of it in my day, and Marlene still has a spot or two for it in her garden these days. And we've both made our fair share of rhubarb jam, and rhubarb wine too, over the years. I'd like to see what the so-called professionals do with it. Go on, off with you two young things now."

Bud and I waved as we left, then sat in silence during the taxi ride back to the B & B. Even when we got out of the car, Bud's expression was tough to read, which, given what I do for a living, was unusual.

"Penny for them?" I said, as we walked toward the front door of Anen House, watching the taxi wind its way down the hill.

"I tell you what, Cait," Bud replied thoughtfully, "given what's running about in my head right now, you'd have to pay a lot more than a penny for my thoughts. What a night: I wasn't expecting all…that. Well, okay, I don't know quite what I was expecting, but it certainly wasn't that."

Me neither…but I wouldn't have missed it for the world.

I looked at my watch. "It's not eleven o'clock yet, Bud. How do you fancy a bit of a chat? You know, pool our thoughts? Run through the suspects, and so forth?"

Bud wandered to one of the plastic chairs that surrounded the little table on the smoking porch and sat down, heavily.

"Are you going to smoke before we go in?" he asked distractedly.

"Sure, I'll join you there," I replied, digging around in my evening purse for my ciggies. I lit up and puffed away.

Lovely.

The cool night air made me shiver a little. Bud got up, took off his jacket, and placed it on my shoulders.

Just like they do in the movies.

"Thanks," was my completely inadequate response, given the significance of his actions, in my eyes. Okay, it was only one word, but I did at least try to fill it with all the pent-up emotion I was feeling.

"You're welcome," he said, still distracted.

A tense silence followed.

Unusual for us.

Eventually, Bud blurted out, "It's all wrong, Cait. With everything we've learned so far, I just cannot bring myself to believe that Annette's death was anything other than a suicide. I can't. You have to agree. Surely you must see it my way now?"

I thought carefully about what to say next. I, too, had been mulling over the events of the evening – what I'd seen, heard, and read on the faces of the people at the cocktail party – and I knew what I had to do.

"Okay, Bud. I'll shut up about murder until I see the paperwork that we've asked Ellen to rustle up for us. I won't press my case, but I will continue to dig around. When I've seen those papers, then we'll discuss how to progress."

Bud stroked his chin.

I can sneak another ciggie, if I'm quick.

My comments seemed to satisfy Bud, who turned to glare at my glowing cigarette. "You're going to finish that, are you?" he asked acidly.

"My addiction, my body, my time," I replied.

Shut up, Cait.

Bud leapt from the little chair and exploded, "This is not the weekend I'd planned, nor hoped for, Cait. Not at all. It was supposed to be fun. Okay, a bit of prying, a bit of helping Ellen come to terms with some tough stuff. But these people? They're all off kilter in some way. Everyone's dysfunctional. That place was a powder keg tonight. Nothing feels…right." He snapped, "Are you coming in now?"

I stubbed out my smoke. "Yep, coming with you, right now."

I trotted after him, holding out his jacket for him to take.

As we stopped between our doorways at the top of the stairs, Bud turned to me and held me close. "Look, let's get some sleep, and we'll talk in the morning." He kissed my forehead.

"See you before breakfast?" I asked, hoping he'd rally.

"What time is breakfast again?" He sounded exhausted.

"Pat said it starts at eight, so I suppose we should be down and ready to mingle by seven forty-five, don't you think?"

"Sounds about right," he replied. "I can't see me being ready for much of anything before that. So I'll see you right here, at seven forty-five. Okay?"

"Of course," I said, as he closed his door.

92

Bottled Water

I, too, shut my door behind me, and went into the spacious, sparkling bathroom to take off my makeup. It's not my usual habit, but I try to make an effort when I'm sleeping on pillowcases that someone else will have to launder. Staring at myself in the brightly lit bathroom mirror allowed for a few moments of self-reflection – figuratively and literally. The former can sometimes be uplifting; the latter, not so much. I might not mind the idea of having an interesting landscape etched on my face late in life, like Marlene Wiser, but I'm not enjoying the journey toward it one little bit.

Comparatively fresh-faced, I clicked off the lights in the bathroom and the bedroom to get a better view of the moon that was poking out from behind a cloud in the black sky, catching the ripples on the lake. It was a delightfully tranquil scene. I stood and drank it all in for a few moments, which allowed me to calm down, and to decide that sulking – and being cross about Bud's mood – wasn't going to get me anywhere.

I decided to do something positive, and get on with analyzing the evening's events, so stepped away from the distracting sight beyond my window and sat at the little desk on the far side of the room. All the furniture at Anen House was old; it looked as though each piece had been lovingly polished for many years. I wondered if these were all original Newman belongings…which immediately brought me back to reality.

The Newmans: did Annette Newman kill herself, or was she murdered? And if she was murdered, who did it, and why?

Okay, Cait – get organized.

I pulled a notepad out of my suitcase, and immediately wished I'd brought my laptop. I didn't know why I hadn't, unless I'd been focusing on being with Bud and indulging in food and wine, rather than looking into a possible homicide. I suspected that was it – I, too, had been looking forward to a fun weekend.

I sat down, found a pen and my specs, and wrote: Asphyxia (cause), due to carbon monoxide poisoning, created by inhaling truck exhaust fumes (manner) across the top of the page. Then I drew a line down the middle of the page; on one side I wrote, MURDER and on the other, SUICIDE.

It's always sensible to take stock, before analyzing.

On the MURDER side of the page, I listed everything I could think of that related to the murder theory:

1. METHOD (NOTE: Psychologically, not this method!)
- Difficult to stage such a murder
- How did murderer get Annette into the truck?
- Drugs or wine to induce unconsciousness?
- Lifting Annette when unconscious? Strength needed
- Would there be another way to get Annette to sit there?
- Would Annette really type a suicide note? Was it a fake?
- 20–30% of suicides leave notes – how many are typed?
- Autopsy: contusions, lacerations, puncture wounds?
- Autopsy: any signs of smothering prior to final asphyxia?
- Murderer had to get to and from scene unseen/unheard
- Seems like no one could have done that – nosey Wisers

2. MOTIVES:
- Annette knew about cannabis wine? Threat to Sammy & Suzie Soul – Suzie's attitude at party
- Raj Pinder wanted to get half of Mount Dewdney business – did he really not know about her will?

I was stumped; there didn't seem to be any more reasons for anyone wanting to kill Annette, that I knew of.

I pretended I was Bud and raked my hand through my hair. It didn't help.

I scribbled, Must find out more about Annette herself. Where's all her stuff? Is it here at Anen House? Build a VICTIM profile.

Then on the SUICIDE side of the sheet I wrote:

1. METHOD:
- Classic female suicide method – passive, restful
- Coroner reports, especially toxicology/drugs?
- Handwriting poor, so typing note was natural?
- Why sister's truck?

2. MOTIVES:
- Note says "can't do my job perfectly" – why not?
- Acting oddly? Raj, Serendipity, Wisers – YES; Ellen – NO
- Missing meetings – why?
- Canceled tastings – why?
- Missed Moveable Feast events – why?
- Bought old clothes at thrift stores – why?
- Avoided the Wisers – why?
- Changed her will – why? Exact wording?
- Coroner would seek family doctor input – insights there?

I felt frustrated; the list idea wasn't helping, so I decided to use another weapon in my armory – recollection: maybe I'd experienced something at the party that would help?

I've read dozens of books and academic papers about memory, and try to keep up to date on what neuroscientists are discovering about the ways human brains work, physiologically speaking. However, there still isn't a single body of work, or a clear set of theories, that help me understand why I can do what

I can do. So I'll just keep doing it, even if no one understands it…or even if they say it can't be done.

I screwed up my eyes to the point where everything starts to get blurry and began to hum; with this method I can be back at a place I once was, and take a long, hard look around. I can't visually stop events in their tracks, as though I've pushed the pause button, but I can keep looping back to re-examine a moment. I can do this for all of my senses…as long as I experienced something in the first place.

One thing the experts do at least agree upon? We humans encode, or remember, much more of what's going on around us than we believe we do. However, to prevent our brains from drowning in a sea of stimuli, we select those things we choose to perceive and ignore those things we don't feel the need to notice at the time: it's called selective perception. We've all done it: we obliterate the sound of a clock ticking in a room; we don't notice the noise overhead when we live under a flightpath; we stop noticing the music in the background at the supermarket. It's natural. It's what allows us to function.

For me, while I might ignore certain inputs when they're happening, I can go back and experience the whole event once more – which can be very handy when you're helping to solve a crime, as Bud quickly discovered when he first saw me "perform".

I took myself back to the moment when Ellen exclaimed that someone had killed Annette, and that she was quite sure the killer was in the room…

Okay – get blurry, Cait, and hummmmm...

I'm standing so close to Bud that I can catch his aroma – Eternity aftershave balm. The wineglass I'm holding is the same temperature as my body, the roundness of its bowl resting comfortably in my left hand, and in my right hand is the still-chilled china spoon from which I've just eaten the snail caviar. Its taste is lingering in my mouth. It's pleasant. Unusual. Earthy.

Beside me stands Ellen, across from Bud. She's almost spilling her drink as she gestures. She's breathing heavily as she speaks. Her face is set in an expression of…satisfaction. *Odd.* She's gloating. She's showing off. She speaks.

Just as she does, the sounds that have been echoing in the room die down. She's speaking more loudly than when she was talking within our group. She's making an announcement. Even though the other noise in the room has stopped, she still keeps her voice at a high level.

She wants people to hear her, and the silence that befalls the room is a lucky break for her.

"Bud's here to find out who killed Annette, right, Bud? And I'm quite sure the killer's here tonight."

She tosses her head in triumph. Her breaths are shorter now, she's exuberant. Her eyes are shining.

At the end of her first sentence, there's a sound from Raj. He's facing me, standing beside Serendipity. They are blocking my view of the rest of the room.

Yes, a definite "Oh" from him as he sucks in his breath.

His expression says…surprise.

Surprise at the idea that Annette was killed? Or surprise that Ellen knows?

It makes a big difference.

Look closely, Cait, read him…

No, I can't tell what he's surprised about. When Ellen speaks again, does his expression change? Yes. Now he looks disbelieving. His mouth is forming a silent "No," there's a shadow of a shake to his head.

Okay…Raj's micro-expressions are the key.

He's truly surprised at first, then his disbelief is colored by something. I can see the expression in his eyes change. Got it...*it's pity*. He's feeling pity for Ellen as she speaks her second sentence.

Interesting.

Now I look at Serendipity: Ellen's first sentence brings an expression of surprise and horror to her face. She clenches her glass more tightly, she leans back from Ellen a little. She's literally taken aback. But she's not just leaning away from Ellen, she's leaning toward Raj. At Ellen's second utterance, she glances sideways, rapidly, at Raj, then back to Ellen. Is she seeking a cue from him, and is that just because these two are a couple? Or is it because she suspects Raj?

Her eyes flash a momentary rounded stare; she's frightened about something...a thought that's slipped into her head, and maybe it pertains to Raj. But, at the same time, her grip on her glass relaxes. *Odd.* She's releasing tension by looking at Raj. She's receiving comfort just by seeing him. They're obviously very close. I believe she's...*pleased?*...by the expression she sees on his face. Yes, she's relieved that he doesn't believe what Ellen is saying.

Interesting.

Now I must look beyond our direct circle, into the dim room.

Closest to us, and therefore the best lit, are the MacMillans. This is before I have met them face to face: what are my initial impressions? They're standing apart from the rest of the guests, and they're very close together, standing side-on to me, about twenty feet away. I can't hear anything they're saying before Ellen's exclamation, but just as Ellen opens her mouth, Sheri MacMillan's expression is easy to read: she's angry. Nostrils flared, lips squeezed tight, corners of her mouth turned down, chin puckered, brows drawn together: *hurt, and angry.* Her eyes are downcast, her face is toward me as she turns away from her husband. Her shoulders are down, her head's down, she's down...*she's lost one of their skirmishes.*

Rob MacMillan, standing opposite her, is a picture of cruel dismissal and anger: sneering upper lip, one nostril flared, staring eyes, glaring at his wife. He's won. He hates her. He sees her as nothing.

I know that look.

Angus used to look at me like that just before he would raise his arm to hit me. That's the expression I learned to flinch from, all those years ago, in that loveless, destructive phase of my life – in those months before I chucked him out of our flat, and then he managed to worm his way back inside, only for him to wind up dead on the floor the next morning, and for the police to end up dragging me into a car, protesting my innocence, which I continued to do…until they had to agree with me.

It's a truly terrible look. And she knows it, too.

I feel sympathy for Sheri.

But I mustn't. I must focus. Now's not the time to think about Angus. He's dead. He's gone. I'm here, doing this. I push the thoughts of him from my mind.

As Ellen speaks, what do the MacMillans do? How do their expressions change?

He whips his head to look at Ellen. His dismissive expression doesn't change immediately; he doesn't like Ellen. As she speaks, his face shifts subtly to show that he's now expecting her to say something that's not worth hearing, and, as she finishes, he rolls his eyes; he's thinking she's a stupid woman.

On the other hand, Sheri's head snaps up and she gives her attention to Ellen. She looks frightened. Is that a hangover of an emotion she feels for her husband? *No.* She clasps her drink to her body; she's frightened for herself, but not because she thinks her husband might strike her. I can tell that because, as one hand recoils toward her breast, her other reaches toward Rob. She's seeking his protection. She's frightened that what Ellen has said will somehow harm her.

Interesting.

She looks away from Ellen and her husband, toward the other people in the room. Now I can't see her face, but her shoulders hunch, and I wonder if she's doing what I'm trying to do – checking to see if there's a killer in the room. The folks she's looking at are the Souls, the Wisers, the Jacksons, Vince Chen, and another man and two women I never got to meet. I can't see the three unknown people at all – they all have their backs to me before Ellen speaks, and turn their heads only when she does. I can only see the sides of their faces, and only partially at that, because of the dim lighting.

Back to my immediate circle.

By the time Raj speaks, his pity for Ellen has subsided, and now his entire body is telling me that he's totally amazed that Ellen has just said what she's said. His body is rigid, his neck muscles taught; he's confused, almost angry. He's frowning as he speaks.

As he makes his comments Ellen's looking…triumphant.

She's almost gloating at Raj's amazement.

Now Ellan straightens herself up, like a warrior going to do battle, and tosses her hair in the most feminine motion I've seen her yet make. Her eyes are ablaze.

As she speaks to Raj, assuring him that she knows what she's talking about, her nostrils are flared, her eyes glittering. Her manner is shocking to Raj, I can see the change in his eyes. He's even more confused.

Now Serendipity speaks. She takes a half-step toward Ellen, and her manner matches Raj's original stance: she's angry. She's telling Ellen off when she speaks to her.

Her expression says...exasperation.

When she says that Annette had been acting oddly for weeks before her death, her shoulders settle a little, she's being dismissive. At Ellen's rebuff, she doesn't falter. As she's listing the different examples of Annette's odd behavior, she's counting them off on her fingers…angrily waving her hands in front of Ellen. Because she's taller than Ellen her hands are right in front of Ellen's eyes.

Now it's Ellen's turn to be dismissive. As she says the word "garbage", she tosses her head again, juts out her chin, and her lips form a sneer. She's literally rubbishing Serendipity.

Now Raj steps in, trying to insert himself – physically – between Ellen and Serendipity, who have moved closer to each other. His tone is soothing, gentler than before. His eyes are pleading with Ellen to accept what he and Serendipity are saying. His hands are raised in supplication. He's trying to ratchet down the tension, while still making his point.

Then the Jacksons butt in, and I'm no longer seeing any specific reactions to Ellen's point about Annette's death anymore.

The next thing to happen is that Suzie Soul makes her way, unsteadily, across the forty feet or so between our groups, waving her glass and shouting as she approaches. She's clearly drunk: her face is a sneering mask, her lipstick smeared, she's holding her glass tightly, she's spilling her drink. She's walking in an almost straight line, but crossing one foot in front of the other as she progresses, surprisingly quickly. She's long ago mastered the alcohol and towering heels combination, but she's swaying. No one is paying her any attention except her husband, who's looking panic-stricken as he follows her into the light. His arms are flailing. He's trying to grab her, but she's keeping ahead of him and pulling her arms and shoulders away from his grasp. As she speaks, all eyes turn to her.

Or do they?

No.

Raj doesn't take his eyes off Ellen.

He still looks aghast.

Suzie Soul waves her glass toward Ellen and shouts, "You're a lush, Ellen Newman. Put your glass down and go home to your sorry, pathetic little life."

Suzie's over-full lips seem to be curling, her nose seems to be wrinkled, and her teeth are certainly on display, but it's hard to tell what's due to plastic surgery and what's a real expression.

One thing I can see is that she's lost pretty much every micro-expression a face can usually have...they've all been nipped, tucked, sliced, and filled away. But her eyes speak volumes: she's not focusing on Ellen, due to the drink, but she's full of hate. Why would Suzie hate Ellen so much? Now I must consider Ellen's reaction to this.

When it happened, I turned to look at Ellen as quickly as I could. Now, in my mind's eye, I do it again...and I can see the last suggestion of disdain on her face. But Ellen replaces disdain with dismay very quickly.

Interesting.

As she reaches us, Suzie continues with, "And take your damned cop with you." She's looking at Bud as she says this.

He looks surprised, and leans away from the woman. Suzie is now almost showing her top gum; I think her upper lip would be completely curled if it were still capable of such a movement. She's pointing toward Bud with an angry hand, her decorated, false fingernails glinting. She's pushed past Serendipity, who, although much taller, has given ground between herself and Raj to her mother, who's on a mission. As she enters our circle, we all lean back from Suzie a little...all except Ellen, who moves toward her, in an almost threatening way. It's at this moment that Sammy Soul reaches his wife's arm and grasps it.

Now all the attention in the room has completely shifted to the Souls: every reaction from this point on relates to this latest outburst, so there's nothing more I can see that's of use.

I stood beside the desk, and drank down a bottle of water, trying to drown my feeling of dissatisfaction.

What have I learned?

Well, a few things were of interest; I'd file them away to tell Bud.

But have I spotted the reactions of a murderer?

As I snuggled into the comforting, downy bedding, I was quite convinced that someone had killed Annette, but I knew that I was probably no closer to proving it than I had been when we'd arrived.

You only got here a few hours ago, Cait…give yourself a break, and get some sleep.

And sleep I did – but I had terrible dreams about Angus, which was a very bad thing.

Irish Breakfast Tea

When I woke, I felt dreadful. The first thing I was aware of was that I'd obviously been crying in my sleep; my eyes were sore and puffy, my head was stuffed up, and I felt anything but refreshed. As I examined the damage in the bathroom mirror, fleeting images from my dreams haunted me. I hadn't had a night when I'd dreamed of Angus, with all the pain that involved, for months. Not since Bud and I had decided to give our relationship a go.

I haven't missed those dreams.

As usual, after such a night, I wasn't feeling positive or chipper. The clock told me it was six thirty, so I showered, did the best I could with my makeup, blow-dried my hair, then pulled it into its everyday ponytail. I struggled into the stretch khaki pants I'd bought in a moment of delight at having lost five pounds – which I'd obviously regained, judging by the snugness with which they were fitting. At least the multi-colored stripy shirt I teamed them with covered most of my lumps and bumps.

You're as ready as you're going to be, Cait.

I wasn't really looking forward to a gourmet Irish breakfast in the company of a group of murder suspects, then I glanced at the underwhelming list of motives for murder that I'd written the night before. I was starting to think that my initial instinct had been wrong: that Annette Newman had probably killed herself after all.

I hate being wrong.

It's funny how time flies when you're getting yourself ready to face the day; I was taken aback to see that it was already seven thirty, then was truly surprised to hear a knock on my door.

"It's me, Cait. Can I come in?" Bud spoke just loudly enough for me to hear.

I opened the door and smiled. "Of course you can."

Bud looked me up and down, a concerned expression furrowing his brow. "Bad night?" he asked gently.

"Is it that obvious?"

"Only to me – no one else would know. Sorry…"

"It's okay, I know what you mean," I sighed.

I do…I look a right mess.

"I didn't sleep that well myself," Bud added, trying to be sympathetic. "Comfortable bed, sure, but uncomfortable thoughts. I'm beginning to think that coming here was a bad idea."

"Why so?" I sat on the edge of the bed, and Bud plopped himself onto the chair beside the desk.

Bud sat quietly for a moment, then said, "I think Ellen's inability to accept that Annette took her own life is the only reason she's shouting about murder. There's no evidence that her sister was killed, and it would have been an impossible murder to carry out. Besides, no one has a motive. But…I was thinking…Ellen's not stupid…so even she must grasp all that. She's just in deep denial, still, and I believe that Annette killed herself, so I think that the only real help I can give her is to firmly tell her that her sister clearly meant to take her own life, and that she has to somehow accept all the evidence and move on."

"I agree," I said.

Bud looked surprised. "You think Annette really did kill herself? That a woman with a keen sense of smell would have done it that way? After everything you've said?" He spoke as though he suspected some sort of ruse on my part.

I shrugged. "I've been working through it too, Bud, and I think it's a distinct possibility. Annette – for some reason we don't know – loathed herself so much that she chose that specific method. She drank a whole bottle of wine, taped up the truck windows, and sat there breathing in noxious fumes until she lost consciousness, and died. I don't know why she wouldn't have chosen to take a simple overdose, for example, but there it is. We might have to accept that we'll never know why, the same way Ellen will have to accept it. So…I agree with you."

"Good," replied Bud thoughtfully. "Right, we need some quiet time with Ellen to talk to her, but, in the meantime, let's go and see what this Pat Corrigan has for us by way of an Irish breakfast. I can't believe it, but I'm starving. You okay?"

"Yes," I said, smiling…meaning that I felt a million times better than when he'd walked into my room.

Bud kissed me on the cheek as he gallantly ushered me onto the landing. Just as we came down the stairs, the Wisers entered the front door, which was being held open by a scowling Lauren Corrigan.

Good mornings were exchanged as Lauren helped to relieve the Wisers of their outerwear. The sun was glinting on the lake below, and the sky was already a cloudless bright blue, even so, the Wisers seemed to be bundled up in clothing that suggested they might be off to tackle Everest. They took off rugged walking boots and layers of cotton, fleece, and waterproofs, and a backpack each. It seemed a little over the top for simply walking up the hairpin road.

I asked, "Have you two come straight up the hill from your house?"

They both laughed.

"Oh heavens, no," replied Marlene Wiser, still grinning, as she handed a second scarf to Lauren. "We thought we'd better work up an appetite, so we came around the back way."

"The back way?" asked Bud. Now he was curious too.

"This house is on top of a hill, right?" replied Gordy. Bud and I nodded. "If you continue around the bend in Lakeshore Road down there for about five minutes, rather than coming into the Close, you get to a trail that'll take you up around the base of the hill to its backside – and I don't mean it that way, Marlene." He grinned wickedly at his wife. "Then you can follow the trail up to the top of the hill, and then to this house. It takes a while, because the terrain is rocky and uneven underfoot, and the old apple cart track's crumbled away long since. But we're used to it, and it's a nice little hike."

"Apple cart track?" Bud was holding a discarded backpack.

"Yes," replied Gordy, "behind the hill…on its backside." He grinned again, like a naughty schoolboy. "There's a natural depression, not quite a cave, but a big gouge out of the side of the hill. Fred Newman, that's Ellen and Annette's father, was always a man for making the best of things, and he fashioned a structure that covered this bite out of the hill that he'd found, and used it as an apple store. In fact, that's how I came to know him. When he needed less storage because he was growing more grapes than apples, I rented the space from him. We'd haul our apples up in our 'apple cart', which is what we called the rusty old pickup we used back then. We'd bring the apples up to the store for the winter then bring them down again to sell. Over the years since we stopped using it, the little road we'd worked out just got worn away by the weather. Now there's almost nothing left of it. Like the orchards, eh, Marlene?"

"Oh, Gordy, don't start on that again." The woman rolled her eyes as she looked lovingly at her husband. "You're obsessed with those orchards. They're subdivisions now, with a lot of people very happy because they have lovely new homes to live in. Come on then, where's this food we're all waiting for?" She spoke cheerily, turning toward Lauren Corrigan. "We see so many folks coming up here for breakfast, but this'll be our first time, you know."

"I'm aware," replied Lauren Corrigan grumpily. She didn't have a chance to add more because just then the front door was opened by Rob MacMillan, showily allowing his wife to enter ahead of him. She looked as though she'd had an even worse night than me: her eyes were red-raw, as was her nose. Of course, she might have developed a sudden head cold, but I reckoned I recognized the signs of a night of tears.

"Come on, Colin, don't dawdle," she said in motherly tones, looking up at the six-footer who was trailing behind her. Colin MacMillan's thin frame supported a head that seemed too big for his narrow shoulders to carry…a vision aided by a thatch of thick, mousey hair. His pock marked skin spoke of battles with acne, and the shortness of his sleeves and jeans suggested a recent spurt of growth. One earbud dangled loosely around his neck, the other was lodged firmly in his right ear. He projected an air of terminal boredom.

"Take your shoes off," his mother instructed him as he crossed the threshold.

"Leave the boy alone," rumbled Rob MacMillan.

I decided to follow the Wisers toward the dining area rather than engage with the MacMillan family; I didn't feel up to it. Bud ambled along with me.

Lauren called, "There's pots of tea in the lounge. You can all go in there out of my way for now. Help yourselves."

Clearly, she was being her usual, hospitable self.

Sure enough, a sideboard was bedecked with cups and saucers, milk jugs, sugar bowls, and several pots of tea – each wearing a natty little knitted jacket.

"Oh – I haven't seen striped tea cozies like those since I used to stay at my gran's house," I commented with pleasure.

"I make them," Lauren said, with pride. "I'm a big knitter."

I felt glad to find something that might help me connect with the woman.

I said, "Really? My sister is, too. She lives in Perth, Australia now. Loves to knit. She can knit anything. Even creates her own patterns."

Lauren was transformed: her face lit up with enthusiasm, and her voice was very different from her usual, bored tones when she gushed, "Oh, me too. It's such fun. And the yarns you can get these days, why, it's nothing short of a miracle. There's a couple of very good local yarn stores here, you know. You should visit them. They have a huge selection – a lot of the special stuff, like hand-dyed silks, that sort of thing. And the people who run them are so accommodating. The tea cozies are just little things that I've made to add a bit of a mood for our breakfast guests, but I make a lot of other pieces too. My project pages on Ravelry.com are quite busy."

I got the impression that Lauren had mistaken my sister's hobby for my own; personally, I don't know the first thing about yarns and patterns…other than what my sister's told me when we talk on the phone, or swap e-mails. I never got the hang of knitting, even though Gran tried to teach us both. With my sister it took. With me? Well, let's just say that digital dexterity is clearly not my forte, because all my knitting efforts looked as though I'd crocheted them, they were so hole-y. I was hoping that Lauren wouldn't force me to feign interest and dredge up a whole list of things – like the comparative merits of circular knitting needles, the benefits of bamboo over metal, and the joy of using hand-made stitch-markers – which seem to engage my sister, Siân, but not me.

Luckily for me, Lauren rushed off to attend to the needs of the Jacksons as they arrived, though she did so with a happier demeanour than she'd been presenting to the world earlier on.

Bud whispered, "Amazing what giving one little compliment to someone can reveal, eh?"

"I'm pleased to know Lauren gets pleasure from her hobby, because looking after this place doesn't seem to float her boat."

"No," agreed Bud, "I think that working here is more about letting her husband follow his passion, as a chef."

"Ah yes, the glow of joy we can experience by giving those we love the chance to be true to themselves," was the pious comment made very close to my ear by Grant Jackson, who, once again, had managed to creep up behind me, unheard.

"Good morning," I said, forcing a jollity into my tone that I didn't feel.

Grant placed his hands together as if in prayer, bowed his head and whispered, "Namaste."

I rolled my eyes – inwardly – then braced myself for some sort of pseudo-spiritual onslaught. Sadly, the man lived down to my expectations.

"It's so important, Cait, that we polish each of our fourteen Critical Facets every day," he intoned with more pious unction than I'd have thought possible. "Giving is one of those Facets, which, when it's matched with its thirteen partners, can lead us to a richer, more fulfilling life, in harmony with ourselves, our loved ones, and the cosmos. Are you aware of the Faceting for Life movement?" He was looking directly at me.

"Sorry to interrupt, Grant, but I need a quick word with Cait about something important that's just come up." Bud smiled politely as he took my arm and steered me toward the staircase.

I flashed him a grateful smile. "Thanks, I thought I was going to get…"

Bud stopped me and nodded toward the cellphone in his hand. "It's from Ellen."

I could tell there was a text message on the screen, but I had to push his arm farther away so I could bring the blur into focus.

Screwing up my eyes, I managed to read: "Can't make it. Not feeling good. Get someone to bring you to the vineyard office after breakfast."

I noted, "I'm not really surprised she's not feeling well. She was very drunk last night."

"True," was Bud's pithy reply.

I spotted Lauren taking a bear-like fur coat from Sammy Soul, who seemed to be accompanied by – *of all people!* – Vince Chen. Suzie Soul was nowhere to be seen. Then the door opened again, and it looked as though a bus had arrived. First in was a group of four – obviously a mother, father, and two daughters – all smiling and rosy cheeked. Mentally referencing Ellen's notes, I took them to be the du Bois family, who owned and operated the *C'est la Vie* Restaurant down on the waterfront in Kelowna. They hadn't been at the previous evening's festivities, due, I suspected, to the fact that they had a business to run. I was looking forward to the dinner at their place: Ellen's notes had informed me that they were known for their cassoulet and duck confit, two of my favorite dishes. Rushing in behind them came Serendipity Soul and Raj Pinder, and they were followed by a man I'd seen at the party the night before, but whom I hadn't had the chance to meet.

At that moment, Pat Corrigan appeared from the kitchen, beating the base of a large copper pot with a wooden spoon. Everyone stopped chattering and gave him their attention as he walked to the staircase and gained some height by standing on the bottom stair.

"Welcome, one and all, to Anen House Bed and Breakfast. Ellen can't be here, which is a shame, but she sends her best, and she'll be with us all for lunch. My beautiful and talented wife, Lauren, and I welcome you, and wish you a hearty breakfast. Some of you here are great chefs, some of you are gourmets, and some are gourmands aspiring to become gourmets…" laughter rippled around the room, "…so I hope that my humble spread tickles your fancy and pleases your palate. Now, you all know that we Irish are famous for our sayings, and there's many I could choose from at a time like this…" another ripple of laughter, "…but I'll keep it simple and I'll offer but one small prayer on behalf of us all: 'May you enjoy the four greatest blessings: honest work to occupy you, a hearty appetite to sustain you, a good woman – or man – to love you, and a wink from the God above'. Now – let's eat!"

Once again Pat beat a rhythm on the pot with his spoon as he ran off to fling open the huge serving hatch at the back of the dining room.

I couldn't have been happier: Bud was beside me, and in front of me were hot plates holding Pat's award-winning sausages – three different types – bacon, eggs, mushrooms, black pudding, white pudding, potatoes cooked three different ways, British-style baked beans in sauce, and fried tomatoes…all just begging me to dig in.

Having piled up my plate, I plopped myself down at a table, delighted to see the big basket of Irish soda bread, salted and creamed butter curls, and homemade jams at its center. I carefully tucked the yellow and white chequered table napkin into the open neck of my shirt, spreading its corners wide, to cover as much of my top half as possible; food that misses my mouth never makes it as far as my lap, so I know it's best to be prepared, even if I do look like a small child.

Bud took a seat opposite me, but by then I was concentrating on my plate, and its magnificent contents. It had been an age since I'd eaten black pudding, and I couldn't believe how flavorful Pat's was. I know that blood pudding isn't everyone's cup of tea – as Bud's face indicated he watched me savoring every morsel – but I grew up eating it, and I miss it. As my tastebuds danced from one delicious mouthful to another, Bud took things more slowly, seemingly getting as much satisfaction from watching me, as from his own plate.

Even though I became completely immersed in the joy of eating, I realised pretty quickly that I had to slow down, or I'd just keep going until I exploded, and I didn't feel that the first proper meal of the Moveable Feast was the right place to do that. So I chewed more slowly and finally paid attention to the tablemates that Bud and I had acquired. I was dismayed to realise that it was young Colin MacMillan next to me, and one of the two du Bois girls across from him.

Two sullen teens, what could be worse?

"Come on, there's a load more black pudding waiting here for all you weaklings who need some good, strong blood in ya," called Pat jovially from his kitchen.

I guessed that, maybe, Bud wasn't alone in having left that particular item where it was, but I couldn't resist, so up I went and took three more slices on a fresh plate, an action which garnered a round of chuckles in the room.

"You see," shouted Pat, as I made my way back to our table, "I knew it would be the Welshwoman who took it. It's only we Celts who know the delights of a good blood pudding."

As I took my seat again, and Lauren brought us a fresh pot of tea, I finally decided to try to engage with our young tablemates.

"Isn't it all lovely?" I asked, between mouthfuls. It was probably the wrong thing to say to them; unsurprisingly, my question drew no response, but at least I got a muffled "Mmm…" from Bud.

"Are you Welsh?" asked Colin MacMillan a few moments later, seemingly apropos to nothing. As he spoke, he put down the fork he'd been using to torment his scrambled eggs, and opened the zipper on his hoodie to reveal, surprisingly, a striped shirt and a hand-tied bow tie.

"Yes, I am," I replied, relieved to break the silence at the table, but not sure what to say next. Nodding toward his neckwear I added, glibly, "Bow ties are cool."

Colin MacMillan beamed. "Fancy some fish fingers and custard?" He giggled.

"Please…unless you've got some jammy dodgers," I replied.

Bud looked at me as though I'd lost my mind.

The young du Bois girl's eyes opened wide, and she swiveled them toward Colin, then me.

"Really?" asked Colin eagerly. "You really like The Doctor?"

"Doctor? What Doctor? Doctor who?" Bud sounded completely baffled.

Colin, the young girl, and I all burst out laughing, which was difficult for me, because I had a mouth full of baked beans at the time.

I tried to calm myself, but Bud kept repeating "Doctor who? Who are you talking about?"

Once I could breathe, I gave Bud a rapid primer regarding the BBC TV series that's been on the air since the 1960s featuring a time lord, a TARDIS, and a host of enemies that had terrified me as a child.

When I'd finished, Colin added, "*Doctor Who* was made by BBC Wales, and the CBC, for a while."

I smiled. "It was brought back to life – or should I say 'regenerated' – by Russell T Davies. I met him once or twice, many years ago. We're both from Swansea."

Colin was clearly impressed that I'd met the man who must have been his idol. He gushed, "Annette Newman and I used to talk about The Doctor a lot. She liked *Doctor Who* too. This was her house, you know."

"Yes, I know. By the way, I'm Cait and this is Bud. Did you know Annette well?"

"You liked her, right Colin?" offered the young girl sitting opposite the boy. It seemed that, like me, she was trying to engage him…indeed, her expression told me she quite liked him, but his informed me he hadn't an inkling that she was interested. "I'm Poppy du Bois, by the way," she added.

Colin nodded. "Yeah. Annette was pretty cool. She used to talk to me. Lots. I was sad when she died. She liked Star Trek too, and Star Wars, and even Stargate Atlantis, and she said she wished she had more time to get into more stuff like that. She had lots of cool books about history. We talked about different things. We even went to the movie theater together a few times. Mom thought it was weird. But it was cool."

"So you like mythologies?" I ventured.

"Yeah," smiled Colin. "She gave me a hardback copy of *The Lord of the Rings* for my birthday one year, and told me I had to read it all and then we could talk about it. It's really good. Though I didn't like *The Hobbit* as much; that's more like a little kid's book."

I was enjoying the chance to finally gain some insight into the real Annette Newman.

"When she killed herself, my dad said she deserved it," added Colin, taking both Bud and me by surprise. He looked around the room as he spoke, careful to keep his voice so low that no one at the tables nearby could hear him.

"What did he mean by that?" I, too, lowered my voice.

"Oh, I don't know," replied Colin, "he gets all weird about things, for no reason. He's not cool at all. About anything. He didn't like me coming here to visit. When it was her house. It was different back then. All her stuff 's gone now. She had some cool stuff."

"Where did it all go?" I asked.

"Ellen took it away and put it in that store they've got on the hillside. I guess that's what she was doing driving her truck back and forth all those times. She didn't, like, announce it, or anything, but I see lots of things when I'm out on my bike."

Bud finally engaged in the conversation with a quiet, "The apple store, around the other side of the hill?"

Colin nodded. "They call it an apple store."

Bud added, "Gordy Wiser was saying that the track to it isn't there anymore, there's just a trail. How'd Ellen manage that?"

Colin shrugged. "I guess she just used the four-wheel drive thing on her truck. It took her a lot of trips. Did it all on her own. Right after Annette died. Like, *right* after. Then everyone started coming around here – helping her fix the place up."

"And you saw Ellen do this?" Bud asked. Bud was almost whispering.

Colin nodded.

"Colin sees lots of things that people do," added Poppy.

"Don't say it like that," whined Colin. "You make me sound like a creep. Or a stalker. I'm not. I just get around."

"And you notice things because you're interested in people." I said it lightly, to encourage him to continue.

Colin nodded, but didn't add more.

I asked, "And did you notice anything odd about Annette before she died? Or about anyone else, afterwards?"

Colin pushed a mushroom around his plate, then looked up and said, "A couple of months before she…died…she put her garbage in her car and drove it to a dumpster downtown. That was weird, because she usually dropped it at the Wisers' for pick-up. Garbage trucks won't climb this hill. And when she drove home from the vineyard in Ellen's truck that last day, she was talking to someone, on her cellphone. I could tell she was upset because she was waving her hands around and crying."

As Colin spoke, several ideas began bumping around in my brain, but instead of asking about any of them, I chose to say, "Did it surprise you that Annette killed herself?"

Colin gave my question some thought. With a maturity that belied his years, he said quietly, "Yeah, it surprised me. She was the one with hope. Ellen's the one without it. When we talked the day before she died, she was real excited about having found a signed James Sandy snuff box that some guy in Newfoundland was going to sell her. She'd been trying to find it for years. She said it was, like, the 'grail' of her collection. Of anyone's collection, she said. She didn't seem down at all. Not like the day she died."

I asked, "You talked to Annette the day before she died, and she was excited about buying a signed James Sandy snuff box? She collected snuff boxes?"

Colin's face lit up. "Yeah, she was interested in all sorts of things, but she really liked snuff boxes. She showed me her collection lots of times. I had to wear white gloves to hold them. She knew the history of every box, and she had a bunch of books with photos and illustrations. She said it was 'ironic' that she loved snuff boxes, 'cos she used her nose to earn her living and, like, snuff's not good for your nose, except to get you to sneeze. She never used snuff, just loved the boxes. She had dozens and dozens of them. Most of them were silver. She kept them all in a glass-fronted cabinet, in there." He nodded toward the area that was now the lounge. His eyes were dewy.

Colin MacMillan looked sad when he turned again to look at me. "I miss Annette. She…understood me…a bit. Mom and Dad don't really…get me…"

"I don't think there's a single teenager in the world whose parents get them, Colin," I said, trying to be sympathetic. "It's a generational imperative: teens rebel, parents worry, and try to impose rules. It's what happens. I bet your parents were the same when they were your age."

Colin rolled his eyes. "Right."

"My parents are the same way with me," piped up Poppy. "I mean, the restaurant's okay and all that, but they still treat me like I'm a little kid. They're always going on about drugs at school, and stuff like that."

"Yeah, mine too," agreed Colin. "But Dad drinks all the time when he's here, which isn't very often, and Mom drinks all the time, period. But because we're surrounded by vineyards, and because every other person here makes their living out of wine, or knows someone who does, we're not supposed to think of booze as a drug. Annette thought it was funny…the way people talked about wine. She couldn't understand why people couldn't smell or taste it like she did. She made fun of them all, all the time. But she didn't make fun of Raj. She liked him. They used to fly off to things together…like at the same time, to the same place, to do their tasting thing, but not, like, together-together. That's what she said, anyway. Then she stopped going. That's when she did the thing with her garbage. Weird. I miss her. I wonder where all her snuff boxes got to? It seems a shame if Ellen just dumped them into a box in storage. They were nice."

And worth a lot of money, I'm guessing.

It was at that table, with a cup of very strong Irish Breakfast tea in my hand, that I decided to trust my instincts: Colin MacMillan had just given me three very good possible motives for Annette's murder, some insight into how it might have happened, and one very good reason why she wouldn't have killed herself. I threw my earlier doubts out of the window, and decided I was back on the case. My eagerness to see the papers Ellen was due to get together for us flooded back, because I had a feeling that – somewhere within them – I'd find a further clue to the real motive for Annette's murder…which could lead me to the culprit.

All I'd have to do then would be to work out how someone had managed to get Annette to sit in Ellen's truck until she couldn't breathe…or else had lifted an already-unconscious Annette into the truck. No one on my list of suspects looked as though they could pick up more than a bag of potatoes, and some of those trucks are so high that I need a stepladder to get into them…and I'm not usually hauling a deadweight.

Already the prospect of solving the puzzle was exciting me, and I couldn't wait to get started.

Poor Bud.

Kopi Luwak

As the breakfast crowd began to rise from their seats and take their leave – shaking Pat and Lauren's hands, and thanking them heartily as they departed – I was anxious to have a chance to compare mental notes with Bud. When I gave him the nod, he was up and moving toward the staircase in pretty short order.

As we made our way upstairs, I could hear Colin tell his mother that he'd like to stay for the luncheon at their home later that day, after all. She gushed with gratitude, and they left with her all but patting him on the head.

It wasn't until I was leaving my bathroom that I realized that Bud and I hadn't made arrangements for someone to drive us to Ellen's office, as she'd suggested. I crossed the landing and knocked on Bud's door, which he opened so quickly I suspected he'd been standing right behind it.

My very reasonable opening gambit was, "We didn't organize a lift to Ellen's. I'm sorry, it slipped my mind." He pulled my arm, and the rest of me, into his room, and shut the door. "We learned a lot about Annette this morning," I added brightly.

"Now you're trying to put lipstick on a pig," he observed wryly. "As far as I can see, the only things we learned about Annette were that – for some reason – she once took her garbage downtown; that the day she died she had a row with someone on the phone, and was upset; and, finally, she collected little boxes. The first two point to unusual behavior immediately prior to her suicide, the third…well, I guess it just tells us she had a hobby."

"Okay," I replied, trying to slide into the topic graciously, "I see where you're coming from, but I interpret those pieces of information differently. For example, the garbage thing: what was in her garbage that she didn't want anyone to find?"

"Who would find anything in her garbage?" was Bud's puzzled retort. "I mean, who would even examine her garbage – except, maybe, the garbage collectors?"

I nodded, but wouldn't be dissuaded. "We don't know, though maybe we can infer, that the assiduously attentive Wisers might have hazarded a peek. But Annette obviously thought it was important, so it should be important to us. As is the argument she had: who was she arguing with, why was she reduced to tears, and what might it mean in terms of a possible murder?"

"Cait, let it go."

"But it tells us is that she was upset…"

"Exactly," interrupted Bud. "And maybe upset enough to kill herself."

"Nope. We don't know enough about the argument, so we should look into it." I wasn't going to be sidetracked. "There's also her collection of snuff boxes. If she had a good, large collection, especially of silver boxes, it could have been extremely valuable. We need to find out if stealing that collection, which Colin says has disappeared, might have been a motive for murder."

Bud crinkled his eyes at me. "Come on, Cait – Colin's a kid. Just because he hasn't seen the collection since Annette died doesn't mean it's 'disappeared'. It's much more likely that Ellen's put it into storage with the rest of her sister's stuff – though…well, that is an interesting point, in its own right."

I recalled how Bud had pressed Colin about the possibility of Ellen hauling her sister's belongings to the old apple store. "Yes, what was all that about? Why ask so pointedly about that?"

Bud scratched his head. "Well, when you were cooing about the canapés to someone last evening, I asked Ellen about the furniture in this place – you know, the nice, old stuff." I nodded. "She told me that she'd kept as many family pieces as she'd needed for setting up the B & B, but that she'd 'got rid of' the rest of Annette's things. I was really asking on your behalf, because I know how good you are at building a profile of a victim from their belongings, and I thought that if you could root through Annette's stuff, you'd be able to build a better picture of her."

I pounced. "Ah, so you do think she might be a 'victim', after all."

Bud tutted. "Hardy-har. What I mean is…why wouldn't Ellen just tell me she'd stored it all? Why would she bother to lie about that? It makes no sense."

I gave it a moment's thought. "Okay, I'll play devil's advocate here: it might just be a sign that Ellen can't let go of her sister. You know…like I am with my parents' ashes? The way they're still sitting in urns on my mantelpiece."

Bud smiled – not unkindly. "Yeah, that is a bit odd, Cait, you have to admit. I mean, it's been a long time now." He shifted from one foot to another as he spoke.

"I know it's been a long time, and I also know that my parents' ashes are where they are because I can't let go. That's not unhealthy. It doesn't mean I'm odd. Plus, there's nowhere for me to put them. Mum and Dad never visited me in Canada, so there's nowhere here that was special to them. I didn't want to leave them behind in Wales, where there'd be no one to tend to a memorial, and I've told you that my sister didn't want them with her in Australia, which was fine by me. I think that having them on my mantelpiece is just the right spot for them. For now. And don't let's even go to the place where you heard me talking to them about you; you were supposed to be asleep, so it was your own fault that you overheard anything. But we're not talking about me…I'm just using that as an example of how people choose to hang onto things. So yes, maybe Ellen wasn't ready to get rid of Annette's stuff: Colin said she made those trips to the old apple store very soon after her sister's death, so maybe that's how she dealt with 'saving her sister'...she 'saved' her belongings."

Bud shrugged. "Why would she lie about it? She told me she'd 'got rid of them'."

"What if she thinks you'd see storing them as an indication that she hasn't come to terms with her sister's death?"

"You're saying that Ellen lied to me, to stop me from thinking that she really believes her sister killed herself?" I nodded. "I guess it's a possibility," said Bud thoughtfully. "However, I still think that the right thing to do is to confront her with that."

"Okay, but don't forget that now we know there's a back way that someone could have got to, or from, Anen House, without anyone who lives in Anen Close being any the wiser. And that's a big game-changer. One of my major stumbling blocks, on the murder front, was how anyone could have gained access to the scene of the crime. Now I know how that could have happened. All I need to do next is work out how someone could have got Annette to sit in the truck until she was dead – and that's where the autopsy will come in handy. How about we get ourselves to Ellen's office, then we'll see if she's got the papers we asked her to hunt down, and I just get one more chance to see if there's anything concrete to go on?"

My "pretty please" voice usually works.

Bud laughed. "You can stop the super-cute smiley face, Cait," I did, "and tell me why you've shifted from agreeing with me, just before breakfast, that Annette probably did kill herself, to being back to believing she was murdered."

"I had a moment of weakness this morning," I sighed. "I was feeling pretty low, and doubted my instincts, which I shouldn't do. And now that I'm beginning to get a little insight into Annette, I realize we don't know the woman – the woman she really was – at all. Initially, you had a pretty thinly drawn picture of her from her sister, no more than a sketch of a perfect woman, whom no one would want to harm. And what have we learned about her so far? She liked science fiction and fantasy; made fun of people who lacked her own skills; collected expensive snuff boxes, and read extensively about history. She even chose to spend time mixing – thoughtfully, by the sounds of it – with the young and the old. We also know that she was acting out of character for the last several weeks or so of her life, and she actually spent a lot of time with Raj Pinder, to whom she willed her half of the family business. We haven't even been here a day yet – so I think we're doing okay…but we could do better. Surely there are enough odd facts coming to light that it's worth spending just a little more time digging around, before you do your big 'grief buddy' thing with her sister?"

Bud had moved his scratching hand from his head to his chin. A good sign. "Okay, I'll give you that," he said, almost grudgingly. "However, if we're going to go visit Ellen, why don't we just take my truck? I know she said to get ourselves a ride, but maybe everyone with a vehicle has left by now. What do you think?"

"I don't know who's still downstairs and who's gone already, but I can see the little parking area behind the house from my bathroom window, and our rooms are mirrors of each other, so you should be able to see it from yours too." Bud trotted into his bathroom as I spoke.

"Are there any cars there?" I asked.

"There's one. A white Prius. Don't know whose it is, but if we're quick, we might be in luck. I guess if she said to get someone to drive us to her office, Ellen must have some sort of plan. She seems quite keen on plans."

"Okay, if you pop down I'll just – you know, run back to my room for a minute. I'll join you."

"Too much tea?" quipped Bud, as I left his room.

A few minutes later I was refreshed, jacketed, and found Bud at the foot of the stairs with…the Jacksons.

Oh joy!

"Grant's very kindly offered to drop us off at Ellen's office before he and Lizzie head back to their store," said Bud, smiling a little too brightly.

"Super," I replied through almost gritted teeth. "We appreciate it."

Please let it be a very quick journey.

"You're welcome," replied Lizzie, blinking at me through her owlish spectacles. "We felt a little guilty driving up the hill from our house first thing, but we knew we'd want to be back at the store for a while before we headed to Sheri's for lunch, so it made sense to not have to walk back down to collect the car. Of course, we don't like to use the car more than we absolutely have to. You know…the environment and so forth."

Here we go.

We chatted politely as we headed toward the car. "You've made a very sensible choice of vehicle…for the environment," I said as I watched Grant Jackson unlock the hybrid.

"Yes, it's a good one," he said proudly, "and only a few thousand on the clock when we bought it from Ellen. It's got a good few years in it, this one."

"This used to be Ellen's car?" I asked, desperately trying to keep the subject away from anything to do with Faceting for Life.

Grant's neck flushed. "No, it was Annette's. But not the one…you know, that she…not that one. She did…that…in Ellen's truck. I don't think we could, you know…" Grant flushed right up to his hairline.

"Drive the vehicle that Annette killed herself in?" I offered.

Bud glared at me.

Lizzie sounded thoughtful when she said, "When we leave this world we leave an imprint, and the imprint of poor Annette's final desperation will always be in that truck, which Ellen insists upon still driving."

She gathered up the layers of pale turquoise satin, chiffon, and velvet clothing that she'd bedecked herself in as she grappled with her seat belt.

She added, "Poor Annette. She had a lot of back problems before she died, and, of course, everyone knew she'd cancelled several tastings, so I suspected that her sense of smell was awry too – both clear indications that her root chakra was completely unbalanced. I told her to wear red, and even gave her a bloodstone to keep with her. But the ultimate failure of the root chakra is suicide. And I couldn't save her."

Good grief.

Grant Jackson managed to find his wife's hand among her multi-layered clothing and held it gently in his. "We failed her, Lizzie. We tried, but we failed. We should have tried harder. I should have recognized the signs when she asked me for help. I did what I thought was right, but I didn't understand what it meant." He kissed his wife's hand. "Lizzie's right, guys. Annette was definitely doing things in those last weeks that weren't normal for her…and she was obviously grappling with something significant. Unfortunately, I didn't connect with that. No…no – she wouldn't allow us to connect, or to help her to spiritualize her life in any way. We tried and failed. But that won't stop us trying with others, *for* others, right, my dear? Right?" He kissed his wife's hand again, or – more specifically – the large, green, crystal ring she wore.

I wondered what Bud and I were in for on the journey, but, as Grant pulled out of the parking lot and began to head down the road toward his own house at its base, I didn't have to wonder for long. He was clearly an evangelist for his belief system, and all Bud and I could do was nod politely as he rattled on…and on…and on.

"I gather you know nothing about Faceting for Life," he began joyfully, "which isn't unusual, eh Lizzie?"

"That's right, Grant," she replied, sounding equally jolly.

Bud squeezed my hand. As a warning?

"This is such an ideal opportunity to tell you a little about it," began Grant.

Oh, just shoot me now.

He chirped, "And you'll have even more of a chance to learn all about it when you come to our humble restaurant for lunch tomorrow. Briefly, it involves the concept that there are fourteen Critical Facets that we need to attend to each day of our lives, in order to allow ourselves to exist harmoniously with our surroundings. They are: playing, achieving, developing, creating, loving, connecting, giving, relaxing, organizing, spiritualizing, vitalizing, indulging, dreaming, and laughing." As an aside he added, "I don't expect you to remember them all, of course, but I'm sure we have a pamphlet somewhere in the car that you can take with you."

Lizzie added, with enthusiasm, "And what we do is make sure we attend to each Facet, each day, and give it a good buffing. Facet and Face It, you see? By ensuring that we make a conscious effort in each of these fourteen parts of our life, every day, we become at one with the whole cosmos."

I'm literally biting my tongue, back here, Lizzie.

I could tell that Bud knew how much I was dying to speak, and he squeezed my hand even tighter…but I couldn't hold back any longer.

I asked, "So Faceting for Life is a simple lifestyle choice, and you just, sort of…do it all on your own?"

I heard Bud tut as he let go of my hand in disgust.

Both the Jacksons laughed.

I wonder if that's all the laughing you'll have to do today to have buffed that particular Facet.

Lizzie said, "Oh no. We're not strong enough to do it as well as we might, completely without help and guidance. That's what we use 'The Gem' for."

Okay, I'll bite…

I asked, "What's 'The Gem'?"

Grant replied, "That's the place in Sedona where we Facetors can meet, live for a while, learn from each other, and fortify ourselves with supplies that help us in the outside world. It's where we met, eh, Lizzie?"

His wife nodded, and smiled at him lovingly, and he gushed on. "Lizzie had been there many times, but it was my first pilgrimage. She was so much more powerful than me, and I learned a great deal from her. We Faceted together for many days and, eventually, we both knew that our future path should be walked together. That's when Lizzie sold up in Phoenix and came to Canada, and I sold up my little business too, in Vancouver. We set up the store, the restaurant, and Lizzie's healing practice, right here. Together."

Bud chipped in with, "I've been told that you help people give up smoking, Lizzie. Cait could do with your help on that front, right, Cait?"

Thanks, Bud.

Lizzie turned as much as she could in her seat to look toward me. "I certainly can. I use a blended program of hypnosis, crystal healing, chakra realignment, and aura manipulation. I'm very successful. It only takes seven sessions. When are you leaving? I could fit you in today, if you like?"

I tried to sound as enthusiastic as possible. "We're leaving on Monday, but I'll certainly bear it in mind for our next visit."

Lizzie turned away from me. "It only took five treatments for Serendipity to quit, though she's still due to have her final two, next week. She's been without the poison in her system for almost a month now, and I'm so pleased for her – she's taken to it so well. And I thought I'd had a success with Marcel du Bois, though I understand he might be backsliding a little. It all went well to start with, but, being at that restaurant, he's got so many opportunities to have a sly smoke there."

I was puzzled. "But, surely he can't possibly smoke at the restaurant?"

I'm only too well aware of all the places you cannot indulge these days.

Lizzie waved a hand. "They have a place out back where the smokers all congregate, and they sometimes leave their cigarettes before they've finished them."

I still didn't get it. "And?"

Lizzie seemed a little flustered. "Well, you see, my particular hypnosis element focuses on stopping a person from wanting to light a cigarette, or cigar. If you don't light it, you won't smoke it, see? I mean, it's bad enough as it is, without smoking someone else's stub, right?"

"Yuk, that's true," I replied. Even I didn't like the idea of sucking on a butt end that had already been in someone else's mouth…and a filthy ashtray, too.

Lizzie ploughed on. "Ellen eats at Marcel's restaurant all the time – it's pretty much underneath her apartment on the waterfront. She mentioned to me that she's seen Marcel pick up the discarded butts folks leave out back and take a drag on them before he stubs them out properly. In fact, his wife, Annie, was just telling me at breakfast that he's taken on the duty of 'making sure the ashtrays are emptied' with what she called 'enthusiasm'. I think I'd better have a quiet word with him, and pretty soon at that. Another failure for me, Grant."

Her husband replied, "No, no, dear, he's almost there. If he hadn't ducked out of that final session with you, you'd have cracked it for him."

Lizzie looked somewhat pacified. "Yes, just one more and I'd have been able to fully balance his crown chakra, then he'd have been fine."

"Yes, of course," I said, "shame to not finish, really. So it's probably better to not start, if I can't finish. I don't want to go back to work and start following students around campus waiting for them to discard their cigarette ends."

My little "joke" seemed to fall rather flat.

"We're here," announced Grant. We swung off Lakeshore Road and onto an unmade side road that headed straight up the vine-planted hillside to a large, unattractive, corrugated metal structure.

"That's the winery?" I must have sounded surprised. "The Mount Dewdney Family Estate Winery? I was expecting – well, not this."

I hadn't meant to sound rude, and was relieved when it appeared the Jacksons took my comments in their stride.

Lizzie smiled as she spoke. "The Newmans have kept it basic. Unlike the Souls who've turned their place into some sort of pseudo-Provençal monstrosity. They've got the golf course as well as the vineyards and orchards to buffer themselves from the rest of us, but all that other stuff they've built – the concert hall, the huge clubhouse, and the restaurant? Dreadful. At least the Newman girls kept it simple, and honest. It's just the working winery, with a small shop attached, and a patio for parties and barbeques in the summer. With them, it was always about the wine. With Sammy Soul? Well…you never can tell what his next money-making scheme will be. That man's chakras have probably been totally undermined by all those drugs he took in earlier decades. You'd think he'd listen to me, wouldn't you, Grant? I mean, all that stuff he wrote about in his music back in the day – it all sounded so…spiritually aware. You'd think he'd understand that I could help him."

Grant nodded as we pulled up in front of the door of the small, unassuming wood-built tasting room and store. It abutted the massive green metal structure that housed the winery.

"Thanks ever so much for the lift," I said, as I rushed to get out of the car.

"Sure thing," replied Lizzie. She handed me a pamphlet about Faceting for Life through her open window. She smiled.

"Thanks again." I returned her smile and waved…hoping they'd take the hint.

"Quick, let's escape," I whispered to Bud.

"Where do we go? Into the store?" He waved and smiled at the silently receding car.

Creepy how those hybrids do that.

"I suppose so. Let's try it." I pulled him toward the door.

Inside the small structure, the atmosphere was calm and inviting; it felt homey, somewhere you could linger, and relax. Three of the four walls were covered with niches, each holding a bottle of wine. There were no chairs, but a high counter with stools ran the entire length of the fourth wall. Behind it stood a woman in her thirties with cropped, bright blue hair and a welcoming expression. I recognized her as one of the women I'd missed the chance to meet at the previous evening's cocktail party.

"Welcome to Mount Dewdney Family Estate Winery," she said. "How can I help you today?"

"We've come to see Ellen," replied Bud. "She's expecting us, but we're not sure where to find her."

"Ah, are you Bud and Cait?" We nodded. "Oh great, I'm Bonnie. Ellen said to send you right up to her office, inside the winery, proper."

We thanked Bonnie, who returned her attention to polishing glasses as we dutifully followed her instructions. Upon entering the main building, a sign reading OFFICE directed us upwards.

I didn't dare look down as I climbed the unenclosed stairway, ignoring the huge metal containers, miles of pipe work, and rows and rows of barrels below us. I made it to the top without feeling too giddy, but I wasn't looking forward to descending the stairs later.

"You okay?" asked Bud, concerned. He knows I have a thing about heights.

Nope…but there's nothing you can do to help.

I shrugged, then we knocked, and entered Ellen's office. The room was large, and lined with that dreadful synthetic wood-paneling that was so popular in years gone by. My first impression was that it was creaking at the seams: collections of wine bottles – some full, others empty, some labeled, some unmarked – stood dotted among neatly stacked boxes and crates, with little piles of labels strewn about everywhere. At the center of the stacks was an immaculately well-ordered desk, and there sat Ellen, her back to the window that overlooked the serried ranks of vines on the hillsides beyond. She was facing the boxes, angled away from the door.

Odd choice.

Looking up, she smiled weakly. "Hi." She spoke quietly, then rose and nodded toward a shelf that held some pretty complex coffee-making equipment.

"Coffee? It's kopi luwak."

"You're kidding?" I exclaimed. "Just your everyday office coffee then, eh?"

"It's my little indulgence," Ellen replied, looking a bit guilty as she grabbed the pot. I eagerly accepted the cup Ellen offered, as did Bud, then we took the seats opposite hers that Ellen had indicated.

"It's amazing, isn't it," I said brightly, "that the folks who gather the beans for this coffee are quite happy to go poking around in civet dung just to harvest them?" As I spoke, I wafted the steam upward, then I took tiny sips of the piping hot fluid. It was magnificent: robust yet mellow, earthy but at the same time almost chocolatey, and syrupy, in an intriguing way.

Bud had already placed his emptied cup back onto the desk. "Dung-harvested beans?" He sounded horrified.

"If it makes it any easier to swallow," my eyebrow was playing around my face by now, "it's the world's most expensive coffee bean. Costs hundreds of dollars a pound, right, Ellen?"

"Like I said, my indulgence," she replied quietly.

"Do you roast it yourself?" I asked.

Ellen glowed as she sipped. "Every morning, at home. I have an old batch roaster there, from the 1940s, and it does a great job. I just roast enough for the day, though I roasted some extra for you guys this morning."

I was surprised. "Where'd you manage to find an old roaster like that? They can't be easy to come by."

Ellen looked at me across her precious coffee. "It's funny you should ask, because I actually got it from Grant Jackson. When he sold his antiques business in Vancouver to come here, he brought a bunch of stuff he thought he might find useful, or decorative…you know, for the restaurant? When I saw the coffee roaster on display there – gathering dust – we both agreed I could give it a better home, so he let me have it at a very reasonable price."

"Lucky," I nodded. "Was that the sort of stuff he used to sell in his last business, then?" I asked. "Kitchenalia?"

Ellen shook her head. "Oh no, that was more luck…for me. Someone had brought it into his store, trying to sell it, just when he'd decided to close down and open the restaurant here. He usually dealt in silver – you know, candlesticks and such like. Apparently, he was very knowledgeable about silver. Not that you'd think it to look at him – all that jibber-jabber he's into these days."

Bud decided, in my moment of contemplation, to take the bull by the horns and asked boldly, "Ellen, were you able to dig out Annette's will, the coroner's file, her final note, and another sample of her signature by any chance?"

Way to go, Bud.

"I did." Ellen reached into a drawer near her feet and passed two folders, plus a single sheet of paper, to Bud. She also handed me a large board that was clearly the artwork for the label for the *Annette Pinot Noir Ice Wine*: a part of the label was Annette's signature. She added, "That signature was taken from Annette's last birthday card to me. It's definitely hers."

I looked at the board, then placed it carefully back on the desk. Bud handed all the other papers directly to me, then engaged Ellen in a bit of small talk about the office and its contents, as well as the winery below, earnestly leaning on the desk as he did so.

As Bud chattered, I popped on my glasses and read through the paperwork, in my usual manner. At one point Bud asked Ellen why she had so many bottles of wine in the room, and wondered aloud how many there were.

I couldn't resist: "There are eighty-three bottles, sixty-seven of which are full."

Ellen stared at me.

"It's a thing I can do," I said. "I'm sorry, I shouldn't have interrupted, but sometimes I can't help myself. Okay, back to my reading."

A glance at Bud showed me he was displeased.

Breaking eye contact with me, he tried to re-engage Ellen with more fervor, but with no luck this time.

Ellen said cooly, "It seems that Cait does all your reading for you, Bud, which makes perfect sense, given her background."

Bud and I exchanged a glance. A glance which could not have gone unnoticed.

"I Googled you," said Ellen, looking directly at me. "Why on earth did you say that you teach marketing, when you're actually quite well known as a professor of criminal psychology?"

"I panicked," I said, panicking.

"I don't think it was very nice of you to lie to me," continued Ellen, sounding more than a little hurt. "I thought we trusted each other, Bud. I thought that meant something."

Bud was blushing. "I'm sorry. Cait thought it would be better if she was incognito, so to speak, if she and I were going to be on the lookout for murder suspects. The folks here might all know I'm a retired cop, but, if they thought that Cait was just my 'plus one', they might open up to her…more than they'd open up to me."

"And have they?" asked Ellen, reasonably enough.

"Not so much," I said, not straying too far from the truth. "It seems there isn't that much to open up about."

"I see." She added, "And what about those files? I'd rather you didn't take them out of this office. Would you like some time to read them?"

I smiled. "No thanks, all done. Would you like them back?" I pushed them across the desk in her direction.

Ellen looked at the papers, then me, then Bud. "Well, if you were only going to glance at them…" She sounded quite disgruntled.

I said, "I have a few questions, if you don't mind?"

"About what?" She was still obviously miffed.

"Let's start with the coroner's file," I began.

"Okay." She added curiously, "How can you have read it all so quickly?"

I hate discussing my special skills with anyone, so I muttered, "I read fast, but that's beside the point." I continued, "First of all, because this was a clear case of suicide, there was no full autopsy, right?" Ellen nodded, and Bud looked a little surprised.

I turned to him. "It's apparently quite usual, Bud, in this region. In these times of tight budgets, the coroner works closely with the family and the physicians of the deceased to understand their general state of mental and physical well-being at the time of death, to help decide if a full autopsy is needed or not." Bud still looked unconvinced. I sighed. "Come on, Bud, you've been with homicide and the gang squad for so long now. When was it you were last involved with a suicide? Ten, fifteen years ago?"

"I guess it must be about that," he grudgingly agreed.

I pressed on. "Times change, and policies change. Nowadays, if it's clearly a suicide, and there's no reason for the coroner to suspect anything else, there doesn't need to be a full autopsy." Bud shrugged. I turned my attention back to Ellen. "The file says your family physician reported that he hadn't seen Annette in over a year, and that he wasn't aware of any medical issues, and that you weren't either. Is that right? Annette was in good health at the time of her death, as far as you knew?" Ellen nodded. "The file also makes it clear that your sister's body bore no marks of violence, restraint, or trauma. She hadn't been held against her will, beaten, hit, or wounded at all, right?"

"Correct," replied Ellen, sounding apprehensive.

I nodded. "The coroner's examination confirms that she died of carbon monoxide poisoning, and wasn't moved after death: blood tests prove the CO levels, and rosy lividity on the rump, lower back, and the lower portions of the legs and feet was evident. She definitely died while sitting in the truck. So, if she didn't kill herself, Ellen, how do you think someone convinced her to sit in that truck until she died?"

Ellen appeared to give the matter some thought for a moment, then said quietly, "She could have been drugged."

"The coroner ran a normal toxicology test; they took samples of blood, urine, and vitreous fluid, and discovered alcohol in Annette's blood, but that was it. No drugs, the report says."

Ellen pounced. "Well, maybe she was so drunk that she passed out…and then someone carried her to the truck and placed her in it."

I was doing my best to be sympathetic, yet firm. "You'd expect to see some marks on the body if that's what happened, Ellen. It's terribly difficult to carry an unconscious person without banging or bumping some part of the body, and she'd have been alive long enough for some bruising to have formed. Besides, it says here that Annette weighed one hundred and sixty pounds. It's no mean feat to lift that weight. You'd either need to be very strong…"

"…or there were two people!" Ellen seemed quite excited.

"So now we're looking for a murderous team?" Bud asked. I knew he thought I was playing right into his "it was suicide" corner.

"Oh dear," said Ellen, looking confused.

I said, "Now we come to the coroner's search of Anen House. Nothing was found to indicate that there'd been a struggle; nothing was out of place, or broken. And you yourself told him there was nothing missing."

Ellen sounded distracted when she replied quietly, "No, there wasn't. Nothing missing."

"But that's not all you told him, is it, Ellen?" I added.

Bud was on the edge of his seat now.

Ellen shook her head. She must have known what was coming next.

I sat back in my chair and spoke softly. "Ellen, that morning – when you found your sister's body, and the coroner interviewed you – you told him that Annette had been acting oddly for weeks, didn't you?" Ellen nodded, her eyes downcast. "You told him that you weren't surprised that she'd killed herself, didn't you?" Again, Ellen nodded. She seemed to be shrinking in her seat as I spoke. "You told him you were in no doubt that the signature on the note was your sister's, and that it didn't surprise you that she'd typed it, right?"

Bud was almost wriggling with anticipation next to me.

I added, "You also told the coroner that Annette must have planned to kill herself that way because she'd specifically borrowed your truck that evening."

Ellen broke down and sobbed.

"I don't get it," whispered Bud as Ellen hunted about in her desk drawers, trying to find a tissue. "What's that about borrowing Ellen's truck?"

I whispered back, "Annette drove a hybrid, Bud. The one the Grants now own. Can you imagine how long it would take to kill yourself with one of those things?"

"Right." He cleared his throat. "Come on Ellen. I think you've just got to face it: Annette meant to do it. She'd been planning it for weeks; she changed her will, borrowed your truck, typed the note, drank the wine, and…waited. I'm so sorry."

He got up and walked around the desk. Ellen rose from her seat, blubbing and shaking as she sobbed.

Bud put his safe arms around her. "There, there. It's difficult, I know Ellen. You must see it now. Poor Annette meant to end her life. It's really quite clear." He pulled back to let Ellen take some deep breaths.

She looked completely deflated. "Oh God…poor Annette. I wish I'd asked her what was wrong. I knew she was acting weirdly. I…I knew something wasn't right, but she wouldn't talk to me about it. And then, when she…when I found her…it was such a shock. But afterwards, I just…couldn't believe it."

She drew a breath, and blew her nose. Finally regaining a little composure, she spoke softly. "Oh Bud, Cait, I'm so sorry. So very sorry. You're right. I have to come to terms with it. I must. If I'd known what she was planning, maybe I could have talked her out of it. If only I'd gone to the house earlier…if only I'd…"

"Ellen, you've read that file, like I have," I said in my most sympathetic voice. "You know she was dead before midnight, and you got there at eight in the morning. An hour here or there wouldn't have made any difference."

"Alright then," replied Ellen angrily, "if I'd gone there the night before. If I'd gone to her then…*then* I could have saved her."

"No, Ellen," I said, more firmly this time, "It wouldn't have made a difference. You told the coroner that Annette specifically asked if she could borrow your truck that afternoon, so she must have had a plan, right?" Ellen nodded. "We know that she was having a bitter argument with someone as she drove up to the house that evening…"

Ellen exploded with, "What? What do you mean? What argument? With who? Who saw her in my truck?" The words tumbled out of her, then she stopped and blew her nose again. Quite thoroughly.

I said, "It doesn't matter who saw Annette. All that matters is that we know she was having a row with someone, and she was very upset."

Ellen angrily interrupted me. "I bet it was Marlene or Gordy Wiser who saw her; they're always sticking their noses in where they aren't wanted. Typical." Ellen clenched her little fists.

I was just about to tell her that it wasn't the Wisers but young Colin MacMillan who'd seen Annette talking on her phone that evening, when Bud piped up, "Ellen, it doesn't matter who told us. What does matter is that you have to start to come to terms with things. You remember what we learned about the stages of grieving? How we all talked about that process?" Ellen nodded. "I suggest you take some time to gather yourself and think through how they apply to you, and Annette's suicide."

I stopped myself from pointing out that psychologists are divided on the topic of stages of grieving, because I thought that

– on balance – it probably wasn't the right moment to toss around an academic chestnut.

Bud suggested, more brightly, "How about Cait and I get Bonnie, downstairs, to organize a tour of the winery for us, while you take some time for yourself? We can either all go to the MacMillans' for lunch together, if you're feeling up to it, or Cait and I will organize getting ourselves to their house alone." Ellen nodded. Bud looked at his watch. "Hey, it's only ten forty-five now, there's lots of time before we have to get there – it's a one o'clock lunch, right?" Again, Ellen nodded. "Okay – that's decided then, right?"

Finally, Ellen looked up, and managed a weak smile. "Yes, that's a good idea. You go on…I'm sure I'll be fine. I mustn't miss the luncheon as well as the breakfast, so tell Bonnie to give me a call when you're done, and I'll meet you at the tasting room. I'll just calm myself, and get myself ready."

Bud and I took our leave of the once-again sobbing Ellen, and I tottered down the staircase, concentrating on my feet and willing myself to not fall. I was relieved when I finally made it to solid ground…but I was still a bit shaky.

Bud put his arm around me. "Good job up there, Cait. It was tough, but someone had to do it. You made Ellen face facts, by simply stating them. Well done. I'm proud of you." Bud gave me a lovely kiss, which was very nice, but, sadly, undeserved.

When he released me from his strong arms, I made a big show of straightening myself up, then I said, "I really enjoyed that kiss, Bud, but I hope you don't want to take it back when I've said what I'm about to say."

Bud looked apprehensive. "And that would be?"

"Well, I rather cherry-picked the bits I wanted to highlight from the coroner's file, to allow Ellen some sense of acceptance."

"But…?"

"Okay. To begin with…yes, Annette weighed one hundred and sixty pounds, which means that if she'd drunk that entire bottle of wine – the empty bottle they found beside her in the truck – and even if she'd done it over several hours, she'd have had a blood alcohol level of something over 0.10. Annette's actual blood alcohol level was only 0.015; that's the equivalent of drinking a glass of wine over about an hour, not a bottle of wine over an evening. Certainly not drinking a bottle in the way you might expect a suicidal woman to do it – by the neck, and in big hits. Also, there was no trace of wine spillage on her clothes: just try drinking wine straight out of the bottle – especially if it's a final, defiant act – without getting a drop on you. I'm pretty sure it can't be done."

"And?" Bud could tell I wasn't finished.

"The coroner mentions that he asked Ellen about an empty cabinet in the living room of Anen House, and she said it had contained Annette's snuff box collection, but that Annette had sold it all, a couple of weeks earlier. Ellen was right, there wasn't anything missing, but it begs the question: Why did Annette sell her cherished collection?"

Bud's reply was pithy and pointed. "Because she was planning to kill herself."

"I think she might have sold it to be able to afford the James Sandy snuff box that Colin told us about. As snuff boxes go, a James Sandy – signed, and with a good provenance – might have been worth the sacrifice, to a collector like Annette."

Bud looked skeptical. "Now you're an expert on antique snuff boxes…and this James Sandy person?"

I smiled. "Don't ask how I know all about James Sandy, because I read it…somewhere…at some point in my life. Anyway, there's always been this rumor that there was a signed box, made by Sandy toward the very end of his short life in 1819, and fashioned from the wood of the bed in which Robbie Burns died. Sandy was from Laurencekirk, a man who overcame physical challenges to invent – or at least perfect, depending on which source you believe – a very specific sort of airtight hinge that allowed snuff boxes to be made from wood. His special hinge led to an entire box-making cottage industry developing in early nineteenth-century Scotland. If Annette had found it, it's a unique piece; it could be worth a lot of money. And I mean a *lot.* You'd only need two collectors bent upon owning it to bid each other up, and there you are. Collectors are like that: they begin with a hobby, something they enjoy…then they learn more, and gather more objects about them then. Eventually, it becomes an increasingly important part of their life…and, sometimes, it even ends up defining them. Finally, for many, there's that one elusive, exquisite, or perfect piece that they'd give almost anything to own. It's not dissimilar to criminal psychopathy in many respects."

Bud sounded a bit dismissive when he replied, "Oh, come on, Cait. Signed boxes? Robbie Burns? Smoke and mirrors."

"I understand why you might say that, but what you don't know is that the coroner also recovered a receipt from Annette's purse that showed she'd made a cash deposit of twenty-five thousand dollars into her bank account the day of her death. That's a lot of cash."

Bud nodded. He started to scratch his chin. "I wonder where she got that sort of money."

"Bud, the snuff boxes are gone, the cash has appeared, she told Colin she'd found the 'grail'. It's a noteworthy pattern; so I'd group those facts together. And, while we're at it, the suicide note had a spelling mistake in it." Bud looked suitably curious. "Yes, it was word for word what Ellen told us it was, but whoever typed it had typed the word 'perfectly' as 'prefectly'. The words 'Love always' and the signature 'Annette' were handwritten. Now, just trust your local, friendly psychologist on this one: anyone, and I mean anyone – however much distress they might be in – *anyone* would check their suicide note. They wouldn't allow their last words to not be exactly what they meant them to be. I just don't buy it, Bud. The more I find out, the less this adds up."

"You're on a roll, Cait, so keep going." Bud sounded…*tense.*

"Annette's will. The new one?" Bud nodded. "It says she leaves everything to 'Rajan Michael Pinder', then it gives his address at SoulVine Wines. Then it adds, get this – 'and thereafter to his firstborn child'. Annette basically tried to entail her half of the winery to Raj's first child, after him, when he's gone. Now, I'm no lawyer, but I have a suspicion you can't do that, legally, but there it is…and Ellen hasn't contested it. The will was one of those pro-forma things you do yourself, and in the whole of the typewritten document – which I believe we can assume was typed by Annette herself – there's not one mistake. Oh – and guess who the witnesses were." Bud shrugged. "The Wisers. *If* they actually signed, it, they must have 'forgotten' to mention that when we were asking them about Annette's behavior in the run-up to her death."

"Still," pressed Bud, "that new will alone points to the intent to kill herself. Right?"

"It could be a forgery. Or…someone who benefitted by it knew about it," I replied.

Bud looked puzzled. "Only Raj Pinder benefits by the will. Do you see him as the murderer?"

"I'm not ruling him out, just because I like him," I replied hesitantly, "but now, whoever is his 'firstborn' stands to do well out of it too."

"He doesn't have any kids, does he?"

"Well, not that we know of, but he might have, back in the UK, or he might be planning one soon – which would bring the mother, and her family, into the picture."

"What do you mean, 'planning one soon'?"

"Oh come on, Bud; Raj and Serendipity? You must have noticed: she's trying to give up smoking, which might mean she's getting ready for kids…"

"Raj and Serendipity aren't a couple." Bud sounded quite certain. "Are they?"

"Oh dear, for a cop, you sometimes don't see the things right in front of you, do you?"

"Cait…it's all so confusing. Why are you doing this to me?"

"I'm not doing it to you, Bud; I'm just looking at the information and working out what it means. And, you're right, it is confusing, which a straightforward suicide shouldn't be, and probably wouldn't be – which is why I'm now more certain than ever that it was a murder."

Bud sighed. "Then why did you say all that stuff up there, to convince Ellen that you thought it was a suicide? I can't wait for the answer to this one." He was almost smiling.

"Because Ellen Newman has found out that I'm a criminal psychologist and I don't want her telling anyone else. I want her to think we're off the case…relaxing and enjoying the Moveable Feast, and that then we'll just go home quietly afterwards. I don't want her opening her mouth and putting her foot in it, like she did last night. I will find out more. I will push this. Someone killed Annette Newman, Bud, and worked hard to make it look like a convincing suicide. Because everyone thought it was a suicide, there was no full autopsy. Now there'll never be one, because Annette was cremated a week after her death. That's a pretty clever murderer, Bud. We've got a whole lot more leads to follow now than we did this time yesterday, don't you agree?"

Bud looked worried, but at least he'd stopped messing with his hair. "This doesn't seem to be as cut and dried as I thought," he agreed. "There are too many unanswered questions, and too much weirdness surrounding Annette's death for it to be a simple suicide – though I should warn you that I'm not giving up on the possibility that she did kill herself…forced to a place where she saw it as her only move. So, maybe manslaughter, not murder – which doesn't mean a lack of culpability on the part of a possible perpetrator, and it might even constitute a more devilish form of seeing someone dead."

I reached around Bud's neck and gave him a big kiss on the cheek. "Oh, I love it when you use words like 'culpability' and 'perpetrator', because it means you're coming around to my way of seeing things. Not that I'm happy that Annette was killed, but – oh you know what I mean."

"On this occasion, yes, I do," he replied, smiling wearily, "but don't take that for granted, because sometimes I have absolutely no idea what you're up to, or why you're up to it."

"Good. That'll keep you on your toes, then."

"True," was Bud's pithy response. I pulled him toward the tasting store to find Bonnie and arrange tour of the winery before it was time to leave for lunch.

The sun was getting higher in the joyous blue sky, and there were a couple of cars parked in front of the store. I felt as though the snowy piles we'd seen at the side of the highway just twenty-four hours earlier were a world away, and wished I hadn't a care in the world…and that I could just enjoy a wonderful break in this magical micro-climate for a few days.

But I was back on the case, and now, with Bud on my side, I had no doubt that we'd work out what had happened to Annette Newman, and why.

I have absolutely no intention of letting anyone get away with murder.

A Flight of Reds and a Flight of Whites

As Bud and I approached the Mount Dewdney Family Estate Winery's tasting room, we had to literally jump out of the way of Colin MacMillan, who was free-wheeling down the hill toward us on his bicycle, happily screaming "woo-hoo", and furiously ringing his bell. Despite the fact that it was still early in the year, a trail of dust shot up from his wheels as he passed. Bud and I spent the next couple of minutes brushing its remains from our clothes.

Finally making our way into the tasting room, Bonnie greeted us with a friendly grin. "He's a devil on that bike, isn't he? Haven't seen him here for an age, now he's back again." She returned her attention to a well-dressed young couple who were paying for a case of wine.

Bonnie whispered, "Back in a minute," as she passed us to help them out to their car.

Bud looked at his watch. "It's gone eleven: do you want a trip around the winery, or do you fancy a tasting?"

"Let's see how long a trip will take?"

Bud agreed as Bonnie bustled back into the room. Keeping an eye on another couple who were standing at the bar sipping from their tasting glasses, she said, "Good meeting with Ellen? How's she doing? Didn't look very good when she arrived. Raj hasn't shown up at all. Lots of sore heads after last night, eh?"

"Raj was at the breakfast at Anen House," I offered, "but I don't know where he went after that. Does he come here every day? Does he have his own office here – or does he share with Ellen?" Picturing the desk isolated amid the boxes upstairs, I couldn't imagine where he'd fit into Ellen's space.

"No, he's not here every day, because he's often away, at weekends and that, so then he'll take the odd weekday off to compensate. Not that he has to punch a clock or anything. I mean, he owns half the place. He's got his own office, downstairs, in back of the winery. Of course," she drew conspiratorially close. "Ellen and Annette used to share the office upstairs, but Raj said he'd prefer his own space. I don't think Ellen liked that." Bonnie's voice had dropped so low that she almost mouthed her last comment.

"Why's that?" I asked. Bonnie was obviously dying to tell us everything she knew – or thought she knew.

"Well," she whispered, checking to make sure that the tasters were still sipping, "I think Ellen's a bit over-protective of Raj; she's always making sure she knows where he is, and what he's doing. She fusses around him like I don't know what. I don't think he's keen on it, but he's polite. Always. Such a gentleman. And that funny accent? Oh, he says some real cute things sometimes. And he's pretty easy on the eye too, eh?" She winked at me as she nudged my arm.

Bud observed, "Ellen's a few years older than Raj, right?"

Bonnie rolled her eyes in my direction and said, "Ah, bless him." I smiled and shook my head.

Sometimes it's hard to believe you were a cop for all those years, Bud.

"But enough chitchat," said Bonnie, with a grin. "Fancy something to taste?"

"We wondered if we might have time for a tour of the winery?" ventured Bud.

"The next organized tour is at noon," said Bonnie, looking at the clock on the wall. "It takes about an hour, and you'd end up here for a tasting."

"Oh dear, we need to be at the MacMillans' by one," I replied. "Could you tell us something about the wines and let us have a tasting here, now?"

Bonnie looked delighted. "Oh, absolutely." She handed us each a laminated card. "Why don't you two have a look at the wine list while I help this couple? Then I'll get you sorted out, okay?" Bud and I nodded our agreement.

We read for a few moments; everything sounded delicious.

"So how do you want to do this?" asked Bonnie upon her return. "We usually serve three or four wines for a tasting, but you're friends of Ellen, and I don't think that either of you will be driving, right?" We nodded. "Okay then, how about a Full Flight of Five? Each."

I asked, "Can I do all red?" I couldn't imagine she'd say no.

"Oh yes, whatever you want – some red, some white, all red, all white – it's up to the customer. By the way, this is on us. Ellen's orders."

Bud said, "In that case, if Cait's going to do all red, I'll do all white…then we can always taste each other's if we want."

I nudged him. "You think I'm going to share?"

I can't believe you're thinking it, let alone saying it.

We turned our attention to the glasses Bonnie lined up in front of us. Ten glasses, in total. Although each of the glasses held only a small amount, the overall vision was a bit daunting.

"You'll want to go from light to full for red," Bonnie announced, "and from dry to sweet for whites. Both work from your left to your right. If you look at the list it'll tell you what you're drinking: this is the Luxe Full Flight of Five. It's at the top of the sheet. The tasting notes are there. Now, is there anything else I can do, or shall I just hover and listen in, like I usually do?" Bonnie grinned wickedly – clearly a woman who enjoyed every aspect of her work.

I replied, "I'm sure we'll have a lot of questions. But I can see you're needed by those folks right now, so we'll see you in a minute."

Bonnie moved away to help the potential buyers, who seemed to be trying to work out how to split a case of twelve bottles between five different wines.

I read the tasting notes, noting the author's initials beside each one, and found that the taste descriptions with an "AN" next to them were better at hitting the mark for me than those with an "RP"; I guessed that my palate was more in tune with Annette Newman's than Raj Pinder's. Carefully sniffing and swirling as I went, I dutifully took one sip, washed it around my mouth and swallowed, then took the first true tasting sip of each wine. I worked from one glass to the next.

Finally, as I'd suspected, it was the most robust of the wines that really caught my tastebuds and set them alight: described as having "aromas of blackberry, cherry, plum, and dark chocolate with raspberry, and coffee layering soft smoky notes on the palate," the *Anen Nightshades* really was "a full-bodied red wine that displays soft tannins and a lengthy finish". I loved it. I could imagine sipping it with a steak…or with strong cheeses…or, frankly, all on its own.

Bonnie had rejoined us, and was smiling at me. "You're enjoying that, right?" she quipped. "More?" She offered the bottle of the final wine.

"Just a drop, thanks." I returned her smile. "You should try this one, Bud. I have a feeling we might be taking some of this home with us."

"Go on, then, I'd better see what I'm in for." He waited as Bonnie poured some *Anen Nightshades* for him too. I watched as Bud swirled, sniffed, sipped, sipped again, sucked…and smiled. "Okay, I get it. Pretty wonderful."

"It was the wine that won the most golds for Annette," said Bonnie sadly. "It's a blended wine. That's what she was really known for. There aren't a lot of folks around here who grow *marechal foch*, but we do, and she came up with this wonderful way of making it work with just the right balance of *gamay noir*, *merlot*, and another unusual one we grow called *michurinetz*, which is a Russian varietal. It's the out-of-the-ordinary varietals that give this winery the edge. The Newmans had vision. A lot of people said they were crazy, of course, but I think they just planted different things to see what would work and what wouldn't. They chose all the best terroirs for the right varietals. Genius, really. I'm so glad that folks enjoy it."

I asked, "Have you been here long, Bonnie?"

"About five years, now," Bonnie replied wistfully. "Raj is very good, and he's always fun to have about the place, but it's not the same since Annette – you know…" She trailed off, as most people seem to when they don't really want to acknowledge the death of someone close.

"Were you surprised that Annette killed herself?"

Someone has to ask, so it might as well be me.

Bonnie paused, as if to organize her thoughts, then said with feeling, "I wouldn't have believed it of her. Not for a minute. And *then*? *When* she…did it? Well, that made no sense to me at all. She'd been a bit off for a while, I know, but *right then*? She was so happy. Bursting with it, she was. Like she had some sort of a secret…maybe a plan that excited her – but nothing she ever talked about. You could see it in her eyes, though; dashing here and there she was, like a bird in spring – never still. Moving stuff from her office to her house, from her house to her office. Always hauling things about. All go. Maybe she was just getting everything in order before she…you know. I had to take a couple of days off I was so knocked by it. And Ellen just fell apart; took her weeks to get back to work. Not until after they'd read that will. And then she comes right back in, that very day, with Raj in tow, if you please. All over him, like gin on an olive. He's good at keeping her at arm's length, I'll give him that. Must get lots of practice at it, too, if you believe all you hear. But, for all the attention he gets, he's never been lucky in love."

It was clear that Bonnie heard quite a lot, and I was keen to keep her on topic; she was a treasure trove of information.

"What do you mean, Bonnie?" I asked innocently.

Topping up our glasses, Bonnie drew close and became our instant confidante. "Well, a few years back, Raj was seeing a nice girl. Jane…something. Can't remember her last name. She was from somewhere near Terrace. One of those wandering types, you know? They work at the ski resorts in the winter and the wineries in the summer. We get a lot of them around here – of course." She chuckled. "Came to all the do's together for a while, they did. Good-looking girl. Then one day, she ups and leaves. Raj was very down about it."

I shrugged and sipped…and urged her to continue.

"Then there was a younger girl people said he was seeing. Stacey Willow. I remember that name. Never forget it, I shouldn't think. She was local – from over in West Kelowna." Bonnie glanced over her shoulder and leaned in. "She killed herself because of Raj. At least, that's what folks said at the time." She sighed heavily. "It was just terrible. Raj *said* he hardly knew her, but there's some people around here think they had quite the thing going. She took a bunch of pills. She was alive when they found her, but they couldn't do anything. Pumped her stomach and everything, but she was too far gone."

Bud and I must have registered surprise because Bonnie added, "Too much of the poison in her system for them to save her. No note. Just did it. They don't always leave notes, right? Kid was only in her twenties. Very sad." Once again, Bonnie glanced around again, furtively, then added, "Funny thing was, Raj said he didn't know why people were sorry for him, because they'd only ever had a couple of drinks together, in a group. But, like everyone said at the time, she must have done it because of a boy, or a man, letting her down. No one could think why she'd have done it otherwise."

I shifted topic a little. "Did you ever think there was something going on between Raj and Annette Newman?"

Bonnie shrugged. "Annette left this place to him – well, her half of it, anyway – so it makes you think, right? And they did go away to the same places a lot of times. Had to, I guess. It was their job, after all." She sounded…*disappointed.*

Bud asked, "No one saw them together other than at functions connected to their jobs?"

Bonnie tutted. "No. And Ellen said any ideas like that were all rubbish. She keeps telling anyone who'll listen that the business is better with Raj, and that Annette did the right thing. But…well…I've heard Raj telling Ellen she should go back to the lawyers and ask them about her sister's will again. He just can't seem to settle here. I still think it's all very odd. I wonder what he said, or did, that got Annette to leave him the business." She winked.

Not letting that pass!

"Do people think that Raj somehow convinced Annette to change her will, and then he…what? Do people think he…killed her?"

The couple dithering over their wine selection had clearly come to a decision, and Bonnie indicated she'd better attend to them.

She left us with a quick remark as she walked away, "Not my idea, but Ellen's commented that it's awful that folks say that sort of thing, and then she's off on the warpath."

Once we were alone, Bud commented wryly, "So we're back to Raj, the ladies' man. We should take another look at him, Cait. He's the only one who really benefitted from Annette's death. I wonder if there's someone here at the local RCMP station I could have a word with about that Stacey Willow. At least we've got a full name, and it sounds as though that suicide was fully investigated. I'm just going to pop outside and make a quick call. Can you hold the fort here? Without drinking yourself under the bar?"

"Absolutely, ossifer," I slurred playfully. "The Leith police dismisseth us," I added, grinning.

Bud gave me a "What are you talking about?" expression.

"It's one of those pub things, in the UK," I replied to his unasked question. "If you can say that phrase aloud three times, you're obviously not drunk. Try it when you're outside, it's not as easy as you think. Now leave me alone so I can grill Bonnie."

I blew him a kiss, and Bud did as he was told, muttering and lisping to himself.

"Like some more?" asked Bonnie, offering the bottle again, "Or, how about some of this? With a wild hibiscus flower in it, as a special treat?"

She pulled a bottle out of a wall-hung cooler; it was the same sparkling wine that Bud had brought with him to brunch at my house the week before. With it, she brought out a jar containing something dark, red, and alluring. Dropping a somewhat gloopy-looking flower into the bottom of a champagne glass, Bonnie added a little of the syrup in which the flowers were obviously preserved, then filled the glass with the sparkling wine. I watched, delighted, as the bubbles from the wine fizzed through and around the flower, which gradually unfurled in the pink liquid.

"The flower tastes like a cross between raspberry and rhubarb," said Bonnie, as I sipped. "You eat it at the end, but it flavors the wine."

"Oh yes, it's delicious," was almost all I could manage. "Do you grow the flowers locally?"

"Sammy Soul's looking into planning permission for some greenhouses so he can take it up in a big way. You need tropical conditions for the hibiscus to thrive, you see. These all come in from Australia. Small producer, high-end, family run; it's a good fit with our business. We sell quite a lot of them. Fun, eh?"

They are, indeed, fun.

As I continued sipping, and watching the ever-changing show within my glass, I took my chance to press my earlier query. "Do you think that Raj might have had a hand in Annette's death so that he could inherit half the winery?"

Popping the suitably stoppered bottle and the jar of preserved flowers back into the fridge, Bonnie prepared to give her pronouncement; we were completely alone, so she was able to speak freely. She settled her shoulders, then said, "I know you hear these things about people changing their will, then five minutes later they're dead and the person who gets the cash is the one who's killed them. But that's just in books, and on those TV shows, right? People don't go around really doing that kind of thing in real life. And, anyway, Raj isn't the type. The ones who do it on the TV? You can always tell. Not Raj. There are whispers, but he either doesn't know about them, or he chooses to ignore them. It's Ellen. She's the one. She's like a terrier about the whole thing."

Interesting.

If there was some sort of miasma of gossip surrounding Raj's inheritance and Annette's death, why on earth would Ellen – who seemed to be quite protective of Raj – be asking Bud to look into it at all? Why wouldn't she just let it lie…stick with the findings of suicide, and not make the sort of scene she had done the night before? It made no sense.

Well, not with a few glasses of wine inside me.

I gave the whole puzzle some more thought, but my only real conclusion was that I needed the loo, and Bonnie was kind enough to point me in the right direction. When I re-entered the tasting room, refreshed, Bud was there and making the sorts of motions that told me he needed to talk to me outside. I looked at my watch.

I asked Bonnie. "Could you let Ellen know that we're ready to leave whenever she is?"

"Sure," she replied, as she happily mopped up the rings we'd left on the countertop.

"Is there an area where I can smoke?" I asked, a bit timidly.

Bonnie grinned. "Outside, turn right, keep going; there are some benches and a big old sand bucket. Will you take this with you?" She held up my unfinished glass of now-pink bubbles.

"But of course…thanks."

I still have the hibiscus to eat.

We scuttled outside into the now-warm sunshine, and I pulled Bud toward the smoking patio, where I tossed my jacket to one side, and dug around in my handbag for my cigarettes, lighter, and sunglasses.

Once I'd stopped pawing about – dropping things, then picking them up again – and finally settled myself with my face to the sun, I said, "Okay, spill."

Bud sat very upright on the bench beside me. "I've done pretty well, I think. I called the RCMP station downtown and asked to speak to an old acquaintance of mine, who I knew wouldn't be there. I introduced myself to the guy who answered, and we chatted. It turns out he knew all about the Willow girl, because he'd known her, personally, before her death. Anyway, because there was no note, and no apparent reason for her killing herself, the parents insisted on a full autopsy. Stomach full of pills. She'd ground them up and put them in a milkshake, of all things. Took it home with her from her job at a burger place downtown. Strawberry, in case you're interested. Enough to kill a horse, apparently. Pills, not milkshake. I don't know how much strawberry milkshake it would take to kill a horse." Bud nudged me playfully, then cleared his throat and said, "Sorry, that wasn't…you know. I'm not used to wine before lunch."

Oh Bud…I love you so.

"I know what you mean," I said, puffing hard. "And what about Raj? Was he connected to her at all?"

"I asked about that. The officer said she'd been dumped by a biker-type she'd been seeing, and that he was the sort who'd do it hard – known to them apparently – but she had no close links to Raj. I stopped then, because the guy I was talking to seemed to feel he'd said too much. I didn't get into Annette's case; thought it best to not push my luck."

"Strawberry milkshake, eh? They're so sweet."

"Yes. Strawberry," replied Bud. "Does the flavor matter? I was really only joking about that." He sounded puzzled.

"It might…if she didn't kill herself," I replied.

Bud stood up, immediately raking his hair in frustration.

"Oh, come on, Cait. Stop it. Some girl – who may, or may not, have known Raj Pinder – takes a bunch of pills because she's had her heart broken by some pseudo-gang-banger…and you're thinking she's another murder victim? Why? What particular bee is buzzing in your bonnet now?"

I didn't answer Bud's testy question directly, because it would have taken too long, and I could see Ellen Newman heading in our direction. Instead, I ate the hibiscus, glugged the last of my drink, stubbed out my cigarette, and talked fast.

"Where would any gossip about Raj and this girl have started, if he really didn't know her well? And why would it start? Has someone got it in for Raj? Maybe someone hates him so much they're working on a long-term, elaborate plan, with him in the frame for two faked suicides. Or…is he really responsible for the deaths of two women, and, maybe, the disappearance of a third?"

Before Bud could reply, Ellen reached us.

She looked us up and down and asked, "Do you need to go back to Anen House to change?" She sounded surprisingly bright for someone we'd left dissolving in tears a little earlier.

What also took me aback was the fact that she'd changed her appearance significantly. She looked rather odd: puffed out hair, sporting a vivid jade-green skirt-suit with big, '80s-style shoulder pads, and giant, gold-colored plastic earrings; like something out of a down-market version of *Dynasty*.

Our faces must have shown our confusion.

Patting her hairdo, Ellen said, "You know you're supposed to come dressed in something 'retro', right? The lunch at the MacMillans' house is a 'retro' lunch." Suddenly, her expression changed, and her hand shot to her mouth. "Oh no, don't tell me I didn't put that in your notes?"

Bud and I both shook our heads.

To be fair to her, she looked mortified.

"Oh dear. Let's think for a minute," said Ellen. She did. So did we. "I wonder if I've got anything suitable for you, at home."

Ellen checked her watch, and clearly made a snap decision.

"If we're quick, we can pop to my apartment downtown, and I know just where I've got some things that'll do…for both of you. No one will worry if we're a few minutes late. Come on."

She turned on her heel, and marched toward a big, old, dark gray Ford F250, with a four-person crew-cab and a full canopy.

The truck in which Annette died…lovely.

I felt a bit fazed by this thought as I hauled myself into the cab and buckled up, though Ellen seemed just fine with it all…and then she was off, crunching along the unmade vineyard trail, until we reached Lakeshore Road, where she skidded around the corner…and we raced toward downtown Kelowna.

French Lemonade

I was beginning to get my head around the layout and the lifestyle of Kelowna: Lakeshore Road was the main drag that took you out of the core and to most of the wineries that had sprung up along the east bank of the lake. On this occasion, the job of Lakeshore Road was to deliver us back into downtown Kelowna itself, where the grid-pattern streets presented a mixture of old housing stock, newer apartments, and a core shopping area full of delightful character, set away from the strip malls that appeared to extend all the way out to the airport. Obviously, Ellen was used to negotiating the lunchtime traffic, as she took right and left turns to avoid major junction snarls.

Within about ten minutes of setting out from her office, all three of us were jumping down from the cab of Ellen's truck, now tucked into a rather tight spot in the underground parkade of her apartment building, which was right on the waterfront.

As Ellen marched toward the elevator, she seemed to be in full bossy mode – a role usually appropriated by myself; I tagged along like a good little guest. Emerging from the elevator, Ellen unlocked the door to an apartment. We trooped in behind her, suddenly slowing as we found ourselves turning sideways to negotiate a hallway that had been narrowed by a row of plastic buckets, neatly stacked along one wall, and piled to the ceiling.

"I know exactly what to pick out for you, Cait," Ellen cried excitedly as she dropped her purse onto a small desk that stood in front of the main room's window, facing the glittering lake.

"Great. Thanks," was all I could muster. I was finding the apartment claustrophobic, and I eyed the stacked bins which also lined each of the walls of the room with suspicion.

"But let me offer you something to drink, first. How about some lovely French lemonade? I've got a bottle here, unopened, and I think you'll like it Cait, because it's just like British lemonade – you know, it doesn't have any lime in it, like we always seem to have here. I use it with Pimm's. That's very British, too, right? Annette introduced me to it, and sometimes – when I sit and think about her – I'll make myself a glass and remember how she enjoyed it. Just a minute…" she dashed beyond a pile of boxes to the kitchen area.

Bud looked at me and mouthed, "What's all this?" He surveyed the room, peering wide-eyed into the open plan kitchen.

I mouthed, "Shh!" back at him, as Ellen reappeared with two glasses of lemonade.

"There, that'll keep you busy. I'll give some thought to Bud's get-up while I'm digging out yours. I won't be long – make yourselves at home." She disappeared, sideways, along the corridor toward what I assumed was a bedroom or two.

Bud and I dutifully sipped at our lemonade as we took in our surroundings.

Ellen was – quite clearly – a hoarder, but, unlike many, she was an incredibly neat hoarder. As I glanced around the boxes, I read the labels: Ellen aged 27; Mom & Dad Vacations, 1960s; Ellen Aged 30; Ellen Aged 28, and so on. The multi-colored boxes were all clean, not dusty, stacked not just five high, but two deep, which reduced the width of the room, and therefore the view of the lake, to about eight feet.

Bud couldn't contain himself any longer; he, too, was eyeing the stacks of boxes with alarm and hissed at me, "Scary stuff."

I whispered, "She hoards. I understand her a good deal better now. She just can't let go of…anything, it seems."

"Explain it to me – quickly," whispered Bud. "Is she sick?"

"Okay," I replied quietly, "I'll try, but there are many different types of hoarding, stemming from many different psychological roots, so I'll give you my take on Ellen. She's not compulsively hoarding what we might see as 'garbage'; she hasn't got filthy old bits and pieces, or piles of old newspapers, and it certainly doesn't smell of decay in here. I'm guessing her bathroom is still accessible, and we can see that her kitchen is clean and tidy, though it's stacked with boxes. She hasn't even gone out and compulsively bought fifteen sets of paper napkins or a dozen sets of Christmas lights, in case she 'runs out'. No, Ellen is keeping things from her past, and, it seems, her parents' past, too. Often, hoarding suggests an inability to make decisions: people keep items because they literally cannot make up their mind if it's good or bad to get rid of them, so they hang onto them 'just in case'. However, it looks to me as though Ellen has made a decision – to keep everything that's precious to her about her own history, and that of her parents. There's often a trigger that's traumatic, and I'm thinking that might have been the death of her parents in a car crash, because some of this stuff dates back a good way. It's not surprising she couldn't get rid of Annette's stuff…she can't get rid of anything."

"This isn't safe," said Bud, "not for Ellen, and not for the folks who live below – or even above her. The floor could collapse…or what if there was a fire? Is there some sort of psychological treatment?"

"Hoarding isn't something Ellen necessarily sees as odd; indeed, she might see it as completely normal. Raising the issue would be opening a can of worms she might not even know exists. It's not something that's easily approached. In fact, a cognitive behavioral therapist would probably need to work with her for a long time to tackle this level of obsession and compulsion. Many don't even think that hoarding and obsessive-compulsive disorder are on the same condition scale, though, for me, the jury's out. If, as I'm guessing, the deaths of loved ones was the trigger for Ellen, it might take years of therapy to help her work though her responses to loss. In fact, with Annette's death, it might get worse before there's any chance it'll get better. She has lost every member of her family to sudden death, after all."

Bud took my point. "Okay, I won't say a thing," he said heavily.

"You know what, Bud," I was relating this new insight into Ellen's psyche to the case of her sister's death, "Ellen hoards, and we know that Annette collected, so maybe they weren't 'chalk and cheese', as Marlene Wiser described them – maybe they were both grappling with loss in their own ways. What if this means that Ellen possesses other personality and behavioral traits that are often associated with hoarding?"

"And what might they be?" asked Bud nervously.

"Oh dear – it's a long list and we psychologists don't really know the level to which they always, or only sometimes, present. It's complicated."

Bud chuckled. "Okay, I get it…you need multiple degrees and a brain the size of a planet to do what you do, but just give me the Cole's Notes version, okay?"

"Anxiety, depression, neuroticism, self-consciousness, vulnerability, indecisiveness, impulsiveness, and perfectionism. All jumbled up, in different ways, somehow related and intertwined. We're not sure which, if any, of these traits, have a causal relationship with hoarding, we just know they're observed traits: they might lead to hoarding, or hoarding might lead to them. All we really know is that they're related. Like collecting and hoarding: not all collectors become hoarders, but you're unlikely to become a hoarder without first seeing yourself as a collector."

Bud looked slightly alarmed. "So am I on the slippery slope with my collection of baseball hats?"

"Hmm, let me see…is your collection preventing you from using your home for its purposes? Is it disrupting your life? Is it hurting those around you? Do you only find beauty, fun, or joy in your hat collection, or do you still see it in other things? If it's 'No' to the first three questions but 'Just the hats' to the fourth, you're just about okay…so far…but, maybe, we should talk about that collection more…sometime." I winked at him, and got a grin back.

Ellen was breathless when she returned to the postage-stamp of a living room. I envisaged her lifting boxes in a small, confined space, and reckoned she must be pretty fit; I'd have been puce in the face if I'd been doing it.

She announced, "Here you go – these should work. Try them on for size. Bud – you go to the last door at the end of the corridor, you can change there. Cait, you can have the bathroom, it's first on the right."

Ellen handed me a bagged hanger, which I unzipped. Inside was a dress and a fluffy petticoat.

"It was Mom's. She made it herself," said Ellen softly. "She was short and…about your shape. I hope it fits. What size shoes do you wear?"

"Six and a half," I replied, heading for the bathroom, which turned out to be gleamingly clean, though also stacked with smaller boxes, all of which were white.

"Great…Mom's size," yelped Ellen. "I'll just go find the right shoes and purse."

She sounded absolutely delighted.

A few minutes later Bud and I stood staring at each other in Ellen's living room as we compared outfits. He'd got away with it lightly: a red and cream 1950s-style leather jacket, obviously originally worn by a much bigger man, a pair of Ray-Bans, and his own jeans and shoes. He looked quite dashing.

But me? The bathroom mirror had told me a part of the story, and Bud's expression told me the rest. I was wearing an early 1960s dress, with three-quarter length sleeves and a buttoned-up bodice which actually fitted over my boobs, though it flattened me a little. The full, gathered skirt skimmed my knees and was held out by the petticoats beneath it. White kitten-heeled shoes, a small white purse with a gold clasp and gold chain handle, and lacy white gloves finished off the outfit. The whole thing wouldn't have been too bad if it hadn't been for the pattern of the fabric: it was light blue, bedecked with massive yellow roses, each surrounded by white daisies.

People will think I've been upholstered.

Ellen walked around me, as best she could within the limited space, and said, "You remind me of Mom." She burst into tears.

Ellen wasn't the only one who felt like a good cry; all of a sudden, this "retro" lunch felt like a bad idea.

I rushed to the bathroom to get some tissues. Handing them to Ellen, I asked, "Would you like some water?"

"Thanks," she snuffled. "There are bottles in the fridge."

I headed to the kitchen, circumnavigated more storage boxes, and pulled open the fridge door. A quick survey of its contents suggested to me that Ellen lived mainly on salads and stir-fries...because I couldn't come up with any other reason for anyone owning so many different types of oil. Bottles of sesame, cold-pressed virgin olive, peanut, walnut, hazelnut, avocado, and flaxseed were arranged height order, in dark-glass bottles, each with a carefully handwritten label. Beside them stood a dozen small bottles of water. I grabbed one and headed back to the main room.

While we waited for Ellen to stop crying, I tried to cheer her up by observing, "You've done a good job of kitting us out. Thanks. I wonder what Raj and Serendipity will wear...I bet they could turn up in almost anything and look good. Maybe Serendipity's parents will let them raid their old closets."

Ellen sounded confused. "I don't see why you're talking about them as though they're a couple."

I chuckled. "Oh come off it, Ellen, of course they are…or would that be a bad thing, if they're at competing wineries?"

She sniffed. "Not really. Serendipity isn't wine, she's food. I guess if they were competing vintners, then it might make things awkward. But you're wrong. He doesn't see that much of her."

I was puzzled. "When he 'scoots off to the gym' in the afternoons, he could be visiting her then. She'd be between lunch and dinner at the restaurant at that time of day. They do seem very well matched, physically, and in terms of lifestyle."

"I guess," Ellen replied curtly. "Could you guys make your way down to the truck, while I sort out my makeup?"

I got the impression from the way she'd been dabbing at her eyes that Ellen wasn't used to wearing mascara, and she was right…she needed to give her face some attention.

"Sure," said Bud, "take your time."

Ellen handed the keys for the truck to Bud, and I took a bag containing the clothes I'd arrived in – and we left her to her own devices. Back at the garage, I found it wasn't easy to get into the truck…my petticoats kept doing weird things, seeming to have a life of their own.

Finally, after a few moments of silence, with Bud grinning over his shoulder from the front seat at me, and me not grinning back at him, Ellen joined us, started up the engine and we set off for lunch, hurtling around corners, across intersections, and along Lakeshore Road toward the MacMillans' house.

Does she always drive this…angrily?

As I battled my petticoats in the back seat, I managed to squash my cellphone, nicotine gum, and my cigarettes and lighter into the tiny purse I'd been loaned. I judged that I could probably survive without lipstick for a while.

Harvey Wallbangers and Sangria

When we arrived at the MacMillans' Lakeview Lodge, a few vehicles were already parked along the roadside and in the driveway to what looked like a tiny, one-storey house with gray wood siding and white trim. Bud graciously helped me out of the truck, which allowed me to understand why women had always allowed men to do the same in years gone by: when you're wearing those skirts and petticoats you have no idea where your feet are going. At least I managed to totter over the gravel on my kitten heels toward the front door under my own steam.

Colin MacMillan was there to greet us, wearing a green velvet smoking jacket, a frilly pink shirt, and gray-green dress pants: the Jon Pertwee version of a Doctor Who outfit.

"Ready to 'reverse the polarity of the neutron flow' at a moment's notice, eh?" I quipped, puzzling both Bud and Ellen.

"Absolutely," replied Colin, beaming. "You'll spot Poppy: she's Sarah Jane Smith from the Third Doctor period. I suggested she wear Amy Pond's policewoman outfit, but she said it wasn't 'retro', so she's gone with Sarah Jane. We don't think many people will get it, but it's 1970s clothing, and we'll know, so who cares, eh? By the way, Mom said everyone's to keep their shoes on today, 'cos of, like, the costumes. Some of them are great – like yours." Colin seemed very excited, and clapped a little round of applause at me as he ushered us inside.

As we walked into the MacMillans' house, my concerns about it being too small to host a large luncheon evaporated: the part of the house visible from the street level gave way to a huge edifice. Built on stilts, the house jutted out over the edge of the cliff face, with three floors of space for entertaining, all glass-fronted, facing the lake. A swimming pool, hot tub, and multi-layered decks were set to the side of the house, and the final stairway from the bottom deck led to a wooden jetty at which two boats were moored. Not your average dinghy-type boats, either, but sleek white things with lots of chrome that glinted in the sun.

What a way to live.

I couldn't resist quipping, "Hey, Colin, it's bigger on the inside, like The Doctor's TARDIS."

"That's what I said the day we moved in, but no one got it," he replied. He smiled, waved, and ambled off.

Bud nodded at Colin's back as he left us. "You seem to have acquired a new puppy." That's what we call the students who latch onto me and make it their business to follow me about the university; there's usually one in every class, and sometimes a whole string of them. It seems that I specialize in their acquisition.

I don't know why.

Having arrived late, the lunch was in full swing, and it was apparent that everyone had taken the retro-dressing theme to heart. Bud headed off to chat to the Wild West era Wisers, while I searched the knots of people to find Raj, whom I'd decided would be my target at the lunch. Finally, I spotted him, dressed as a Beatle, standing beside Serendipity, who was wearing a simple white sleeveless shift dress, with a circlet of white flowers in her hair. She appeared clean, cool, and calm…and I was just a little jealous that she looked so perfect. I was saved from having any less charitable thoughts about Serendipity by the arrival of Lizzie Jackson who was dressed as…herself.

"Good to see you. How are you? Long time no see." She grinned. "Hey, you look great. Boy, that dress is just your size, Cait. Wherever did you find it?" She was almost vibrating with excitement.

I smiled politely as I replied, "Ellen rustled it up for me. Apparently, it was her mother's. Bud and I didn't know about the dressing up thing, so we were lucky that Ellen had some clothes at her place that we could borrow."

Lizzie grimaced and said, "Ah, have you just been to Ellen's apartment?"

I replied, "Yes. Have you ever visited there?"

She peered through her round glasses with eyes that became just as round. "Hmm," she nodded. "She came to me about four years ago and asked for some advice about it. You know...the hoarding? Said she'd found someone she wanted to 'make space for' in her life and that she knew she'd have to make some real space for them too. Back then she was quite open-minded about such things, and we talked a great deal. I even showed her some techniques for meditation and self-hypnosis that I thought might help her."

"Something like wakeful dreaming?" I asked.

Lizzie looked both taken aback and delighted. "Why yes, that sort of thing, but what does a marketing person like you know about my field?"

Oops...my cover!

"I once helped promote a line of self-help books, and one of them was about mental reorganization," I lied.

Lizzie nodded sagely. "Ah yes, it's an area where folks can help themselves much more than they think. Ellen and I had a few sessions together, and she seemed to take to it like a duck to water. Surprisingly, she has a talent for using words to calm. I even thought she might be about to join us in the Faceting fold, but something...happened. I don't think that whatever relationship she was hoping for came to anything, and she became, well...as you see her now. Sometimes she's quite scathing about our approach to life. You think she'd have let it go by now. But hey, that was her problem all along."

I nodded; I didn't want to get sidetracked into more Faceting talk. "Is the food good?"

"Oh yes," she replied. "Sheri's totally onboard with our views on food, and she's had help for this." Lizzie nodded in the general direction of the groaning tables as she spoke. "We've loaned her Ray from the restaurant to oversee the prep, and she's got some local girls to help with the serving and clearing. I think it's a great idea to go back to some of those old favorites we used to enjoy in decades gone by. Of course, I love what Ray does with food at our place nowadays, but, sometimes, it's nice to bump into an old friend on a plate, right?" She laughed as she added, "You should go see. It's quite a spread."

"I intend to," I replied quickly, seeing a chance to escape. I waved my farewell as I moved away.

As I wandered across the cavernous room toward the food – and Raj Pinder – I could see that every finish in the MacMillan home was just about as high-end as it gets. Then, on the laden tables, I spotted the retro favorites of aspic-encased salmon, slices of aubergine topped with tomato and parmesan, prawn cocktails, and even a row of fondue pots: they'd really stuck to their retro theme.

"Hey, have one of these!" Colin appeared in front of me holding a tall glass full of an almost fluorescent orange fluid. A slice of orange and a maraschino cherry speared onto a little pink umbrella was balanced on its edge. "Mom says it's called a Harvey Wallbanger. I think it looks disgusting. It's this, or sangria." He wrinkled his nose.

As he pushed the glass toward me, I caught a whiff of Galliano…and it all came back to me: one too many of that exact cocktail during a friend's birthday party in Swansea almost thirty years earlier. I began to gag and pushed the glass away as politely as I could.

"Could I have sangria instead?" I asked, praying my saliva glands would calm down. "But first, the loo?" Colin pointed me in the right direction.

Don't go throwing up just because of your perfect memory, Cait.

Locking the loo door behind me, I took some deep breaths and ran cold water over my wrists. I patted my neck with dampened toilet tissue, and finally managed to focus on memories that would calm my stomach: sea air, freshly cut grass, sunlight dappling through trees onto springy undergrowth – freeing, cleansing experiences…to replace the unpleasant ones.

It usually works.

Eventually, I managed to calm my gag reflex, and I took a moment to gather my thoughts: I had to get out there, find Raj, again, and get him to open up to me, a complete stranger. *Easy.* But first, a smoke. I'd have to ask where I could light up.

Peering out around the bathroom door, I spotted our hostess, who was dressed in a chequered, sleeveless dress that I suspected was of late '60s, or early '70s, vintage. I made a beeline for her, as she fluttered her way between guests.

"Hi Sheri, nice dress," I opened.

"Thanks. Carol Brady did such a good job with all those children, don't you think?"

Ah, the Brady Bunch. Right.

"Absolutely," I replied, like a good little guest. "Wonderful spread," I added, meaning it.

"Thanks," replied Sheri. "It's not exactly gourmet, but it is all fresh, local, organic, and peanut-free, because of Colin, of course." She looked over my shoulder at the table traffic. "I just hope there's enough of everything."

"Oh, I'm sure there will be," I replied. There seemed to be enough to feed a small army. "Is Colin allergic to peanuts, then?" I ventured.

"Yes. Always has been, poor thing. It's not as difficult for him these days, because it's so much better understood. In fact, so many children have the same problem that his school is nut-free now."

"It must still be difficult to eat out," I observed.

"Well, it sure used to be, but there are a lot of places now that offer good, safe choices. SoulVineFineDine, for one, and Faceting for Life, for another. They're both totally peanut-free restaurants. Even Pat Corrigan, this morning, made sure everything was safe. He's thoughtful like that. Well, with both Serendipity and Colin there, he would make special effort, of course."

"Serendipity's allergic too?" I replied. I tried to sound interested.

Why am I talking about this? I want to know where I can smoke.

Shari nodded. "Oh yes, that's why she first became interested in food, and its preparation. She's doing some wonderful things with peanut-free recipes for catering companies."

"Right. She mentioned something to me last night about a range of sauces she's working on, though I didn't realize they were peanut-free because she, herself, has allergies."

Come on Cait – get to the point.

Sheri nodded at a passing couple dressed as Fred Astaire and Ginger Rogers as she said, "Peanut-free, gluten-free, and preservative-free organic sauces. Oh, they're excellent. She had Colin and me over to do some tastings and even he liked them…which is saying something. I worry about him so; he seems to live in his own little world, all those weird fantasy things he likes." She smiled indulgently at the thought of her son.

I patted her arm. "Don't worry. It's normal. And all it means is that he's interested in history, mythology, and nice, old-fashioned tales of good versus evil, where a hero is needed. A friend of mine at the university has had a fulfilling career as a professor of comparative mythologies, and he's written lots of research papers about the use of ancient mythologies as the inspiration for science fiction stories. Colin will be just fine. He's intelligent, articulate, observant…and he's pretty fit, too, with all that cycling he does. Which isn't something you can say about many seventeen-year-olds these days."

By now, Sheri was looking much brighter.

Good, now I can make my break for freedom.

I dared, "Speaking of Colin, I asked him to get me a drink, which I should collect from him. And…I wondered if there was anywhere that I might be allowed to smoke?"

Sheri smiled. "The middle and bottom decks are the smoking ones. It's where you'll find my Rob, no doubt, holding court in the sunshine with his cigars, and beers. A friend of his from West Kelowna hitched a ride across the lake with the Souls on their boat. They might still be down at the pier. At least, I'm guessing that's where he is, because I haven't seen him for ages."

I thanked my hostess, and managed to spot Raj Pinder near the exit. I grabbed a glass of sangria on my way, then made eye contact with Bud long enough to make smoking motions to him as I pointed to the decks.

"Just the man," I said, as I caught Raj by the arm and firmly steered him in the direction I wanted to go. He looked surprised, but didn't object as I added, "Could you spare a few minutes?"

"Okey dokey," he replied, smiling. He followed me as I grasped the handrail of the deck staircase and tried to not look down the cliffside beneath me. "Let me take that," he said, grabbing my drink.

"Such a gent," I replied, not taking my eyes off the steps.

"Well, you're such a lady," he responded, which could have made me smile if I hadn't been balancing on kitten heels, on wooden steps, on the side of a cliff. Reaching the deck was a relief, and I plopped into a patio chair, reached into my tiny purse and lit a cigarette. It took about three seconds. I glugged my drink, then I gave my attention to my escort.

"You alright there, Cait?" he asked. I nodded, puffing. "Only, you don't look too good. Is it the heights that get you?" I nodded again, still puffing. "Aye, poor old Annette were much the same. Mind you, she started to come over all queer for no reason at all toward the end. Flat ground or no, she'd get a look about her that said she weren't feeling well. Maybe that's how depression can take you, I dunno."

I took my chance. "You know Raj, you're a lovely chap. I saw the way you looked at Ellen when she said last night that Bud had come to help her look into who might have killed her sister." Raj opened his mouth to speak, but I stopped him. "I just wanted to ask you a couple of questions about Annette." Raj was beginning to look alarmed. Putting all niceties aside, I added, "Look, it's obvious to me that you and Serendipity are a couple, right?"

Raj nodded, "Well…aye, but please don't say owt. Her parents would go berserk. Well, her mother would, any road. It's awkward. You saw her last night; there's nowt can quiet that Suzie when she wants summat." His Yorkshire accent was oddly calming.

"And what about Annette? Did you and she have a relationship?" I was pretty sure I knew the answer, but asked anyway.

"What makes you ask that?" Raj's expression signaled even more alarm.

"Raj, you're an attractive, single man. You and Annette traveled to a lot of the same places, for several years, had a huge amount in common, and she, too, was single, and not unattractive. It's not beyond the bounds of reason to imagine you two getting together, though I'm guessing that being competitors in the world of wine might have made it difficult to be open about it." I kept my voice low; I wasn't sure how sound might carry against the cliff.

Raj finally nodded. "Okay, but please don't say owt about that, neither." He drew close to me and whispered. "No one knows except Serendipity. I told her, but no one else. It weren't nothing big, just a bit of a fling that didn't last long, just two events really, one in California, one in Niagara. And that were it. We couldn't cope with the sneaking about back here, and the fact that we couldn't talk about owt we wanted to. I were working at Sammy's place back then, of course, and there's stuff as goes on in a winery that you can't talk about to the competition. We agreed, it weren't worth it. We called it off about six or seven weeks before she died. And, no, I didn't break her heart. I know that 'cos she and I talked it through."

"Do you think that's why she bequeathed you her share of the winery?"

Raj sunk into his Beatle suit. "I never expected that, it were a right surprise. I dunno what she were thinking. Floored me. I told Ellen she should argue her case with the lawyers, but no, she says she won't. I feel terrible about it, but there's nowt I can do. It's a brilliant chance for me…but to get it that way? Terrible. I mean, like I said, it weren't nothing serious. Why would Annette do it? Lovely woman…but that?"

The closer I studied him, the more I wondered if Raj Pinder was better at controlling his physical self than most people.

I pressed on. "What about the wording of Annette's will? I understand that she tried to entail the share of the business to your 'firstborn'. Why so?"

Raj sighed. Deeply. "None of it makes no sense. I talked to the lawyer about it, the one that Annette sent the will to, and he said – in front of me and Ellen like – that, what with Annette killing herself, Ellen could contest the will if she wanted, and she might win. He weren't being nasty to me, he just said that he thought he should mention Ellen's options. He also told me that, if I were to keep the inheritance, then I should draw up some papers later on about that weird clause, 'cos it could mess things up if I had more than one kid in't future."

Raj sounded bemused more than anything else. I had just one more topic I wanted to talk to him about.

"Stacey Willow?" It was all I needed to say.

Raj shook his head. "You too? Ellen won't shut up about that girl. I hardly knew her. Her older brother and I played the odd game of footie – you know, soccer – and she were in the crowd a couple of times when we all had a drink afterwards. That were it. Then Ellen's hugging me and saying how sorry she is for me that Stacey's dead…I mean, I didn't have owt against the girl, poor thing, and I'm really sorry for her brother, who took it hard. But Ellen going on about it like I lost the love of my life? Nuts. Aye, nuts."

"So there was nothing between you and Stacey Willow?"

"Nowt. Never."

I'm ninety-nine percent sure you're telling the truth.

"Pretty girl?" I asked.

"Oh aye. Very easy on the eye she were," he replied, smiling wistfully. Finally rallying he asked, "So why are you poking about in all…this, anyway?"

"I promised Bud I'd ask a few questions. You're top of the list of suspects for killing Annette, because you're the one who profited from her death," I said bluntly.

He deserves the truth.

Raj looked horrified. "There's folks going about saying I've killed Annette?" He seemed nonplussed. "No one's ever said owt to me. Not to me face, any road."

"Well, they wouldn't be likely to, would they, Raj?"

"No, I s'pose not," he replied quietly. "I…I had no idea."

My mind was racing; a few things were beginning to make more sense. However, whatever my growing suspicions might be, I still had to work out how someone could have convinced Annette Newman to sit in the cab of a truck that was gradually filling with exhaust fumes.

As he stood, Raj looked down at me with his dark, soulful eyes and whispered, "I liked Annette. She were good at her job, she worked hard, she were fun, and we had some good times – you know? But…it's the real thing with Serendipity. She's the one, I'm sure of it. We've known each other for years, but we never got together until after I left her dad's place, mainly because her mother followed me about all the time when I were there, and it seemed, well…not right, to be going about with her daughter. But we can't say anything yet. We've got to wait for the right moment. So, you know…?"

"I won't say a word, promise," I replied, and I twisted an invisible key against my closed lips, tossing it with abandon over my shoulder. Had it been real, it would have hit Colin MacMillan in the face.

"Hey, I brought you that drink." It sounded as though Colin was shouting, because the conversation between Raj and myself had been so hushed.

"Thanks, you're very kind," I replied to Colin, waving, unnecessarily, at Raj's back. "I've nearly finished this one. It's very good. Who made it?"

Colin sat beside me, in the seat that the escaping Raj had vacated. "Mom. She drinks a lot of the stuff. It's organic wine, of course, from SoulVine Wines, and all the fruit's organic, and local…and she even buys local organic gin to put in it from a place in Pemberton, just along the lake. I guess she thinks that makes it a health drink." His voice was flat.

I had a thought. "Colin, you know you said you saw Annette driving home the day she died?" Colin nodded. "What exactly was she doing? You said she was talking to someone on the phone?"

"Yeah, hands free. She always did that. I can show you." He turned in his seat so that I was looking at the left side of his face. He sat upright and adopted a driving pose. Suddenly he started to flail his arms, shaking his head and making exaggerated howling motions with his mouth. Next, he wiped away non-existent tears with his right fist, intermittently waving his right arm away from me, as he placed his left onto the imaginary steering wheel. It was quite a performance.

"Thanks," I said. "You saw her from the driver's side of the truck?" He nodded. "And about how far away were you?"

"Oh, she drove toward me, then right past me. I was sort of parked, with my bike, just standing there in Anen Close, right next to the sign for the B & B. I don't think she noticed me, though. I was only about five feet away and her window was open, that's how I know she was shouting. Oh – and I just remembered something she shouted…"

I was all ears. "And what was that?"

"She said, 'So you've never loved me, then? Why should I help you?' That's what she shouted."

Very interesting. A lover? An ex-lover? Who needed 'help'?

"Is that good?" Colin was almost panting with excitement and anticipation.

"It might be," I replied slowly. I smiled and stood. "I need to go and get something to eat now, before my stomach thinks my throat's been cut."

We walked up the stairs together, and Bud met us at the top. "I'm glad you're back," he said, smiling enigmatically. "I didn't want you to miss all the fun."

"What fun?"

I peered through the glass wall toward the area where the food had been laid out, to see Suzie Soul – in full Betty Boop regalia – hurling a plate of something at Vince Chen's head. Sammy Soul was trying to hold her back, his Elvis wig askew on top of his bald head, and Serendipity – her little circlet of innocent white flowers now trampled underfoot – was trying to grab her father. Sheri MacMillan and Marlene Wiser both darted toward the airborne plate to try to prevent it from reaching its target. They failed. In a corner, Ellen Newman was sucking her thumbnail and smirking, holding Raj's arm as he tried to pull away from her, toward Serendipity. The whole scene was even more wonderful because I could just hear the Beach Boys' "Good Vibrations" above the crashing of the crockery.

"What on earth is going on?" I asked, not really needing to.

Bud explained. "It seems that – following on from last night's embarrassment – Vince decided to tell Suzie that he's had enough…but she doesn't agree with him. Maybe he thought he'd get away with it easier if he told her in public. Poor guy."

"Yes, poor guy," I replied. "Do you think there'll be any food left when she's finished? I haven't eaten anything yet, and I'm hungry."

Suzie Soul suddenly flung her arms around her husband's neck and kissed him…and he began to physically haul her away from yet another party.

Bud and I walked into the room to see if there was anything left worth eating, just as Ellen tapped her glass with a spoon. I expected some sort of toast, but, no, Ellen had one more lunchtime surprise up her sleeve for us, it seemed.

"Listen up, folks," she shouted. Everyone did. "I know that last night was quite eventful, and today's turning out to have its own very special moments too…but there's something I must say: I had a bit too much to drink last night, and said some things about the death of my sister that I very much regret. I know many of you have now met Bud, and Cait, and Bud's put his considerable experience as a police officer to work. He's looked into matters, and has convinced me that my poor, dear sister, Annette, really did intend to take her own life. Now I hope that puts stops any speculation running around the city, or the industry. I know it's difficult, but I must accept it, and I'm working on that. I feel better now that I've talked it through with

Bud, so, thank you, Bud, and, of course, thank you Cait." Then she raised her glass toward the two of us and drank.

Bud's mouth was open; I'd managed to clamp mine shut.

Our surprise was mirrored around the room; the body language I observed was screaming, "At least she's come to her senses," mixed with, "Maybe she's had too much to drink again?"

All very telling.

Bud shut his mouth and headed to the bar shaking his head. "Coming, Cait?" he called over his shoulder.

"Right behind you," I called back, and I followed him as fast as my kitten heels allowed.

For about twenty minutes, no one talked to us, and we barely spoke to each other, except to mutter about the food. We'd decided, after a quick drink, that it was best to graze. The atmosphere was…difficult, despite Sheri MacMillan's best efforts.

By about three o'clock, most people had already drifted away, and I asked Bud, "Have we got a plan? What are we doing when we leave here? Which, by the way, I think should be soon. We've got a dinner at SoulVineFineDine at eight, after all." I looked at the bowl of sherry trifle I was holding and decided I'd have just one more spoonful before setting it aside…though I knew I'd have to wrestle with my conscience to put down a bowl that was anything other than completely empty.

Bud looked around, "Caitlin Morgan, I want nothing more than to have some time alone with you. Do you think we could arrange that? We need to talk, Cait. I found out some interesting stuff about the Wisers from Ray and Gloria, over there." He nodded toward Bonnie, and the man and woman I still hadn't managed to meet. I referenced Ellen's notes for Bud.

"Ah, that's who they are: Ray Murciano, chef at the Faceting for Life Restaurant – originally from Florida, a Cuban-American, now a Canadian. He built a reputation for his Cuban cuisine when he worked in South Beach, Miami – now building another one for his work with organic produce and the Hundred Mile approach. Gloria Thompson – a Kelowna born and bred flake, according to Ellen. Most of her notes were a pretty scathing physical description. That said, she does seem to be on the overpowering end of the dress code, but, hey, look at me. She works at the Faceting for Life store. Ray wasn't here when Annette died, because he hadn't arrived from the States at that time and, conveniently, Gloria was away on an extended stay at 'The Gem' in Sedona. They're both out of the frame as far as Annette's murder is concerned. But I'm guessing they might both be back in it for Stacey Willow."

"Okay – stop right there, Cait," Bud sounded stern. "Stacey Willow killed herself. That's that. Forget her. She's got nothing to do with Annette. But I'll tell you what has got something to with Annette…"

Unfortunately, he didn't get the chance to tell me, because at that very moment, Ellen pounced and offered to give us a ride to Anen House. Of course we accepted, and we thanked Sheri and Colin for their hospitality on our way out.

As I tottered back to Ellen's truck, which was now sitting almost alone on the roadside, I had to avoid a pool of yuk in the gutter, then finally – once I'd managed to find all the bits and buckles to secure myself – Ellen took off along Lakeshore Road at speed. She was going so fast that she had to stamp on the brakes when we rounded a bend that swung down a steep part of the road and encountered a small, orange car that had smashed against the cliff face of the hill upon which Anen House stood. Smoke was coming from beneath the crumpled front end of the vehicle.

"It's the Wisers. That's their car," shouted Ellen. "Someone call 911!"

At least, I'm pretty sure that's what she said, because at that moment the Wisers' car exploded, hurling rocks and debris at Ellen's windshield. Blinded by the smashing glass, Ellen lost control, and the truck skidded into the roadside ditch, all three of us lurching against our seatbelts.

The world seemed to stop. Eventually, I looked around.

Bud seemed okay, and we nodded at each other.

"Are you alright?" Bud asked Ellen.

She was clearly shaken, but uninjured, it seemed.

The truck was lying in the ditch at an angle, with Bud's door facing the ground. He opened it, but I could see he wouldn't be able to push it far enough to get out that way. I felt for my buckle, popped it, and grabbed the little white purse that had slithered across the seat – my phone was in it. I managed to push open my door – up into the air – and I wiggled up and out.

I finally made it to the ground. "Stay there, I'm going to see if I can help," I shouted at Ellen and Bud.

I heard Bud yelling, "No," as I ran toward the vehicle.

But there was nothing I could do when I got there. It was quite obvious that the two figures in the car were beyond help; the whole thing was ablaze. I just stood there, numb, fighting back the tears and rage. I felt totally and utterly useless. Then I gave in, and let the emotion wash over me.

I remembered the phone call I'd received about my parents' accident – word for word, pause for pause, sob for sob. I remembered the trip back to Wales from Canada, to make the arrangements; the funeral, the hymn singing, the smell and feel of dampness in the church; the crematorium, the softness of the vicar's hand shaking mine. Then there was the reception, the dry sandwiches, the smell of flowers dying in vases. My sister Siân's uncontrollable crying. Our hugs, our shared sense of loss. The smell of the photo albums as we'd sorted through them and divided up the photographs. I don't usually let myself relive it all. It's too painful. Now, I couldn't stop myself.

Finally, I dragged myself back to reality. Poor Gordy and Marlene. How awful. They were such lovely people…so full of…life. I hoped they'd died instantly, before the explosion or the flames, and wondered why they'd have had an accident there, on a corner they must have driven around so many times over the years. Then I remembered the puddle of yuk on the road that I'd side-stepped back at the MacMillans' place.

Brake fluid!

Tea and Brandy

My visualization of brake fluid on the roadside was interrupted by the screeching arrival of Colin MacMillan on his bicycle. He took in the scene from beneath his lime-green cycling helmet, open-mouthed.

He mumbled, "I heard the bang. The explosion. I thought it was you." He was clearly distraught.

"No, we're all fine," I managed, still crying. "Ellen says it's the Wisers' car?"

Colin nodded. "I'll call 911," he said, pulling his cell phone from his pocket.

"No – I'll do that. Could you see if you can help Ellen out of the truck? I'm too short."

"Sure." He picked up his bike, and laid it carefully on the side of the road.

I made the call – *why didn't I stuff a hanky into this stupid little purse?* – and Colin managed to get Ellen out of her truck. He helped haul Bud out, too.

The next half an hour or so was a blur of sirens, first responders, and a creeping realization of the depth of the tragedy we'd witnessed. I took my chance to inform a young officer about the brake fluid I'd seen back at the MacMillans' house; he made notes, looking suitably concerned. Everything seemed to be moving at half speed, me included, and I suspected that the three of us who'd been in the truck were feeling the effects of shock. Luckily, none of us had sustained any injuries, which was something of a miracle.

Pat Corrigan arrived on the scene in his car: the sirens had alerted him to the fact that something wasn't right, and he'd driven down from Anen House to see if he could help. He, too, was horrified by the terrible sight, and its meaning.

Eventually – though the road was still cordoned off – the fire had been properly extinguished, and the medics were finished with us, as were the police…for the time being, they said…so we were allowed to leave. Colin headed homeward on his trusty metal steed, and Pat drove us back to the B & B, where Lauren was anxiously hovering on the front doorstep.

She ushered us into the house, then settled us in the lounge, while Pat explained everything that had happened. It still didn't seem real to me; we'd left the MacMillans' lunch less than an hour earlier. It was all so fast. So…horribly final.

Lauren brought a pot of tea and three brandies. There wasn't much talk, just a general numbness. I drank my brandy before my tea.

"We'll host the wake here, of course," announced Pat, doing his best to lift the gloomy mood, "if that's okay with you, Ellen?"

Ellen nodded. She studied her tea.

"Sure we will," agreed Lauren. "No two people were more full of life. It'll be a grand party. A big one. Such long, loving lives. There'll be a lot of folks that'll be wanting a last knees-up with Gordy and Marlene Wiser."

I absolutely get the Irish thing of wanting to celebrate lives, not cry over death; it's even psychologically sound. However, the thought of a party reminded me about the event we were due to attend at SoulVine Wines that evening.

"Do you think the dinner tonight will go ahead?" I asked.

Somebody has to.

"I'll call the Souls to find out," suggested Lauren.

For all that she was usually a bit of a grump, Lauren certainly came into her own when there was someone to fuss over; she headed off to make the call, and we were all still sitting there, silently, when she returned. "Well, bad news travels fast. They know all about the Wisers and they're going ahead with the plans for their dinner. Serendipity says that everything'll go to waste otherwise, and Sammy Soul thinks it's the best way to honor two fun-loving people. I cannot say that I disagree with him."

We all half nodded. Lauren was in her element. "Now listen up, you three. You've had a terrible shock, so you have, so this is what I suggest: Pat, you'll drive Ellen home…it'll be a while before that truck of yours is on the road again, Ellen, so you should get off to your own place, have a long, hot shower, or a bath even, and get yourself ready for the evening. Bud, Cait, you should do the same. Pop up to your rooms, why don't you, and get yourselves cleaned up, then maybe have a bit of a nap. You don't have to be at the Souls' place until eight, so you've plenty of time. Right. Come on with you all, let's be moving and doing."

She clapped her hands, and we all seemed to snap out of our stupor. She was right, of course; sitting about wasn't going to help anyone, so we all did as she'd suggested.

Bud and I hugged each other, hard, at the top of the stairs, before agreeing we were each headed for our own bathtub.

As I turned to go, he asked, "You okay? Really okay?"

I nodded. "I had a bit of a thing back there. About Mum and Dad. Their accident. Seeing the Wisers'? It brought it all back."

He pulled me into his arms again. "I guessed," he whispered.

"I knew you'd understand. I'm…I'm through that, now." I leaned back, recalling what Bud had said at the lunch. "What was it that Ray and Gloria told you about Gordy and Marlene?"

Bud looked puzzled. His expression cleared. "Right…they'd mentioned to Ray and Gloria, when they were having lunch down at Faceting for Life one day, that they'd taken it upon themselves to collect Annette's mail and that they'd put it in the old apple store with all her other stuff. Apparently, Colin was right: that's where all Annette's things are, and now all her mail, too, it seems."

"And that's it?" I said, somewhat underwhelmed. Bud nodded. I suggested, "Okay then, how about we both go and get cleaned up and sorted out, eh? Give ourselves an hour or two to relax and rejuvenate? At least we have a bath each to use."

He smiled, but looked tired. I wondered how these two sudden deaths might be triggering his grief for Jan: I was only too well aware – both professionally, and personally – that this was exactly the sort of shock to the system that could reignite the initial response to a prior emotional trauma.

I asked, "How are you doing with all of this?"

Bud's smile didn't quite reach his eyes. "It's…well, it's a reminder of just how sudden the end of it all can be. If I needed one. Which I didn't. But…yeah…a bit of quiet time won't go amiss."

Or we could talk…

I decided to not press the matter. "See you in a while."

We squeezed each other's hands before we separated and went to our own rooms.

I stripped off Ellen's dead mother's dress, and dropped it onto the slipper chair in the corner of my room. I hoped that the sound of the running bathwater and the warmth of the billowing steam would begin to ease my sadness. They didn't. I cleaned off the bits of makeup that had mingled with smuts of ash on my face, washed my hair, wrapped it in a fluffy towel and soaked in the deep, old-fashioned bathtub for the next ten minutes, trying to think of…nothing.

Trying to not visualize my own parents in that burned out car.

When my puckered fingertips told me it was time to get out of the bath, dry off, and sort out my hair, I lay on my bed in my waffled robe staring out at the glittering lake.

The permanence of nature; the frailty of life.

It was no good, I wasn't going to be able to catch a nap. I checked my watch: almost five o'clock. I got up, pulled on the clothes I'd planned to wear to breakfast the next day, and padded over to Bud's room.

I knocked, but there was no answer, so I opened the door quietly. There he was, in his waffly robe, sleeping on top of his bedclothes, flat on his back with his hands curled like otter paws. He looked adorable. I didn't want to disturb him so closed his door as silently as I could, went back to my own room, grabbed a pair of flats and my big bag, and tiptoed downstairs, where I headed to the kitchen in search of a Corrigan.

"Hey, you're looking a bit better," said Lauren as she glanced up from the bowl in which she was mixing something yellow and creamy.

"I feel it," I replied, smiling. "Thanks for everything. You're great in a crisis. A bath was just what I needed, though I'm pretty restless now."

"That'll be the shock," she observed knowingly. "Funny thing, shock. My mother was a nurse. Often talked about shock, she did. And it's come in handy at last."

"I wondered if you could help some more?"

"Sure thing, what's it to be?" Lauren wiped her hands on her full-body apron.

"There's an old apple store, behind the hill?" Lauren nodded. "Is it locked do you know? And, if so, do you have a key?"

"To be sure it is, and we do, though why you'd be wanting to tramp down there I don't know." She walked over to a small cupboard on the wall. Inside were two rows of hooks, six of which had keys hanging on them. She pulled off a single big, iron key, which she handed to me.

"Ellen's stored all of Annette's belongings there, and she said I could take a look," I lied.

Lauren shrugged. "Do you know where you're going?" I shook my head. "Go out the back door, past our place, then there's a path that'll take you there. It's only about ten minutes away, and it's quite well done up in there – you know, electricity, a few lightbulbs, and so on. Though that old lock might take some work. It's one heck of a key, to be sure. I haven't seen one like that before. Big enough for you?" She laughed. The key was about six inches long, and its shaft seemed to have been welded into a huge old iron doorknob.

I wonder how big the lock will be?

"Thanks, Lauren," I said, heading to the back door. "If he emerges, tell Bud where I've gone, and that I'll be back by seven – that'll give me half an hour to sort myself out before I leave. You know…put a bit of slap on the old mug."

"You Welsh, always putting yourselves down, you are. You should be more like us Irish and revel in the beauty God gave you."

I chuckled. "I did when I was your age, Lauren, but just you wait and see how you feel about makeup when you're my age. I've got a good few years on you. You're young yet – enjoy the collagen while you've got it."

I headed out past the double-wide, which looked very homey, and found the path Lauren had described. The track wasn't good, but at least I was going down it, not climbing up. Unfortunately, that meant I had to look down the steep incline, so I focused on my feet…which was a shame, because it was still such a beautiful day, though there wasn't much warmth left in the sun, and a few clouds were starting to bubble up in the west.

I really didn't know what I hoped to find at the apple store and, while I didn't know what it would look like, it was quite clear that I'd reached it when I got there. Something like an old log cabin built had been onto the side of the hill, with a spacious, flat area in front of it, and a wide, rugged track leading down the remainder of the hillside. The structure itself had no windows, just one large door, covered with an iron gate. An old padlock secured a bolt to a big metal plate that was set off to one side of the doorway. The padlock was massive.

Come on, Cait, don't hang about.

I pushed the key into the lock and was surprised that it turned easily; the lock fell open. I pulled it off, slid back the metal bolt it had been holding, and popped the padlock back onto the U-shaped hook on the end of the bolt for safe keeping. I pushed the key into my bag and pulled open the heavy gate. It made soft, metallic scraping sounds as it swung open, but there didn't seem to be any problems with the hinges. The wooden door itself wasn't locked, it just had a thumb-lever latch, which was also in good working order. I stepped into the cabin and felt the cool, dry air inside. The place still smelled of apples.

Lovely.

As the light from the northern sky fell onto the smooth dirt floor ahead of me, I allowed my eyes to adjust to the dimness, then looked around for a light switch. Just ahead of me a light bulb attached to a simple wire had a little chain hanging down beside it. I pulled the chain, and the bulb lit. I repeated this three times as I walked further into the cave part of the apple store. Ellen's father had been incredibly clever; he'd managed to turn a natural depression in the cliff face into a wonderful storage space about forty feet deep, including the ten feet or so of the cabin, and at least forty feet wide. It was big, airy, and extremely dry. Ideal for apples. The wooden door swung itself shut, but I patted the heavy key in my purse and looked around, not worried about being able to get out again.

The scene was reminiscent of what we'd seen at Ellen's apartment – row upon row of stacked plastic storage boxes, each bearing a label. At one end was a bit of a jumble and some pieces of furniture, so I headed there first.

A small wooden cabinet caught my eye, upon which there sat a plastic box, filled with mail.

Annette's mail, delivered here by the Wisers.

I picked up the box and realized it was standing not on a simple cabinet, but on a wind-up gramophone player. Recalling my grandmother's old machine – which I was never allowed to use – I opened the door in the front of the cabinet to reveal a stack of hard, black 78 rpm records in tattered paper jackets. I enjoyed feeling their considerable weight in my hands.

Just like Grandma Morgan's.

I pulled the *Moonlight Sonata* from its cover and placed it on the bed, wound the handle, worked out how to lift and swivel the needle-holding arm, and set the record in motion. As I lay the needle onto the spinning disk, a rasping sound, interspersed with clicks, echoed around the apple store, then the long-dead fingers of Paderewski beckoned me to join him on a magical journey. By the time the needle was bumping around in the center of the disk, I was crying my eyes out.

Beethoven's nothing if not cathartic.

I fished about in my bag for a hanky…of course I didn't have one – *note to self, must pack hankies in every bag you own* – so I used my sleeve. Not pleasant, but necessary. I set about finding my specs and began wading through Annette's mail. A lot of it was rubbish, and I wondered why on earth the Wisers would have thought it worth saving, or storing. Some was clearly from institutions I guessed Ellen was now dealing with on behalf of her dead sister, and there was one very intriguing, boxy package. It had been opened. The sender's address was in Newfoundland, and it had been delivered by courier, not Canada Post. I knew what it was before I looked inside. It had to be the James Sandy snuff box.

My fingers trembled as I opened the end of the package that had already been split apart. Inside the outer box was a fat roll of bubble-wrap, which, uncurled, revealed a green velvet pouch. I could feel the snuff box inside, but I hardly dared touch it. Finally, I took the little treasure out of its soft envelope. It sat easily in the palm of my hand and was exquisitely plain, except for the signature which had been, so the story goes, burned into the wood with a hot iron nail. *James Sandy.* I opened the lid, which moved easily and showed a hinge and a liner without a single dent or abrasion. It was as close to perfect as a used item could be. I peered into the packaging again, and found a plastic wallet. Inside, protected against the elements, was a letter written in spidery copperplate that was difficult to read in the dimness of the old light bulbs. I could at least tell that the signature, James Sandy, was the same as on the snuff box.

Yes, a grail for a collector, to be sure.

I wondered how much Annette had paid to be the proud owner of a box she'd dreamed about, and I read through the copy of the paperwork that bore the logo of the courier company that had delivered it. Then it dawned on me…someone must have signed for this package; the courier wouldn't have left something this valuable on the doorstep. The signature on the paperwork was Annette's. *Annette's!* It appeared to be exactly the same signature as those I'd seen on the suicide note, her will, and the facsimile of Annette's signature that Ellen had shown me on the artwork for the wine label. However, the date of delivery was two days after Annette had died.

How could Annette have signed for a package two days after she was dead?

I looked at my watch: six o'clock…I couldn't dawdle. I picked up the snuff box and reinserted it into its packaging, shoved it and the signed courier's receipt into my purse – *just as well it's as big as it is* – turned out the lights as I went, then pulled open the big wooden door. The metal-barred gate had swung shut, so I pushed it outwards. It wouldn't budge. I pushed again. Nothing. I tried to peer out, but I could only fit my nose between the metal bars. I rattled the gate. Nothing.

How on earth has it got stuck?

"Hello?" I shouted. "Anybody there?"

Don't be stupid, Cait, of course there's no one there.

I rooted around in my purse for my cellphone, but I couldn't find it. Knowing how the blessed thing can disappear when it wants to, I dumped the entire contents of my bag onto the floor of the apple store and spread everything out, then felt around every inch of the lining. Nope, it wasn't there. The penny dropped…*it's still in the little white purse I took to lunch.*

I felt the bitterness of panic in my throat. Back at the gate again I shouted, "Hello – can anybody hear me?"

My voice rang around the canyon and echoed back to me. It was a very lonely sound.

Apple Juice

My stomach tightened, my breathing became shallow and rapid.

Don't panic, Cait. Calm down.

I shouted louder. "Hellooooooo! Anyone there?"

Once again my voice echoed back at me.

"I'm here," came a quiet reply.

I jumped, then shouted, "Hello – who is it? I'm in here – in the apple store."

"Yes, I know," said Colin MacMillan calmly, and quite close by. "You've been in there for some time. How did you get in?"

He appeared from the deepening shadows beyond the gate. It seemed to be a very odd question, under the circumstances.

I was a bit nonplussed, but regained my focus quickly. "Colin. Hello. What are you doing here?"

"I was just hanging out, down below, and I heard you shouting," he replied innocently.

I could tell he was lying. "No you weren't. You've been following me, haven't you? That's why you seem to be everywhere I am. Colin, it's not right, you know…" I stopped myself; it didn't matter how unhealthy his little obsession with me might be, the important thing was that he was on the spot, and he could help.

I adopted my "firm but fair professor" tone, "Look, Colin, this gate has somehow shut itself and I can't open it. Can you open it for me from there? It's very important that I get out."

"It's locked," he said. "There's a padlock locked onto a bolt. I'd need a key."

"That's okay – I've got the key here." I plucked it from the pile on the floor and pushed the shaft through the iron bars, but the round knob on the end of the key, which I'd thought charming, now made the object too wide to fit between them.

"It won't fit," Colin observed.

"No kidding."

He asked, "What shall we do now? I don't think there's much chance of me being able to break the padlock with a rock or anything. I'm not really that strong. Wiry, you know, but not strong." He sounded deflated. "If I were The Doctor I could use my sonic screwdriver." He smiled wistfully.

"Well, you're not The Doctor, and neither of us has a sonic screwdriver, because they don't exist. Fantasy is all well and good, in its place, but sometimes you just have to face up to reality and deal with it, Colin. And the reality is that I need to be somewhere that isn't here. Now."

I wasn't as angry with Colin as I was with myself, but that wasn't what he was getting out of this conversation…and he didn't deserve that. I took a deep breath.

"Colin, I'm sorry. I'm not cross with you, I'm cross with myself. Just give me a minute to think." I did. "Have you got a cellphone with you?"

"Of course," he replied, sounding hurt, "but there's no signal here."

"Let me see," I said, then added hastily, "I'm sure you're right." He was. No reception. So no phone call to Bud.

"Would you be able to run up to Anen House and get Bud?" I knew he'd be there, and he'd probably still be asleep.

"Sure, but how will he open the lock?"

I thought it might hurt the boy even more if I pointed out that Bud had a good deal more strength than he, and might well be able to smash the lock…so I didn't say it.

He added, "Bud's quite old. Like Dad, or older even."

I bridled. "That's a little unfair, don't you think? Older can mean wiser, and can mean more able. I think I'm getting better the older I get. There's a psychological proposition that many of we…marketers…agree upon that…"

I stopped talking, hoping I hadn't blown my cover story.

"You don't have to lie, I looked you up," sighed Colin. "You can't really pretend to be someone else and hope to get away with it when you use your real name and you're all over the internet, Doctor Morgan." He shook his head.

It was my turn to sigh. "Okay. Busted. It was my way of trying to get people to open up about Annette's death without knowing they were talking to a criminal psychologist. I apologize for lying. Now, can we please get me out of here?"

"Sure," he replied. "How?"

I thought about it again. "Colin, can you take a photo of the lock out there with your phone?"

"Sure." He pouted. The flash snapped in the gloom.

"Okay, now hand it through to me." He passed the phone through the bars, and I could see the whole lock and bolt arrangement. It was exactly as I remembered it. "Great photo. If you take that up to Bud, he'll see that there are screws in the panel that's holding the bolt. If he can bring a flat-head screwdriver, and maybe some of that stuff that helps with releasing rusty screws, we could be in business. We won't open the lock, we'll just remove the whole panel. It's not a sonic screwdriver, but it was you who gave me the idea, Colin." I hoped my praise would cheer him up.

He brightened a little. "Okay. But how about I just ask the Corrigans if they have a spare key?"

I laughed. "Yes, you're quite right, Colin. But I'm pretty sure they don't have one. In the key cupboard there were ten hooks in two rows, four had bunches of keys on them, no one key of which was big enough for this padlock, and on two of the other hooks were this key and one other, single key, that was much smaller. Of course, they might have one elsewhere, so – yes – why not ask? Let's adopt a belt and braces approach, and do both, okay?"

"Eidetic memory, eh?" asked Colin.

I nodded. *Bright boy.*

Colin shrugged. "Several of The Doctor's incarnations have worn both a belt and braces, thereby ensuring a reduced risk of losing their trousers." He giggled. I hoped his levity meant that I'd regained some favor in his eyes.

"Colin – go, please? It's important. Quick as you can, right?"

"Sure thing," he said, and off he went.

It would take Colin about ten minutes to get to Anen House, ten minutes to wake Bud and find the bits and pieces…quicker if there was a spare key…and ten minutes to get back. I checked my watch, then switched on all the bulbs, determined to do something useful with the half an hour I was likely to be stuck there. I reckoned it would be a good idea to root around in Annette's belongings and hope to find something, *anything*, that would help me understand what had happened to her.

It was clear that someone had locked me into the apple store…probably when I was floating away on a cloud of Beethoven-y loveliness. But who even knew I was there?

Only Lauren Corrigan…and she couldn't have killed Annette because she was in Ireland at the time. I guessed she might have mentioned it to her husband – who was also not in the frame for the same reason as his wife – so what on earth was going on? Maybe the lurking Colin had seen something; I'd have to ask him when he returned.

I spotted a plastic storage bin marked Annette – Books #1. *That might be interesting.*

To get to it I could see I'd have to move two bins from above it, both of which were marked Annette – Kitchen Cupboard #2. I reached up and shifted the top one. *Whoa – heavy.* Plopping it onto the floor, the lid loosened, and I could see that the contents were spices, herbs, packets of seasonings, and a slew of tetra packs of apple juice. Why would Ellen keep all that?

I pulled out a couple of the little packages of juice and stuck in the tiny straws I peeled off their sides. I sucked…the juice was pleasantly cool. The taste of apples revitalized my awareness of the smell of the place.

Back to business: who locked me in?

What about Colin? He obviously knew I was in the store…he'd been following me everywhere. He knew who I really was, and that I was looking into Annette's death; he could have locked me in. He'd admitted seeing Annette on the day of her death, and no one else had verified his story, so he could have been making up the whole thing. *Only* Colin had suggested that Annette had been having an argument with someone. *Only* Colin had mentioned the snuff box. In fact, the more I thought about it, the more the pieces fell into place. Colin liked Annette – he "hung out" with her. Bonnie had said Colin always used to appear around the Mount Dewdney winery during Annette's time there; clearly, Colin had been following Annette the same way he was following me about the place. He'd probably been even more obsessed with her: Annette had given him gifts, he'd been a visitor at her house – so many links between a fragile, sensitive, over-protected teen and an older woman who might not have known that he was infatuated with her.

I pushed a rickety chair against the wall, to give it a bit of help with holding my weight. If I sat down and used my skills, I could do this. I could join the dots.

Take a deep breath, and begin.

I hummed, closed my eyes, and took myself to the place where I can allow thoughts to float freely, having decided to undertake the "wakeful dreaming" that I'd mentioned to Lizzie Jackson. All I had to do was think of each person in turn, and allow them to gather about themselves those things which were "theirs," without my overlaying any sort of judgment upon the process.

Annette's face, the face I only know from a photograph, comes to me first: she's holding a tiny wooden box in one hand, and a giant garbage bag in the other. She's laughing. She's dressed in rags. Now she's running toward the truck in which she died and floating into the cab.

Ellen? Ellen's scowling, she's crying, and trying to stuff something large into a storage box, but it won't fit. What is it, Ellen? Ah, it's Annette. Of course. Annette won't fit into the box because it's too full of empty bottles of wine, snuff boxes, wine labels, and a giant scroll, which is obviously Annette's will. Pages and pages of notes about "suspects" are floating in the air around her, fluttering at her feet.

Raj Pinder floats toward me next: he's holding a giant wine bottle and crying. "It's perfect," he says, then he's fighting off Suzie Soul, who's just appeared as a snake with a cat's face. She's coiling herself around Raj's legs. He can't escape. She eats him.

Sammy Soul appears with a giant reefer between his lips, puffing away and chewing marijuana leaves at the same time. Serendipity is shouting at him – "Don't eat the leaves!" She's dressed like a picture-book angel, wings and all, and she's flying up to the sky with her father running along the ground trying to catch her. She's scattering a trail of what I know are snail eggs, but they look like tiny little snails, each with Raj Pinder's face.

I conjure up the Jacksons next: Lizzie is wearing a huge, faceted rock around her neck, it's weighing her down, but she's repeating a mantra – "Look into my eyes, my eyes, my eyes" – and smiling. Grant is tiny, like a little scuttling insect, but in almost human form. He's running around on the ground beside Lizzie shouting loudly, but she can't hear him, only I can: "Face It. Face It. You know, you know it. Face it." Now Grant is chasing Sammy Soul, who hasn't got a reefer anymore, but he's scattering cigarettes as he runs, still trying to catch the diaphanous gown of his daughter.

"Don't light it. Don't light it," calls Lizzie to Grant as he picks up one of the now-tiny cigarettes.

Colin, Sheri, and Rob MacMillan appear in a puff of smoke. "Time travel is great," says Colin to his parents, who start screaming at him that they want to go home. He's crying now. His father's wearing boxing gloves and starts to punch himself in the head. His mother is crying too. She's stroking Colin, petting him like she would a cat. Colin's hair grows very long, and he starts to trot toward me. He's panting like a puppy, but the sounds coming out of his mouth are the sounds of Doctor Who's TARDIS as it lands.

"I have to have it." Annette has broken out of the storage box that Ellen is trying to stuff her into. "I have to have it!" She's wearing a gasmask, and she's running toward Grant Jackson who's trying to hide from her giant feet. He grows to her size, and there he is, holding a large candlestick in one hand, a coffee roaster in the other. Annette grabs the candlestick from him and proceeds to bash away at the stacks of plastic bins that are suddenly surrounding her. They start to topple. Everyone is being hit by giant storage bins...

I stopped, and pulled myself together. It was a start. What had I learned? Anything? What had I felt? I sensed...obsession. Why? I gave it some thought.

Everyone had an obsession: Annette and her snuff boxes; Colin and The Doctor, and probably Annette...and now me; Raj and the perfect wine; Serendipity and the perfect food; Sammy Soul and his wife; Suzie Soul and her lovers; Grant and Lizzie Jackson and their Faceting; Sheri MacMillan and her son; Rob MacMillan and his escape; Gordy Wiser and his orchards; Lauren Corrigan and her knitting; Pat Corrigan and his sausages. Marlene Wiser – poor Marlene – seemed to be the only one who hadn't been caught up with something that was their distraction, or their focus…or maybe adopting six children was obsessive?

I allowed my mind to wander back to Colin MacMillan: his sad home life; his other, fantasy world; the kindnesses Annette had shown him; their connection; his obsession. He knew about science, and he had access to Annette's home. She'd been acting strangely – had she offended him in some way? Would she have known if she had? How would Colin react?

I was questioning…judging. Was I now taking a step too far? Being too judgmental? I was nervous that I'd just sent Colin away, and he might never come back.

I want a cigarette. Is that why I pictured all those cigarettes?

I got up from the chair and walked over to the contents of my bag which were still on the floor in a heap. I gleefully saw that the pile contained a squashed cigarette box with two smokes in it and a limp book of matches. I gathered up the other bits and bobs and put back them where they belonged, then I looked around; I couldn't really see any harm in lighting up. The door was wide open, even if the gate was locked. The relief I felt as I inhaled the first puff was tremendous.

I'm an addict. I admit it.

I looked at my watch; thirty minutes had passed. Bud should be arriving at any moment…if Colin had actually gone to get him.

I walked back toward the box of books I'd been intending to get to when I'd sidetracked myself with the apple juice. I pulled down the other kitchen box that was on top of it, and finally achieved my goal. I didn't know what I'd expected to find, but what I saw was a pretty comprehensive collection of books about silver antiques. I picked out one or two, and wandered back to the spot near the gramophone, under a lightbulb. Inside the front cover of one of the books was an inscription: "To one of my best customers, G. J."

Of course…Grant Jackson…why hadn't I thought of that before? *The candlesticks!*

Just then I heard a crunching noise beyond the gate.

"Hello?" It was Colin's voice.

Quick as a flash I was at the gate. "You're back." I was relieved.

"Yep," he said.

"Where's Bud?" I asked impatiently.

"He wasn't there," he replied. He added proudly, "I brought a screwdriver and some WD-40."

"What do you mean, Bud wasn't there?" I might have sounded a little terse.

"It's a long story, so I'll tell you while I try to undo this, okay?" Colin sounded as though he was speaking to a child.

I sighed. "Yes, right, okay. Sorry. I'm just a bit stressed."

"I might be only seventeen, but I am possessed of a modicum of perception," said Colin loftily.

That's me put in my place.

"What's happened to Bud?" I had to know.

I peered as far as I could out of the gate, but all I could see was Colin's left side. His tongue poked out, and he was clearly struggling with the screws. I could smell the oily chemicals of the WD-40 wafting on the cool evening air.

Colin spoke calmly. "Ellen came back to Anen House with Pat in his car. She asked Bud to drive her to the winery in his truck to collect some ice wine that she'd promised to take to SoulVine Wines for the dinner tonight. They'd left before I got there, because she had to get to Serendipity's restaurant before the other guests showed up. Lauren told Bud you weren't due back at the B & B until seven, so he called your cellphone and left you a message. Pat's a bit tied up right now, but he said he'd drive you over to West Kelowna when you're out of here. He offered to help, but I said I could manage."

I took it all in. Ellen was pretty good at getting people, especially Bud, to help her out. But that's what Bud's like. Damsel in distress and all that.

Well, I was a damsel in distress right now, and I could have done with his help a bit more than Ellen needed it.

But you don't know that, Bud.

"Are you talking to me, or yourself?" asked Colin.

I hadn't been aware I was saying anything aloud. "Myself," I replied.

"Good," he sniped back.

"How's it coming along out there?" I asked.

"Just two more." I could hear the effort in his voice.

I stood as calmly as I could. I hate waiting, and it's especially annoying when I'm not in control of the situation…where putting pressure on someone else does anything but help.

I sighed. "What about you and Poppy du Bois then, Colin? I reckon you'd be spending your time much more wisely with her than following the likes of me about the place."

The sounds of Colin's exertion stopped.

"What do you mean Poppy? And what do you mean follow you?" He sounded quite put out.

"Oh, come on, Colin, you've been following me about. Did you see who locked this gate, when you were skulking around out there?"

"I wasn't skulking, and I didn't see anyone. And what do you mean about Poppy?"

Ah, so you are interested, after all, eh?

"I think Poppy quite likes you, Colin. You two have a lot in common: same class at school, similar interests. I guess you spend quite a bit of time together."

Colin was clearly back at work. "Yeah, but she has to help out at the restaurant, you know? They all work together. Like a proper family. She's okay. She's pretty cool for a girl."

I thought it best not to press the matter, but I'd planted at least the germ of a thought that might spur Colin to take up with a girl his own age, rather than obsessing over me – or any other inappropriate adult – and mooning about the place. I didn't want to say anything any more concrete…after all, who ever knew a teen who'd do something if they thought an adult wanted them to do it?

"Hey – got it. Last one now," exclaimed Colin.

"Good job," I offered by way of encouragement. "I'll check that I've left everything in good order here," I added.

"Okay, just a few more turns and I'm sure it'll be out," Colin called, sounding hopeful.

I darted back into the cavernous apple store and glanced around. I picked up my bag and peered into it. Had I collected everything off the floor? I cast my eyes about the place. Yes. Did I have my cigarettes and matches? No, I'd put them down next to the box of mail. As I reached for them, I knocked the plastic box onto the floor; the mail scattered everywhere. I gathered it up and popped it back into the box. I looked around for a larger flat surface for the big box, and spotted a table – it would do. I picked up a couple of photographs printed on large glossy sheets that were lying there.

Who prints out photos these days? I only do that when I'm giving them to someone else, as a gift, or memento.

I gave them my attention before I placed them on top of the mail. One was the same as the shot that Bud had shown to me at my house a week earlier – the one that had introduced me to the Newman sisters. Someone had drawn hearts above each head. The other one also had hearts drawn above the two women, but was a slightly different shot. It had obviously been taken a few moments before, or after, the one I'd originally seen. I popped my specs back on, held one photograph in each hand, and studied them.

I focused first on the expressions on the sisters' faces, then on their body language: in the photo that Bud had shown me, Annette was closest to the camera, smiling happily, her arm around Ellen's shoulders. Ellen was trying to look happy too.

In the other photo, the one I was seeing for the first time, Ellen and Annette were looking at each other, rather than at the camera. Annette's entire body said "happy": her arms were outstretched, upward and toward her sister; her face, even though I could only see a side view, was gleeful; her mouth was open wide in a smile, and her head was thrown back in joy. Ellen? Well she'd been caught in an instant of pure disbelief. Her mouth was also open, but in an "o" of shock, not delight; her arms were also raised, but her hands were on their way to grasp her face; her shoulders drooped in defeat, she was curling in on herself.

And there was one more significant difference between the photos: because this photo showed a side view of the sisters, I could see that it wasn't only Annette's bra that didn't fit. Her shirt and pants were pulling on her, too.

And that was it. I didn't need any more "wakeful dreaming" to help me work out who had killed Annette Newman, and Stacey Willow, and poor old Gordy and Marlene Wiser…or why…or how. Everything slid into place like a pattern in a kaleidoscope.

Annette Newman's bra didn't fit…and I'd known that a week ago.

Oh, Cait Morgan, you are so stupid.

"It's open!" called Colin proudly. "You can come and push now."

I picked up the photos, stuffed them into my purse, tugged the chains to turn out the lights, and launched myself at the gate. It began to shift. A moment later, I was out, and trying not to panic.

"Can I use your phone to call Bud?" I asked Colin.

"It doesn't work here. I think we established that, right?"

I had to smile at my stupidity.

The boy shook his head, as he added, "Eidetic memory? Right."

I held my forehead.

"You're thinking?" he asked.

I nodded. I was also trying to keep calm. "Right-o, Colin. You've rescued me – thank you so much. Now we have to get back to Anen House as quickly as we can, then to SoulVine Wines. Let's go. We'll talk on the way." I knew I was barking at him, but it didn't matter. "You lead, and can you use your phone to light the path a bit? It's almost dark."

"Sure can," he replied jauntily.

As we trudged up the hill in the darkness – which was a lot more difficult to do than to wander down it in daylight – I sorted through all the facts in my mind, and knew I wasn't wrong about things…which wasn't good.

I must get hold of Bud as fast as possible.

"Once we get up to Pat and his car, how quickly can we get to SoulVine Wines?" I asked, panting as I plodded.

"This time of day, it's about twenty minutes to half an hour from here by road. It could be longer, depending on the bridge."

I did my best to control my mounting concerns by telling myself that at least I could phone Bud from the B & B and tell him what was going on. That would help. It *should* help.

"There is a quicker way," added Colin.

"What?" I spoke too sharply.

"Our boat. If Pat gives us a ride to my house, we can just zip right across the lake. The Souls are opposite us. It'll only take five, ten minutes."

"Will we need a car on the other side?" I wasn't sure exactly where the dinner was taking place, geographically speaking.

"No. We just tie up at their jetty and walk up the steps to the restaurant. Didn't you see it opposite our house today?"

"I suppose I just didn't know what I was looking at."

That's at least two examples of you not understanding what you were looking at in the way you should have done, Cait.

"You'd have a life jacket on the boat I could use?" I asked, now huffing, as well as puffing; the track seemed to be a lot steeper than I recalled.

Colin stopped and looked back down the trail at me, smiling, "Can't you swim?" he chuckled.

"No," I admitted. "I grew up by the seaside, yet managed to go my whole life without learning to swim. But you should always wear a life jacket, whether you can swim or not. Right?"

"Yes, 'Mom'," sighed Colin. "Are you okay in boats?" he asked after a brief pause.

"No, not really. But I'm sure I can keep it together for ten minutes, as long as that's all it is."

"If Mom let's me drive, it could be five," he said, laughing.

"Colin, your Mom can drive…or your Dad – I don't really care, so long as whomever is in charge gives me a life jacket, hasn't been drinking, and gets us there quickly."

"Well, the not drinking thing is a bit of a challenge," said Colin. "I didn't see much of Dad today, but when I did, he was knocking back the beers with his mate Dave from West Kelowna. They work together sometimes in Calgary, and when he visits, all they do is drink. And Mom? When I left to foll…to ride down to Kelowna, after lunch, she was hitting those cocktails pretty hard, and she hadn't stopped when I went back and told her about the accident, or when I left again. I've got all my certificates, and I don't drink, so I really can drive you there in the boat. If Pat can get us to it."

So there I was, about to put my life in the hands of a sad, lonely, and obsessive teen…but with no other choice. I looked up at Colin's back, and at the climb that still stood between me and a place where I could at least call Bud.

Good heavens, I'd thought we'd be closer…how far have we come?

I looked back over my shoulder at the path behind us and could see we'd come a good way. As I turned around and looked up again, I felt myself sway with giddiness. I missed my footing, my ankle rolled on a rock, and I came crashing down onto my knees and side. I put out my arm to break my fall.

I heard a crack, then swore…a lot.

Pinot Noir Ice Wine

"Don't touch me. Don't try to help. Just let me take my time and get up on my own. I can do this." I was telling myself as much as I was telling Colin that I could get to my feet without his help. I didn't really believe me, but he seemed convinced.

He stood back, held up his cellphone to throw a little more light onto the path for me, and made encouraging noises.

It took a few moments, but I managed it. It was a good job I was wearing pants, because at least they'd saved some of the skin on my knees and thigh. I'd ripped through the left sleeve of my shirt, and my elbow was badly grazed, which was nothing compared with the greater discomforts of a broken wrist and a turned ankle.

I put my weight back on my damaged side as gently as I could and found that if I kept the weight on the ball of my foot, rather than my heel, it was bearable.

Come on Cait, you have to move.

I cradled my floppy left wrist in my right hand.

There you go, left wrist broken – again. That's twice in one year. Brilliant. Another six weeks in plaster.

I was angry with myself. I didn't talk…just gritted my teeth and hobbled up the steep path. Fortunately, Colin MacMillan had more sense than to ask me how I was doing. He lighted my way, as best he could. After what seemed like an age, we finally reached flatter ground and I could see the Corrigans' home ahead of us and, beyond that, the lights of Anen House.

I stopped for a moment to catch my breath, but knew I couldn't give up.

"Does your phone work here?" I asked Colin abruptly.

He checked. "Yes, I've got a signal. Can I punch in Bud's number for you?"

I nodded, gave him the number, and took the cellphone from him with my good hand. It rang. And rang. Finally, Bud answered.

"Hello? Hello?"

I could hear laughter, voices, and the clattering of a kitchen.

"Bud, it's Cait. Can you hear me?"

"Cait?"

"Yes, Cait!" I shouted angrily. "Go somewhere where you can hear me – it's important."

"Okay, okay, keep your hair on," replied Bud jovially. "Hey guys, gotta take this, back in a minute," he called to…someone.

I stood silently beneath the star-pricked sky, blood starting to trickle down my arm, my wrist thumping, my ankle screaming, and I listened to Bud humming as though he were "hold please" music.

Usually, it's entertaining. Right now? Not so much.

I could feel the adrenaline charging through my veins. I could see my breath puffing in the cool night air.

"Hey, so how's it going?" he finally asked.

"Bud, you know I love you, right?"

"Oh-oh, this can't be good."

Perceptive.

"I can't get there for a little while, Bud. It doesn't matter why. But I need you to do something and it's important. In fact, it could be critical. Got it?"

"You're with someone and you can't say exactly what you want to say?"

Highly perceptive.

"Correct," I replied.

"Are you in danger? Do I need to come to you?"

You're good.

"No and no. I will get there. But between now and then you're Serendipity Soul's shadow. Got it?"

"She's in danger?"

"Uh-huh."

"Got it. I'll go right back to the kitchen. I'm on my way now. When will you be here, and are you okay?"

"Thanks Bud. I'll be there as soon as I can. I'm fine. Bye. Got to go."

"Got it. I'm on it."

I love it when you're Bud, Bud.

I could relax a little, but not too much. "Right, let's get into the house, then Pat can drive us to your boat," I said, handing Colin's phone back to him.

"You cannot be serious," he said. "You can't go on the boat like that. You can't walk. You can't balance. You won't even be able to get onto it, let alone cope with all the bouncing around."

You're right.

I said, "Okay then, change of plan…let's get Pat to drive us over. Come on, let's go." I hobbled toward the back door I'd sauntered out of not two hours earlier.

"Pat, Lauren…need some help, please," called Colin, racing ahead of me.

As I approached the door, I saw the concerned look on Lauren's face turn to horror when she caught sight of me.

"Oh, sweet Mother of Jesus!" she cried as she ran toward me. "Pat, call 911."

I replied, as firmly as I could, "No…please, no. Stop right there – please Lauren, just while I catch my breath. Where's Pat? Pat, you too, come closer, but stop there." They both did as I asked, but each looked at the other with alarm.

"Lauren, Pat, Colin, I need you all to help me, please…and by doing that you'll also be helping someone who might be in danger. I can't say more than that. Not now. You need to trust me on this one. Lauren, you told me earlier that your mum was a nurse; did she teach you how to strap up an injured – probably broken – wrist?" Lauren nodded. "Good. Could you find something that you can use as a bandage for support, please? And I think a large tea towel will do fine for a sling." Lauren nodded, and she was gone.

I continued, "Pat, I need you to drive me, Colin – and Lauren – over to SoulVine Wines, please. We might not be back for some time, so you'd better make sure that everything here's safe to leave, okay?" Pat nodded and headed to the kitchen.

Finally, I turned to my young helper. "Colin, you've already done so much, but I need you to come with me, right? You're not to leave my side. Not for a minute. Okay?"

"Why?" asked Colin.

"I can't tell you that."

"Okay, that's cool," he replied, and shrugged. "Can I help with the bandaging?"

"Let's go in and see how Lauren's getting on with the supplies," I replied.

Lauren and Pat were brilliant, and Colin was as helpful as he could be. I declined painkillers but allowed Lauren to wipe the grit off my face, as well as strapping up my wrist. Then she very kindly offered to help me in the bathroom.

Because I knew that Bud was on the case across the lake, I tried not to mind too much that it took us fifteen minutes to get out of the house, and another half an hour before we reached the grand, gated entrance to the SoulVine Winery and Country Club. However, if the movement of the car was anything to go by, my poor body just couldn't have coped with bobbing across the lake on a boat; Colin had made a good call on that one. Nevertheless, the time we'd lost was a real concern to me; every extra moment it had taken us to reach our destination presented an additional moment of danger to Serendipity.

Finally, we crunched along the wide driveway that led from the road toward the clubhouse and restaurant complex. It was huge: four stories tall in some parts, just one in others. Dozens of windows were brightly lit, and a golden glow pooled on the grass and manicured plantings that surrounded the building. Pat brought his car to a standstill under a two-storey copper awning that sat atop a magnificent pair of gray stone-clad columns. It took all three of them to get me out of the car.

I could feel the swelling really getting a grip on my left wrist and hand, and the throbbing in my ankle was now building into a continuous pain. I'd seen myself in the bathroom mirror at Anen House, and I wasn't a pretty sight. I had no doubt that Bud would go ballistic when he saw me, and then again when he realized the extent of my injuries. But how I looked didn't matter…what mattered was that Bud had stuck to Serendipity like glue, and that Colin never left my side.

As I hobbled through the glazed double doors, I could hear laughter echoing in a distant room. I looked at my watch. It was almost half past eight. Everyone must have arrived by now.

Pat and Lauren's entrance into the private dining room was greeted by a small cheer, Colin's with some puzzlement – especially from his mother – and mine with gasps of astonishment. As I looked around the room, I took the time to read every face, knowing I couldn't afford to make a mistake: Serendipity, Raj, Sheri, Grant, Lizzie, Ray, Gloria, Sammy, Suzie, and Ellen all looked completely – *and totally believably* – shocked by the sight of me.

Bud looked horrified. "Cait – what's happened to you?" He rushed to my side. I winced. "Don't panic, I won't touch you," he said softly. "What have you done? Broken your wrist? Again?"

I nodded. I wasn't going to let myself cry, but the relief I felt just from being with Bud was pretty overwhelming.

"Is your head okay? No concussion?"

"All in *perfect* working order," I replied, meaningfully.

Bud's eyes showed me that he understood. He whispered, "We should talk. Or should I call the cops first?"

I nodded, ever so slightly. I whispered back, "Can you get them here, tell them I'll be revealing something they'll want to know about the Wisers' 'accident', and then just get them to hover? You know, use your Bud-power on them. Also, can you do it without leaving Serendipity?"

He winked. "I'll sort it."

It was clear that my arrival had rather changed the atmosphere of the evening, and what an evening it should have been. The room was magnificent: the chandelier alone must have cost a bomb, and the fact that the oak-paneled walls glittered with Sammy Soul's collection of framed gold and platinum records, as well as several guitars dotted here and there, brought the whole thing to a different level.

Under any other circumstances I'd have been blown away merely by the food that was on display: if her presentation was anything to go by, Serendipity Soul was, indeed, a highly talented chef. She'd used the colors and textures of her dishes artistically: fish, shellfish, meats, vegetables, fruits, and pâtés were attractively displayed beside cheeses, fabulous breads, and glittering plates, all in multiple layers. It was a truly breathtaking, and tempting, sight. But I couldn't have managed to eat one single mouthful of it…and that knowledge was driving me nuts.

Sheri MacMillan was the first to approach me. "Why don't you come sit over here?" She waved an arm toward one of the little tables dotted around the room. "I can give you a hand."

"No, Mom. Cait doesn't need any help, she can manage quite well on her own." Colin sounded terribly grown up; apparently more so to his mother than to me.

"Yes, dear," she replied, looking shocked.

Colin made sure I had a clear path to reach the table, pulled out a chair for me, and turned it at an angle, so it was easier for me to sit. As I settled myself, I could see Bud and Serendipity leave the room through a swing door. I guessed they were headed to the kitchen. I knew I had to buy time.

Everyone fussed around me. The story was that I'd tripped, while on a walk, but hadn't wanted to miss the evening. Besides – I emphasized – I looked a lot worse than I felt.

Ellen was particularly attentive. She brought me a plate of food, which looked so delicious that I wondered if I might even manage to eat a few morsels from it. Suzie Soul brought me a glass of water – which I gratefully drank down – and a glass of champagne, which I couldn't face…surprisingly, for me.

Sammy stood beside his wife and smiled with an expression of great pride. "What do ya think of the room? Quite a collection. Lotta years on these walls, man. Lotta years. And a lotta miles. Touring. Recording. My history. Suzie loves this room, don't ya, Babe?"

"It's truly a great honor to be here, Sammy," I replied. "That's one of the reasons I didn't want to miss this evening. I knew that whatever you and your family had out here, it would be special."

Having proved I could at least form a sentence – however alarming I might look – Sammy seemed happy to stay and chat. He took the seat next to me.

"You're interesting," he said bluntly.

"How so?" I asked, intrigued.

Does he know who I really am, too?

"A marketer and a cop? Odd couple. And since you two guys showed up, man, everything's gone a bit mad. It's not usually like this here – all drama. It's usually pretty quiet. But since you got here, my Babe's been a bit off, you've had this fall, and then there's the accident, of course. Man, that's a bad vibe. Nice people. Gordy was nearly ten years older than me. I hope I've got that much juice when I'm his age."

I looked at Sammy. Not even a decade between him and Gordy Wiser? Gordy had raised six children, built a business that supported them, educated them, and had then set up him and Marlene for the rest of their lives…all with his bare hands, his knowledge of the soil and the seasons, and the sweat of his brow. Sammy Soul had taken his sweat, and his hands, and had made a guitar scream like only he could. He'd built all this. Such different paths…but maybe they weren't so very different under their skins.

I also looked over at Suzie. She and poor Marlene really couldn't have been more dissimilar. What a difference: chalk and cheese.

That was what Marlene had said about Annette and Ellen, and it set me thinking about the truth of that observation. As I did, I realized I was crying. I wasn't sobbing, but an unheralded tear was rolling down my cheek. I didn't even bother to reach for my bag – what would have been the point?

I asked, "Anyone got a hanky I can have, please? Or a paper napkin?" Ellen, Sheri, and Suzie each passed one in my direction.

What's the collective noun for paper tissues? A rustling?

I dabbed at my face silently, and was relieved to see that no one wanted to make eye contact with me, except Colin, who was right beside me, watching my every move.

I pushed the used tissue into my bag, and turned to find Ellen hovering beside me with yet another glass in her hand.

"It's ours," she gushed. "A pinot noir ice wine. Not the *Annette*, of course, that's not ready, but this was my sister's most award-winning ice wine. Please have some? We're all going to drink a toast to Marlene and Gordy in a minute."

I can't refuse, can I?

Ellen held out a big, heavy-looking, cut-crystal glass…which was odd for an ice wine glass – they're usually small, because the wine's so rich, and costly. My head was thumping. The room was warm, and stifling. I could smell the seafood on the plate in front of me mixed with Sheri MacMillan's sickly perfume, and, for some weird reason – as I took the glass from Ellen, with my one good hand – I suddenly fancied some chocolate. And not just any chocolate…nope, quite specifically, *Reese's Pieces.*

Bizarre.

Sammy Soul moved to the center of the room just as Bud and Serendipity re-entered it. Bud flashed fifteen fingers at me.

Okay, I have to busk for fifteen minutes. Somehow.

It looked as though Sammy was about to help me out on that front, because he tapped his glass with one of the many rings on his fingers and a hush fell over our weird little gathering.

"Hey, though you might think I do a lot of this stuff, I don't, right, Babe?" He grinned at his wife, and she wriggled coquettishly in his general direction. "I kinda let my guitar do the talking for me all those years, but today is different. Special. Man, they were cool dudes, right? Gordy and Marlene? Him always moanin'. Her always fussin'. They loved each other, man. Loved each other. All those years together. All those kids. Kids are tough. Except my angel here, of course."

There were suitable mutterings around the room.

Sammy continued, "Tonight was gonna be my Serendipity's night. The night she did her thing, and we all went 'Wow', and she got to be the rock star. 'Cos that's what she is. A star. I know she'd want me to say what I'm gonna say. All this," he waved his arm expansively toward the food, "all this, is nothing, compared with the lives we lost today. It's fabulous, my angel, but Marlene and Gordy were fabulous too. They'll be missed. So, hey, come on guys, raise your glasses and let's have a toast. Cait – stay, don't get up" – he looked directly at me, as did everyone else. "Now, here's to Gordy and Marlene Wiser."

We all raised our glasses, and repeated the toast loudly and with gusto: "Gordy and Marlene Wiser!" We all drank.

"Well, that's mighty nice of you folks, but you could have waited till we got here."

It was Gordy Wiser's voice.

He was standing in the doorway. Beside him stood Marlene.

Sheri let out a little scream.

Colin grinned, and said, "Cool."

Lauren crossed herself, and cried, "Jesus, Mary, and Joseph."

"It's a miracle, so it is," added her husband.

Sammy dropped his glass.

Suzie swore, loudly.

Ellen gripped the edge of the table.

"How wonderful!" exclaimed Lizzie.

Grant began bowing, bobbing, and muttering.

Raj gasped, "By 'eck!"

Serendipity beamed and clapped her hands joyfully.

Bud mouthed something unrepeatable.

I felt the room swim…my head hit the table, then…through a mist…

"Give her air, give her air," called Lauren.

"Someone bring her a glass of water. I think I need one too," shouted Sheri.

I managed to sit myself upright, my head lolling like a baby. I tried to focus on the Wisers, who were rushing toward me.

"What's been going on?" asked Marlene, looking concerned. "We're sorry we're late, we got caught up at *C'est la Vie*. We only popped in there for a quick cup of coffee this afternoon, and we ended up running into some old friends. We haven't even been home to change for dinner. Sorry, Sammy dear, you'll have to take us as we are."

"But you're dead," I said, bluntly.

Someone has to say it.

"You bumped your head, dear," said Marlene, peering into my eyes. "I think you should see a doctor."

"Cait's fine," said Bud firmly. "She's right. I…we…saw you. This afternoon. Your car. It crashed. Exploded. At the base of the final bend leading to Anen Close. It went right into the cliff face. It burned. I saw you…sitting in it."

Bud was clearly flabbergasted.

A look of horror crossed Marlene's face. "Our car?"

Bud nodded.

Everyone nodded.

Sheri handed me a glass of water. I took it and sipped.

"That's bad. Very bad," said Gordy. "But we weren't in it. We decided to walk home, change out of our costumes, then walk on all the way down to the waterfront. It was such a lovely day. We thought you all knew. We told Rob."

"You told Rob?" exclaimed Sheri. "When did you tell him? Where did you tell him? I haven't seen him all day, not since Dave arrived with you guys on your boat before lunch." She glanced in the direction of Sammy and Suzie. "Did Dave and Rob come back over to West Kelowna with you on your boat?"

The Souls shrugged and shook their heads.

"I got me and Serendipity out of your place in…a bit of a hurry," muttered Sammy, acquiring himself a fresh drink.

"So where's my Rob then?" asked Sheri.

Oh no…

"Well that's the thing, dear," replied Marlene, moving toward Sheri. She nodded at her husband, who moved closer to Colin.

"We gave our car keys to Rob, in case he needed to move it at all…you know, in case it was in anyone's way. And he said that he and Dave might drive into town, later on. Now, I don't know if that's what happened, but if they did…"

A strangled, "Oh," came from Colin. "It was Dad. Dad and Dave in the car. In the Wisers' car. When it burned."

"Don't be ridiculous." Sheri's eyes searched our group for someone who would tell her it couldn't be so. "Rob wouldn't have driven. Not after all that…not having drunk so much. He's not that stupid. It can't have been him."

"Well, if not him, then who?" asked Marlene Wiser, rubbing Sheri's back. "And where's he got to?"

"Oh, he'll turn up. He always turns up, sooner or later." Sheri MacMillan almost sounded sure of herself.

"Mom, stop it. Stop it. It was Dad. He was drunk, like he always is. It was Dad!" Colin MacMillan was suddenly seventeen, going on ten. "Mom…Daddy's dead. I saw him. I saw it all. He burned. I saw my Daddy burn!" He was red in the face, tears streaming. He was pulling at his hair.

The immense joy we'd all felt at seeing Gordy and Marlene alive in our midst was sucked out of us by the anguish and devastation of loss that we were seeing unfolding before us.

Colin was sobbing on Gordy's shoulder, Sheri was wailing into Marlene's chest, and Sammy was shouting orders to the barman to bring a round of large brandies for everyone…when another disturbance grabbed our collective attention.

The door from the kitchen flew open, and banged against the wall of the dining room; I heard pots tumbling beyond it. Serendipity flung herself into the room, and caught the edge of the tablecloth on the serving table. As she fell to the ground, clutching her throat, the cloth in her hand brought food tumbling onto the floor. Plates smashed, domed lids rang out like mournful bells, food splattered. We all remained paralyzed.

Only Colin moved. He tore himself from Gordy's arms and ran toward Serendipity, screaming "No!"

His arm was raised and something glinted in his fist. As he approached Serendipity's writhing body, her father leapt forward, trying to grab Colin's arm.

"Get away from my angel," he screamed, and lunged for Colin. But Colin had the advantage of youth on his side; all that Sammy managed to grab was…air.

As Sammy hit the floor, Colin stabbed Serendipity in the thigh, hard.

Suzie screamed, and flew at Colin. She threw herself on top of him, a frenzied figure made up of snarling teeth and flashing claws. She pulled his hair and beat him with her fists. Sammy picked himself up off the floor and tried to remove his wife. It seemed she was on top of Colin for an age, but it was probably no more than a matter of seconds.

As Sammy finally managed to pull Suzie away, Colin rolled onto the floor beside Serendipity, who was still moaning and holding her throat.

Colin croaked, "Peanuts – Mom – peanuts."

I suddenly realized what had happened. My wrist and ankle aside, I had to be heard; I stood, using the table for support.

I shouted, "Sammy…Suzie – where does Serendipity keep her epinephrine pen? Quick…Colin needs it. He just used his own on your daughter. Now he needs one too. Fetch it now."

Neither of them answered; they both looked dazed.

"Colin? What's wrong?" Poor Sheri MacMillan was having one heck of an evening. "Are there peanuts? Where are there peanuts? I don't understand."

"Sheri," I addressed the distraught woman directly and calmly. "Serendipity was suffering an allergic reaction to peanuts. Colin recognized the symptoms, and he used his own epinephrine pen to save her. The contact between him and Serendipity has led to Colin having enough of an exposure for him to suffer an allergic reaction himself. That's why we need Serendipity's pen, so it can be used to treat Colin."

I turned to the Souls who were both looking a great deal the worse for wear, and still completely confused.

"She's always got one in her pocket," replied Suzie, snapping out of her stupor. "Why didn't she use it herself?"

"Quick, Bud, check Serendipity's pockets," I called.

Bud was already on it. "Nothing," he said.

I was beginning to get a bad feeling about Colin, who was grasping at his throat and chest as he lay on the floor beside the chef he'd just selflessly saved.

"I've got a spare one," shouted Sheri, coming to her senses and rising to her feet. "Where's my purse? It's red." Everyone scanned the room.

"Got it," shouted Bud. He ran to a table diagonally opposite us, grabbed up a large, red-leather purse, dumped its entire contents onto the table, and pulled an epinephrine pen from the heap. He ran toward Colin and stabbed him in the thigh.

Everyone breathed.

"I'll organize an ambulance," said Bud.

You're so good at being in charge.

Sheri ran to her son's side. The Souls knelt by their daughter. I drank the rest of the ice wine in my glass, and immediately regretted it. Moments later, two RCMP officers stuck their heads into the room, caught Bud's eye, and rushed to Colin and Serendipity. Once they'd done what they could, Bud ushered them outside…and nodded toward me as he left.

The Souls were huddled up consoling each other at one spot on the floor, the MacMillans were crying on each other at another. Everyone else seemed to be downing a drink. Lauren was hovering beside me.

"I wonder, Lauren, could I bother you to give me hand outside, please? I'm going to take this little window of opportunity to go and smoke a cigarette."

I need one!

She tutted. "Sure I will. It's out through that door there, and around the side. Come on with you now."

As I hobbled, she held my good arm, and we made it out quite quickly. I limped toward the large decorative pot that was filled with fine, white sand with a few butts in it, and lit up. As I balanced myself against the edge of the pot, I saw a long stub of a slightly wet-looking cigarette. I picked it up with one of the tissues I'd shoved up my sleeve, and sniffed.

Of course. Clever. Nasty. Gotcha!

If I'd been in any doubt at all about it, that was the final nail in the murderer's coffin.

I asked Lauren for two favors: she nipped into the kitchen and managed to find a sealable plastic bag, into which I dropped the cigarette stub that I'd found; then she handed me her cellphone and allowed me a few private moments. I pulled the piece of paper I needed from my bag and made a long-distance call; I apologized profusely for disturbing the poor man who answered.

Finally, with all that done, I waited for Lauren to return to help me inside, and puffed hard on the last ciggie from my squashed packet.

I had a quiet word with myself.

Alright, Cait Morgan. Time for the show. You'd better be good.

I knew that the paramedics would arrive at some point to take Serendipity and Colin – and me – to the emergency room, but had no idea when that would be…but I knew I had to get on with my task.

As I hobbled back inside, with Lauren's help, Bud gave me the nod. Oh bless him…he had absolutely no idea what I was about to do, and yet I could tell he was supporting me totally and completely.

Love you, Bud.

Okay – now or never Cait.

Champagne and Cup-a-Soup

"Ladies and gentlemen," Bud's voice rang out across the dining room. "Can I have your attention, please? Everyone, please, take a seat. Just while we wait for the ambulances to arrive."

Bud helped Sheri to lift Colin onto a chair at an unoccupied table. The boy flopped there, pale, panting, and sipping water. His mother's love for him was obvious in every look, touch, and movement.

At the next table sat Serendipity, attended to by both Sammy and Suzie. Raj was perched at her side. I hadn't seen Vince Chen at the dinner, and suspected that dodging crockery at lunchtime had been his cue to exit Kelowna and head for the comparative safety of another winemaking region.

Beyond the two "sick" tables was the "dead" table: Gordy and Marlene Wiser sat alone, holding each others' hands, clearly trying to come to terms with the shocks of the past half hour.

Across the room, Lizzie and Grant Jackson were also sitting very close to each other. She was blinking at the goings on through her giant spectacles, he was fiddling with the crystal that lay on his breast. Opposite them sat Ray Murciano and Gloria Thompson, the two people the Jacksons employed at their store and restaurant.

Lauren and Pat Corrigan were at my table, Lauren making sure I had hankies, water, and whatever else I needed, and Ellen came to join us.

Everyone looked surprised when Bud came across the room to help me to my feet, saying, "Cait's got some stuff she needs to talk through with you all. I know she's not feeling her best, so I'm sure you'll all be patient with her."

I cleared my throat, and made sure my footing was as stable as possible, with no weight on my sprained ankle.

I began. "I know you've all met me as Bud's 'other half', but I have to begin by telling you that I've been here this weekend under…false pretences."

The folks I'd expected to shoot puzzled looks did so.

Good.

"Yes, my name's Cait Morgan, and I am indeed a professor at the University of Vancouver, but I'm not a marketing professor, I'm a criminal psychologist. I specialize in profiling victims. And – as those of you who were at the party last evening will know – Ellen invited Bud, who's a retired police officer, to come to Kelowna to look into her sister's death. To be fair to Ellen," I nodded in her direction, "she didn't know that Bud's 'accompanying other' for this weekend visit would be me – well, she knew it would be me, Cait, but she didn't know then what I do for a living. She was just lucky, I guess, that she actually got two investigators for the price of one." I forced a smile.

I'd expected a buzz around the room, and that's pretty much what I got.

Excellent.

"I realize that Bud and I have only spent a very small amount of time with each of you, but we've managed to learn a lot in a short time. Now, with the events of this afternoon and this evening, it's clear that something's amiss here, so it's time for me to speak up – with Bud's support, of course…and with the indulgence of the RCMP, who, you might have noticed, have a presence in the room."

It was clear from the response that several people hadn't noticed that the cops were still hovering at the door. To be fair, there had been rather a lot going on. There was a lot of shuffling on seats.

Also good.

I pressed on. "Now, of course, we're all devastated by the tragic deaths of Rob MacMillan and Dave...um, his friend and colleague, Dave, this afternoon." As voices muttered around the room, Sheri blew her nose loudly, and Colin looked toward me with red eyes, his pale face a mask of despair.

You poor things...

"I also know that you might think that the reason for the accident was that the driver had been drinking. However, when Bud, Ellen, and I left the lunch today, I saw a puddle of brake fluid on the side of the road, close to where the Wisers' car had been parked. I mentioned this to the police." I raised an eyebrow in Bud's direction, and he nodded at me. "They have confirmed that the brake fluid line on the Wisers' car had been tampered with."

Gasps. Open mouths. The Wisers grabbed each others' hands even tighter.

"Oh my God," cried Sheri.

"Mom, he was drunk anyway," responded Colin bleakly.

I held up my one good hand, hoping for quiet. I got it.

"Obviously, the police need to find out who might have done this, and why. I believe I can help them. First of all, we have to wonder if Rob and Dave were the intended victims, and I cannot discount the possibility that – since Rob and Dave were friends who sometimes worked together in the oil business in Alberta – some sort of reason for them to be targeted might have followed them here to Kelowna, from Calgary. However, I think you'll all agree that most people would have expected the Wisers to be driving their own car, heading down the steep curves and bends of Lakeshore Road, toward Anen Close, this afternoon."

Accepting expressions and head nodding all around.

Good.

"So the question is...who would want to kill Marlene and Gordy Wiser? And why?"

This time a round of head shaking, rather than nodding.

Useful.

"Who are the Wisers?" I asked, rhetorically. "Gordy's been a farmer in this area for decades. He and Marlene have raised six children, all adopted, and have secured a future for themselves by the efforts they've made to tame the land and grow fine crops. They're a fun-loving, happily married couple, who, I think everyone would agree, have their little quirks, as we all do." I saw a few smiles, and even the Wisers were nodding. "They're well respected, and well known in the community." More nodding. "One of their little quirks is that they like to know what's going on around them. Keeping an eye on things is second nature for them. Interested neighbors can be very useful." I was trying to err on the side of politeness, but realized I'd have to cross the line at some point. "However, some might see it as nosiness. And nosiness can be dangerous, because a nosey person might see things that others would prefer they didn't. And they might do things that others might wish they hadn't. The Wisers even went so far as to keep collecting Annette's mail after her death… as a way to continue to 'keep an eye on her'."

I'll let that sink in…while I watch you all. Good.

"So what might the Wisers have seen or done that might have caused them to become the target of a killer?" I paused. I didn't expect any suggestions. "This is what brought me to a possible link with Annette's death. You all know the circumstances of that tragedy: Ellen found her sister dead, with a note and an empty wine bottle beside her. It's always been accepted that Annette intended to take her own life. Indeed, when I thought in detail about the reactions to Ellen's little outburst last night, it became clear to me that the idea that someone might have killed Annette was completely alien to most people in the room. That was a most telling discovery. But that's exactly what Bud and I were asked to come here to consider: was Annette Newman murdered? Which brings me to the answer to that question: yes, she was."

The silence that followed was eventually broken by Grant Jackson, who spoke loudly. "At lunch today, Ellen said that Bud had looked into Annette's death and had convinced her it was a suicide after all. I'm confused."

I replied, "Ellen had that epiphany this morning. Later on, Bud and I discovered more facts that led us to believe it was murder after all."

"You didn't tell Ellen that? You didn't tell anyone?" Grant seemed to be speaking on behalf of my entire audience.

I nodded. "Okay, I understand your confusion, because I, too, was confused for a long time. Right up until this evening, actually: but here it is…I know that Annette Newman was killed, and I know a good deal more. I know who tampered with the Wisers' brakes, and why – and who made sure that Serendipity Soul suffered an almost fatal allergic reaction tonight."

Sammy Soul pounced. "Okay – out with it. You're saying someone did that to my angel? Someone poisoned her? Tried to kill her?" The aged rocker was on his feet, once again ready to fight for his child. Maybe even ready to kill for her. He couldn't have been less laid back. All the passion he'd put into his stage presence was still there.

I replied, "Serendipity is quite safe now, don't panic. I can hear the sirens coming. It won't be long until she's at the hospital."

"I'm fine, really I'm fine," said Serendipity weakly. "Sit down, Dad."

It was clear that both Sammy and Suzie were taken aback at the use of this term by their daughter, and it had the desired effect.

And the sirens had their effect upon me; I knew that I had to get a move on.

"If Annette was killed, then maybe the attempt on the Wisers' lives had something to do with that. After all, they were close to Annette; they saw her frequently, they each dropped into the other's homes. She brought them little treats, they knew of her hobbies, her interests, her passions…and they had a bird's eye view of all the comings and goings at Anen House, all day, every day. If they knew that much about her life, what might they know about her death? Now, Gordy and Marlene did mention to me that Annette had become distant in the last few weeks of her life, but, somehow they forgot to mention that they'd witnessed her new will. Why would they forget to mention that?" I peered over at them. "That was an important piece of information, really, wasn't it? Especially since the new will was one of the things that quite a few people in this room used as an example of how Annette must have been getting ready to kill herself. It's an odd thing, that: the will that left her part of the winery to you, Raj."

Now it was Raj's turn to wriggle with discomfort beneath my withering glance.

I added, "To you and your 'firstborn child', that is, Raj, which is even more odd, isn't it? Got any kids? I mean, you're heading for forty, and you've only been here a few years. Plenty of time for you to have had a child or two back in Yorkshire. Anything to say? You are, as I've already told you, the prime suspect here, given what Annette bequeathed you. Did the Wisers know something about you that you didn't want them to share? Did you convince them to sign a fake will, thereby gaining access to what you've told me more than once is a unique collection of grape varietals? Did Serendipity begin to suspect? Maybe she wasn't the first girl who needed to be disposed of. Maybe…"

Sammy leaped to his feet.

Serendipity jumped up too.

"Dad, down. Stop, Cait. This isn't fair to Raj." She turned toward the man she clearly loved and said, "No more messing about. Cards on the table? Now…right?"

Raj nodded, and sat beside Sammy, his head in his hands.

Serendipity said, "Look everyone, Raj and I love each other. We've been together a while, and, whatever you might think, Cait Morgan, I know he didn't kill Annette. He really quite liked Annette. In fact, they'd been together for a little while, back when he was still working here, right?"

Sammy looked shocked, Suzie rolled her eyes, and Raj just kept bobbing his head.

She added, "Raj hasn't got any children…yet. Though…well, we might have some, in the future."

"Are you two…?" Sammy sounded amazed.

Serendipity nodded. "Yes, Mom, Dad, I'm sorry you're finding out this way, but we are – and we always will be – a couple. We've decided. We're old enough to know our own minds, and I don't need your permission to do anything I want."

Sammy shook his head, dazed.

"Raj," I said, cutting across the personal dramas of the Souls, "would I be right in saying that, when you and Annette hooked up at a wine event the first time, you weren't as 'careful' as you might have been?"

Raj shrugged. "I told you, about it, Ser…we was drunk. It were just one of them things."

Serendipity reached out and took his hand. "Raj. I told you…you and Annette having been together? Not an issue."

"But, you see Raj," I continued, "Annette got pregnant. She was pregnant when she died. In fact, it was because she was pregnant with your child that she was killed."

I watched. I saw. I carried on.

"Annette's odd behavior during those last weeks of her life was because she was pregnant: even Bonnie said she was 'dashing here and there like a bird in spring'. A nesting bird. Annette lost a tasting event to you, Raj; there's a lot of research that suggests that taste and smell change during pregnancy. She missed meetings, canceled tastings. She was probably suffering from morning sickness, and knew she couldn't hide her changing abilities when it came to her job. She was, literally, clearing out her house and beginning to prepare for a baby in her life. She started to buy larger clothes at thrift stores, and she dumped her garbage herself, probably because it contained items she didn't want anyone, even garbage collectors, to see – maybe pregnancy test kits, even the debris from cleaning up unexpected attacks of vomiting. She didn't want anyone to know. She didn't even tell you, Raj, did she?"

Raj was shaking his head sadly. "Is that why she changed her will, then? 'Cos she were having my child? It…that child…would have been my 'firstborn'."

I nodded.

"Oh, dear, dear," said Marlene, quietly. "Terrible."

"Yes, terrible," I agreed, "because Annette's killer committed a double homicide: Annette and her baby." I let it sink in.

I took in the expressions of the people in the room. "And yet none of you knew? None of you even suspected? Not you, Ellen, her loving sister, who saw her every day? Not you, Gordy and Marlene, who said she was acting oddly, and yet agreed to sign a new will? Not you, Raj, who continued to see her constantly in and around the locale and the business? Not any of you? Lizzie – you told me Annette was suffering from a bad back, an altered mood, and a changed sense of smell…how could you come up with 'root chakra' and not 'pregnant'? Amazing. No one saw what was right under their noses. All the clues were there, and not one of you put them together to work out that she was having a baby. That's largely because you were all, to a greater or lesser extent, fixated on your own obsessions."

People shifted uncomfortably.

"Of course, there was the complication I had to work through about Annette selling her entire collection of snuff boxes, but that related to her own obsession, and not to the fact that she was pregnant. Grant, you told me that you tried to help Annette, but you let her down?"

Grant nodded. "I did, and maybe even more than I thought, if what you're saying is true."

"Oh, it's true alright. It's also true, isn't it, that Annette – one of your 'best customers', according to an inscription you wrote in a book on silverware for her – came to you and begged you to sell her snuff box collection. In a hurry, right?"

He nodded. "We'd worked together building her snuff box collection over many years. That's how I came to know Kelowna, driving up here with boxes I'd found for her, when I still had my silver and antiques business in Vancouver. She came to me, a couple of months before she died, and asked if I could go back to my old contacts and sell her whole collection. Fast. I told her she'd get a lot more if only she would wait for the right sales to come up, but she said she needed money, and she needed it quickly. I should have pressed her. I should have made her tell me why she needed it. Though," and here he looked puzzled, "I still don't really get it. I mean, okay, she might have been about to have a child, but the winery's doing well. She can't have been short of money."

"She needed the cash to be able to buy her collectors' 'grail'. She told Colin about it, right?" Colin nodded. "Otherwise, like the obsessive collector she was, she kept the whole thing to herself. I'm going to suggest that you sold her collection of silver snuff boxes for around forty thousand dollars, would that be right?"

Grant looked surprised. "How'd you know that?"

Bud's face was telling me he wanted to ask the same question.

"I just spoke to a very nice, if sleepy, man in Newfoundland, by the name of 'Sanderson'. His family name used to be 'Sandy' back when they were in Scotland: such a well-respected name, in certain parts, that it was an honor to be known as a 'son' of the house; hence 'Sanderson'. He confirmed that he sold Annette a signed James Sandy snuff box, made from the wood of the bed in which Robbie Burns died, with a letter in Sandy's own handwriting giving it an impeccable provenance. She paid fifteen thousand dollars for it – which he assures me was a very fair price – and Annette had deposited another twenty-five grand in her bank account. That's forty."

There was a sharp intake of breath from Ellen, to my right.

Ah!

I turned toward Ellen. "Yes, you didn't know that the plain wooden box that arrived at Anen House by courier, two days after Annette's death, was worth that much, did you Ellen? Otherwise, you might not have tossed it into the apple store with all her other mail. All that stuff you hang onto, Ellen? All the years you've been filling storage bins, surrounding yourself with the evidence of your inability to let go? It speaks volumes about you. You're a very unusual hoarder: you're neat; you're highly organized; and, unlike many who see the 'value' in everything – which is why they can't get rid of it – you're a hoarder who sees 'value' in nothing. Not in a small, perfectly formed little box. Not in your sister. In fact, the only thing you do see 'value' in, the only thing you see as 'important' is…you. You are the center of your universe, Ellen. You are the only one with desires that matter. It is only your obsession that counts. You are the person in this room with by far the strongest, most driving obsession. Your obsession is Raj Pinder, isn't it? It has been since he arrived in Kelowna, four years ago. Which was when you went to Lizzie Jackson and asked for her help to 'make room' in your life for 'someone special'. It was because of your obsession with Raj that you've killed four, probably five people, including your own sister, and have tried to kill again tonight."

Complete silence? To be expected.

"Don't be ridiculous!" Ellen jumped to her feet. She drew herself up to her full height and looked down at me. "You're talking rubbish. It was me who said Annette had been murdered. Why would I say that if I'd murdered her, when everyone else said it was a suicide? Why wouldn't I just…shut up and get away with it?"

Everyone looked at me, Ellen's question reflected on their faces.

"That's such a good question, Ellen, and – you know what? – that had even me confused for quite some time. If you'd managed to stage the perfect murder – because everyone thought it was a suicide – then why would you be rattling the cage, asking Bud to come here to look into your sister's 'possible murder'?"

"And the answer is?" Lizzie spoke on behalf of the room.

"The answer is because of Raj. Again, back to Ellen's obsession. Let me explain."

"Please do," said Sheri, "because I want my boy to be off to the hospital – but only when you've explained everything, right, Colin? I have to understand why my Rob is dead, and I don't."

I nodded at Sheri, then at Bud. He understood, and began to move toward one of the two sets of doors.

"This is what happened, and how it happened, and why it happened," I said, suddenly feeling very weary. I took a sip of water. Then one of champagne.

Much better.

"Ellen and Annette Newman lost their parents, tragically, in a road traffic accident. Ellen stepped up and made sure she and her sister were okay. She, and then her sister, built up a successful and – thanks to Annette's fabulous, and gold-award-winning nose – world-renowned winery. About four years ago Raj Pinder comes to town. He's a little younger than Ellen, good-looking, and a bit out of the ordinary for a woman like her, whose major brush with the outside world – her years at the University of Vancouver – made her feel a bit left out of things. It's not an unusual story: Ellen Newman fell for Raj Pinder. What is unusual is the psychological profile of the woman doing the falling." I looked down at Ellen, who had plopped back onto her seat.

She looked up at me: nostrils flaring; face all pink.

She's seething.

"I haven't spent a great deal of time with you, Ellen, but I can see traits in you that suggest a borderline personality: you're a woman of extreme emotions. You will not be denied, you will organize and arrange, you will have your way. And if you don't, you snap. You are clever though, I'll give you that much, Ellen, and you've balanced your impulsiveness with your intelligence very well. For example, you knew – rationally – that you couldn't invite Raj to your apartment with all those storage boxes in it, so you sought help to work through how to get rid of them, because your mental condition wouldn't allow you to simply make a dozen trips to the dump…but it did allow for at least trying some hypnotherapy. It didn't work for you, though, did it? And, because you 'didn't get your way' – in other words, because Lizzie Jackson and her healing powers, and by association Grant Jackson and the whole Faceting for Life dogma, couldn't help you – you didn't just walk away…no, you launched a campaign of vitriol against both the Jacksons, and their beliefs."

Grant and Lizzie shuffled in their seats, muttering.

"But you didn't get Raj, Ellen. It just didn't happen. Sometimes these things aren't meant to be. That didn't mean it was over for you, though, did it? Raj's life progressed here, yours stagnated – with him as your sole obsession. Suzie, I'm going to suggest that you made your play for Raj pretty soon after his arrival at your winery."

I didn't expect a response, so I was surprised when Suzie leaped up and shouted, "So what if I did? He's cute…"

She stopped, put her talon-tipped fingers to her mouth, looked at her daughter, and said, "Oh, sorry Serendipity, baby." She looked deflated.

I carried on. "When you threw those comments at Ellen last night, Suzie, I was puzzled. Did you hate Ellen so much because you thought that she – and when she was alive, her sister – was going to spoil the nice little business you and Sammy were developing in cannabis wine? Or was there another reason? Having put this all together, I'm suggesting that Ellen and you had words about Raj, and that's where your hatred of her stems from. You'd have made an open play for him, and I think that Ellen wouldn't have been able to resist telling you to back off."

"You're right, she did," Suzie replied. "Who did she think she was? She told me that Raj would rather be with her than me. When he turned me down, flat, I was pissed…sure. But I soon found out he wasn't with her, either. Look at her. Who would want her? She's all desiccated. Eaten away from inside. That's where real beauty is born."

The irony of these last words wasn't lost on the majority of people in the room – given they were spoken by a woman whose many procedures had probably gone a long way toward supporting at least one plastic surgeon's child through college.

"Thanks for being so – open, Suzie," I said.

Suzie smiled…sweetly…as she flicked her hair, and sat.

I continued, "And what about Raj's girlfriend, Jane? I'm sorry Raj, I don't know any more about her than that she was a girl who held down seasonal jobs and then…well, could you tell us a little more?"

Serendipity held Raj's hand as he spoke. "She worked at Big White in't winter, then at a winery in't summer. It were just a bit of fun. But she were nice."

I asked, "She 'disappeared'? Is that right? In what way?"

Raj nodded. "She went out one day on her rollerblades. Loved them, she did. She went really fast. At least, that's what she said she were doing. But when I went to her place the next evening to pick her up to go out, all her stuff were gone and she were gone too. Didn't leave no note, no rent, just did a runner. Didn't hand in her notice or nothing. And never a word from her since."

"Did you, or her family, or anyone, report her as missing? I can't imagine you were the only person who knew she'd gone."

There was a bit of fidgeting around the room. Clearly more people than Raj had known about this Jane's disappearance and had done – what, I wondered?

Raj shrugged. "Well, I didn't think it were my place. I mean, like I said, it weren't nothing serious. I did phone her aunt in Terrace and told her, and she said I weren't to worry because Jane were always up and leaving places. She'd done it before, and she usually got in touch when she were good and ready. So I didn't do owt. And it were chaos here, anyway. It were when those fires hit. You know, the really bad ones? We was lucky, over here at SoulVine Wines, but we could see the fires over on the other side of the lake, and thousands were out of their homes. What with all the coming and going, and people's houses being burned down, and folks with nowhere to live, I think we was all just a bit involved with that." Raj hung his head.

"Okay, I think that'll be something for our friends here in the RCMP to look into at some future date. I don't believe that Ellen's carefully planned murder of Annette is where it all started, you see: I believe there might have been an impulsive crime before that, which showed Ellen that she could get away with killing someone. Right, Ellen?"

I looked down at the woman: her arms were crossed in fury; there were spots of color on her cheeks.

I said quietly, "And then of course, there was poor Stacey Willow, right Ellen?"

"Who's Stacey Willow?" Sammy Soul raised his hand, like a schoolboy.

"Let's ask Ellen, eh? What – did you catch sight of Raj, and the sister of one of his soccer buddies, laughing together in a crowd one night…maybe in a bar downtown? Was that all it took that time? A hint of him enjoying himself with someone other than you? Poor Stacey Willow: twenty years old, and drugged to death with pills ground up into a strawberry milkshake. How did you get her to drink it, Ellen? Just befriended her at the end of her shift at the burger bar? Treated her to a milkshake? Popped in the pills, knowing they'd kill her as she slept in the bedroom at her parents' house that she'd had since she was a child. Another 'rival' bites the dust, right?"

The enormity of what I was saying was hitting home around the room. I knew I was beginning to run out of steam.

I looked across at Bud, and he winked at me. I smiled back, sighed, and continued.

"Which brings us to Annette. You had no idea that Annette and Raj had been seeing each other when they were away at wine events, did you, Ellen? You really didn't notice what was going on right under your nose. You didn't notice Annette's changing habits, or body. In fact, a couple of photographs of the two of you that I found in the apple store show the moment that Annette told you she was pregnant, right?"

I didn't expect Ellen to respond, and she didn't.

"In one photograph, the camera has snapped at the moment when Annette is telling you the joyful news, and you are clearly horror-stricken that 'your' Raj has got her pregnant. Your sister, and the man you loved…together? I'm not surprised you were shocked. I suspect it didn't take you long to decide to get rid of your rival – your sister – and the baby, did it? What…did you beg her to not tell Raj – nor anyone else except her big sister – until she'd reached the magic three-month mark? Buying yourself some time, right? Planning how to do it. That was clever, Ellen. Really clever. But how do you get someone to write a suicide note, and then actually commit suicide? Because that's what you did."

"I did not. No one could," said Ellen, with venom.

"Oh, but you did. It was difficult for me to work out how you did it, because it was so clever. I have to admit that when I saw that the signatures on Annette's will, her suicide note, and the receipt for the courier – signed two days after she was dead – were all the same, I toyed with the idea of forgeries: you could have forged Annette's signature on the suicide note, as you obviously did on the courier receipt, and you could even have supplied a birthday card to yourself, written by you, as 'proof' that what I was seeing was, indeed, Annette's hand. What about the will, though? The Wisers had witnessed that signature. I wondered if – for some reason – they were in cahoots with you, and they had willingly witnessed a forged will, and so, eventually, they had to be done away with, too. But, no, the signature on the courier's receipt was the clincher. You didn't know that anyone would ever see that. But then I got it: I've been thinking about my relationship with my own sister, since I began to think about you and Annette, and that's what gave me the answer – you're able to sign your sister's name just as I can pretty much sign my sister's, and she mine. Same schoolteachers, same handwriting lessons, same family – it's not odd. The suicide note? It *was* Annette's signature, because Annette did type and sign that letter herself. Her letter of resignation, right? Not a suicide note at all."

I looked up from Ellen and addressed the room. "For those of you who don't know, Annette wrote: 'Ellen, It's no use, I can't do it anymore. I can't go on. It just won't work. I can't do my job anymore. And if I can't do my job perfectly…except she typed 'prefectly'…then there's no point to any of it. I'm sorry. I know you'll miss me. But that's it. I'm done. Love, always, Annette'. The letter was telling Ellen that Annette was leaving the winery, not life. A typo wasn't the end of the world. It wasn't the last thing she'd ever write, it was just a loving note to a sister. When you saw that letter, you knew you could use it against her, Ellen. First piece of the puzzle: a handy, dandy suicide note. Sorted. Then you had to get to Anen House without anyone seeing you: the fight that Annette was seen having in your truck, the truck she 'borrowed' the day she died? Annette's arms were flailing, she was crying. She was fighting with you. You were in the truck with her. Hidden in the back seat. It's easy to hide in there, you just duck down…I know, because I've been in it. When Annette shouted 'So – you've never loved me – why should I help you?' it was you she was fighting with. A sister who couldn't hide how she felt about her sibling's pregnancy. I got the wording right, eh, Colin?"

Colin nodded.

"Colin?" Ellen sounded shocked.

"Yes, Ellen, it wasn't the Wisers who saw Annette in the truck that evening, it was Colin. He didn't see you at all. You were quite safe. But, once Bud and I mentioned that Annette had been spotted having a fight, in her truck, you couldn't run the risk that you'd been seen. You knew that no one would have seen you leave Annette's house. You took the route down the backside of the hill, a route you've known since childhood, and made your way through the vineyards to your car…or should I say Annette's car? You left it parked out of sight along the way. You assumed it was the nosey Wisers who'd seen you arriving with Annette in your truck, and you certainly know your way around vehicles well enough to be able to cut a brake fluid line; when you were ranting last night, you even threw it out there that it was you who kept the machinery and the vehicles in working order at the winery in the days when you couldn't afford mechanics. Of course, I knew that the real witness had been Colin, but at least I knew he was safe – once I'd worked things out, I kept him close by me. Just in case there was some way you'd discovered that he was the one who'd seen Annette, and very possibly you, in the truck that evening. Now you're safe, Colin. It's all out in the open."

"You, Ellen? You killed my Rob? You cut that brake thingy? Why?" Sheri was wailing, and clearly having a hard time coming to terms with it all.

"Of course not, she's just rambling," replied Ellen dismissively.

I sighed. *Poor Sheri.* "Ellen was trying to kill the Wisers, not Rob, and she tried to kill the Wisers because she thought they'd seen her go up to her sister's house, fighting with her on the way, the evening that she died. Ellen simply slipped out of the luncheon today, snipped the lines, and came back in. She knew that the leaking fluid and the steep hills would take their toll. And they did. It's just that the wrong people were in the car at the time. I'm so sorry, Sheri, Colin. Rob wasn't the target, but he and his colleague became two more victims of this woman."

Sheri and Colin hugged each other close.

Time's getting short. Keep going, Cait.

"So how exactly did Ellen arrange Annette's death? That was a difficult part of the puzzle to solve, because it seemed physically impossible for Ellen to have drugged Annette, then carry her to the truck. If that wasn't how she'd ensured that her sister sat in the truck long enough to become unconscious, then how on earth had she done it? I finally managed to work it out: you taught her how to do it, Lizzie."

Lizzie looked horrified. "What do you mean? I taught Ellen how to kill her sister? How?"

I sighed. "You told me that you use hypnotherapy techniques in your practice, and you mentioned that you'd used hypnosis in your 'healing' sessions with Ellen. You even told me that Ellen had a real talent for it, right?" Lizzie nodded. "She coldly and calculatingly used that talent on her sister. I can see it now: Annette, distraught after an engineered argument with her big sister; Ellen offering to help her calm down by using some deep breathing and relaxation exercises; the ability to then suggest to Annette, when she's in an almost hypnotic state, that she sit in a comfy seat and sleep, quietly. All Ellen needed to do was make sure that the big, comfy seat she led her sleepwalking sister to was in the truck, and the job was done. Annette simply slept, peacefully, shut in the vehicle, with a hastily attached hosepipe run through an almost closed window, until she'd been poisoned. When her sister was dead, Ellen placed the note and the bottle beside her, taped up the windows of the truck, hooked up the hosepipe 'properly' – then ripped it all open again the next morning. Ellen's not stupid. These days, we're all bombarded with so many forensic detectives on TV that almost everyone knows about Locard's principle – the theory that there's always an exchange of forensic evidence when there's contact between two things. So Ellen knew she had to have a plan that could explain away all of the evidence she was about to create. If any of Ellen's fingerprints were found, they were there because of her rescue attempts."

I looked down at Ellen, who was beginning to lose her color.

"You just had to place the duct tape in Annette's hands as you unwound it, to get her prints onto it, and put the bottle into her palm for the same reason. Oh, and that's where you made your one big mistake, Ellen."

I looked at the top of her head. She was ignoring me.

"Annette had nowhere near enough alcohol in her blood for having drunk a whole bottle of wine. A glass, yes. A glass you'd probably have shared as sisters, as a part of the relaxation process, but not a bottle."

Serendipity interrupted me. "If Annette knew she was pregnant, surely she wouldn't have had a drink at all. I mean – the baby…"

I nodded. "Yes, I know what you mean. I'm guessing that, as a professional wine taster, she'd have been aware of the research that shows that a small amount of alcohol, even on a regular basis, doesn't harm the fetus; it's binge drinking that does the damage. She probably happily sipped a small glass that evening with her sister. That was the extent of your plan, wasn't it, Ellen? A murder set up to look like a suicide."

There were puzzled, and horrified, faces all round.

I was flagging. "Yes, that was the original plan, right? Make it look like a suicide, back up the theory of a suicide, and you'd be home clear. You saw Annette as your rival for Raj's affections: she was between you and the object of your obsession. A quick kill, and she'd be out of the way – no questions asked. Well, very few asked, in any case. Not even a full autopsy. Which was perfect, because then no one would find out that she had been pregnant. A finger-tip examination by the coroner wouldn't detect a pregnancy of ten or so weeks, especially given that Annette's body would have been supine for the process. No one need ever know. And that would be it."

I could see that, while people might not like what I was saying, they were beginning to understand how it might be possible.

I pushed on. "But that wasn't it. Because what the very clever Ellen didn't know was that – despite the fact that she hadn't told anyone about the pregnancy – Annette was getting ready to go public, and she'd changed her will. A few weeks after her death, there was the meeting at the lawyers' office, the one where Raj told me that Ellen 'lost it for a while'. You had no idea about

Annette's new will, did you, Ellen? So your immediate reaction was what we'd all expect: you were mad because you'd been robbed of your rightful inheritance. It wasn't why you'd killed Annette, but you'd expected to get the whole winery nonetheless, as your birthright. That was a very telling insight. But you're quick, Ellen, very quick. You almost immediately realized what Annette's will meant: Raj would be working alongside you, every day, in every way. This was your chance. You pounced…going so far as to physically drag him out of SoulVine Wines and off to your winery that very day. Last night, when you introduced Bud and me to Raj, you introduced him as your 'partner', the implication being that you're a couple. Because that's how you see the situation. But Raj wasn't comfortable with the inheritance: he suggested that you contest the will. Even the lawyer suggested the same thing. You see, if Annette's mind had been set on suicide when she'd written that will, you'd have had a good argument against her plan to leave her interest to Raj. And Raj didn't let it go, did he? He kept bringing it up. He couldn't help but communicate his discomfort. So you had to do something to help him to feel comfortable in his new role, as your 'partner'."

Bud cleared his throat and tapped his wrist.

Okay, I get it.

"When you found out the real identity of your online 'grief buddy', you formed a plan. As a grieving sister unable to come to terms with her sibling's suicide, you'd invite Bud to investigate. And Bud was all for it. Clear suicide. No evidence to the contrary. You'd have had an ex-cop say so, in public. Which is why we all got treated to those two little scenes: the sister in denial at the party, the sister now accepting suicide at the lunch. Very nice, Ellen. Raj could rest easy, should rest easy. It would help him settle into his new role as your partner in business, and then – in your mind, at least – your partner in life."

It was clear from the faces, and the tension, in the room that no one was in any doubt any longer. Raj was shaking his head in disgust.

"It all might have worked if Bud hadn't spoken to me about it: I didn't buy the idea that a woman with such a finely tuned sense of smell would asphyxiate herself with noxious fumes. When I realized your obsession with Raj, worked out that Annette was pregnant, and put that together with what I'd found out about the death of poor Stacey Willow, it all made a warped sort of sense…and I knew that Serendipity was in danger too."

Sammy raised his hand again. "Ellen somehow made my angel girl eat peanuts because she found out that Serendipity and Raj have been dating?"

He was trying to wrap his head around the whole thing. I guessed he'd have welcomed the return of a few of the millions of brain cells he'd slaughtered through excess over the years.

"Sort of, and I'm to blame for that," I said, addressing Serendipity and Raj. "I'm so terribly sorry that I put you in harm's way. I should have been brighter, I should have seen Ellen's fixation for what it was, but I didn't. You see, I mentioned my observations about your love for each other to her, without realizing the implications." I looked at the beautifully matched, if terribly distressed, couple and repeated, "I'm so sorry."

"How did she make Serendipity eat peanuts?" Sammy was still puzzled. "I don't get it. Serendipity's always so careful."

"She didn't eat peanuts," I replied. "In Ellen's fridge yesterday, I saw lots of cooking and salad dressings, one of which was peanut oil. When I was outside, grabbing a quick smoke, I spotted a cigarette stub that looked wet. In fact, it was oily, not wet. Ellen had injected it with peanut oil, and Serendipity inhaled it. Probably took a really big, deep drag on it. I know that's what I do when I'm grabbing a quick smoke."

"But Serendipity's quit smoking," said Raj.

Serendipity blushed.

I said, "I'm aware that Serendipity's been visiting Lizzie to help her quit, Raj, and I applaud her for it. Lizzie's hypnotic process allows the person who's quitting to still smoke cigarettes that are already alight, though they won't light them up for themselves. Ellen knew that. In fact, she was the one who told Lizzie that she'd seen Marcel at *C'est la Vie* do exactly that – pick up smoldering butts and puff on them. All Ellen had to do was to inject a cigarette's filter with peanut oil and leave it where Serendipity would be sure to find it – like in the big ashtray-pot at the side of the building here. She could easily just keep repeating the process all evening. After all, who would pick up a discarded butt and puff away at it? No one…except a smoker for whom that was their only option. When Serendipity ducked out to the loo, and then for a breath of fresh air when we were all distracted by the arrival of the Wisers, she saw a lighted cigarette, couldn't resist, and smoked it. We all saw how extremely swift and violent her allergic reaction was. It's one of the most dangerous and deadly ways to experience an allergen – in the lungs like that."

I turned and addressed the MacMillans.

"Colin – if it hadn't been for your quick actions, Serendipity would probably have died. That's what Ellen didn't expect: you weren't due to be here tonight, Colin, and she'd already lifted Serendipity's epinephrine pen from her pocket. I have to acknowledge, here and now, that – while you might not be 'The Doctor' – you certainly are a hero. You put another person's life ahead of your own, even though you were reeling from the news of your dad's death."

"What happened to my Colin? Why was he taken badly too?" Sheri's voice was frail, though she was patting her son's hand, proudly.

"Well, to be fair to Suzie, I think it was quite natural for her to react as she did. All she could see was Colin launching himself at her daughter, and stab at her leg with something. Serendipity would have been exhaling peanut fumes all over him and – being sandwiched between Serendipity and her mother – Colin was pretty close to those fumes. He'd have received a much lower level of the allergen than you, Serendipity, but enough to kick his response to it into overdrive. It's such good fortune that you had the spare pen with you, Sheri."

I looked around. Pretty much everybody looked as drained as I felt…except Ellen.

She leapt from her seat and confronted me. "None of this is true. No one believes a word of it. Besides, there's no proof of any of it."

"Actually, there is, Ellen. I have the cigarette with the peanut oil in it, safely preserved for the police. I'm sure they'll be able to match the oil in the cigarette to the bottle in your fridge…and the residue on your fingers."

Ellen Newman's eyes involuntarily flickered toward her hands.

Yes…definitely gotcha.

I nodded. "Earlier on, I had an irrational desire for *Reese's Pieces*. It was the smell of peanuts that made me want them. I can still smell it on you now. It's difficult to get rid of. That should be enough for attempted murder. And you know what, Ellen? I'm sure there'll have been someone who saw you with Staccy Willow, and – now that the cops know what they're looking for – they'll find something that ties you to her. And if there's an investigation into the disappearance of 'Jane', I'm going to bet that you left some trail of evidence there too; it's likely you were sloppy…she was your first, after all. Unfortunately, I do accept that there might not be any physical evidence to put in front of a jury to prove that you killed Annette, but I think that the circumstantial evidence is building up around her death quite significantly. And there might be something to tie you to tampering with the Wisers' brakes. So, to respond to your first point, Ellen, there is evidence. Lots. And to respond to your second observation – that no one will believe it – well, just look around you. These people have known you for years. Some for your whole life. It looks to me like they all believe you could have done – and indeed did do – what I've accused you of doing. And if they've made that journey in a few, short minutes, imagine the way the case will build against you over days, or even weeks, in court. But, hey, that's not up to me, and it's not even up to the two very accommodating officers from the RCMP who've been listening to all this. It's up to the legal system now."

I'm exhausted.

As Bud stood guard at one door, the two cops made their way from the other toward Ellen. She had nowhere to go. No escape. She ran across the room and launched herself at Raj.

She kissed him, hugged him. "I did it for you, my darling. I did it all for you. All of them, they were all trying to come between us. I knew it was me you really wanted. I could see it when you looked at me. Even when you turned away from me…when you didn't want other people to see how much you desired me. That silly girl Jane – she was always flying around on her skates. I sorted her out. I told her you were mine, and she laughed at me. Laughed – *at me.* I pushed her, and she fell. When she was lying there, rambling and bleeding, it was easy. Who knew that rollerblades have such heft."

Raj was looking in horror over Ellen's shoulder at Bud, who was making "stretch it out motions" at him…and he played along. He put up with Ellen's caresses, and kisses.

"But I never had nothing to do with that girl Stacey," he said. "She weren't nothing to me. Just a friend's sister."

Bud gave him the thumbs-up.

Ellen pulled back. "She was all over you, Raj. All over you. I knew she was after you, it was as clear as day. All I did was send her to sleep. I didn't hurt her. Like I didn't hurt Annette. All I did was get her to go to sleep, too. Her and the baby. Nighty-night. I didn't like the feeling that I'd hurt Jane, you see. You do understand, don't you? That started as an accident, and then she was dead. But when I planned it, I didn't plan to hurt people."

Suzie could stand no more. She jumped up and grabbed Ellen's hair. "You planned to hurt my baby! We all saw the agony she was in. You didn't care! You're mad…"

Suzie dragged Ellen off Raj, held her by the hair, and started slapping her with her free hand. Her fingernails raked Ellen's face. Suzie was screaming incoherently. She was a tiger, protecting her young.

It took the two cops at least a minute to detach Suzie from Ellen: Suzie had lost some fake nails; Ellen's face was bleeding.

Finally…it's over.

Ellen wept as the RCMP officers escorted her away.

Sheri held her son close, then pulled back, looked up at him, and said, "You know your father used to hit me?" Colin nodded, slowly and sadly. He looked grim. "Well," she continued with a forced brightness, "now we're on our own, and no one will ever make me afraid again. We'll get through this, Colin, you and me together. You're the man I want in my life. I'm so proud of you." He bent down, and let her kiss him. "Now, let's get you to the emergency room. On the way you can tell me all about this 'doctor' that Cait mentioned."

As the MacMillans left, I mentally wished Sheri luck with the journey she was about to undertake. When Angus died, it had taken me about five years to stop blaming myself for how he'd treated me. It took another five before the walls I'd built around myself for protection crumbled just enough for Bud to peer in, and save me.

I smiled at Bud as I silently sent these wishes to Sheri. I knew very well he wouldn't be able to read the expression on my face, other than to register that I was tired, and relieved.

In the corner of the room, the Souls had a group hug…and included Raj. "Man, I love this family," said Sammy.

At their table, the Jacksons and their two employees had all joined hands and were chanting something, swaying to and fro. They seemed preoccupied.

Standing alone near the exit, close together, the Wisers looked at each other like teenagers, despite their advanced years.

The Corrigans were discussing what they should do about the business. Lauren calmly pointed out that it was the beginning of the busy season, and they shouldn't let folks down. Pat didn't disagree, but I wondered how long it would be before Pat and his world-famous sausages were the draw at another venue. Not long, I suspected. I mean, who can resist sausages?

I was completely done in; all the adrenalin that had deadened my aches and pains for a while was finally draining away, and I was throbbing – quite literally – from head to toe.

Bud reached out and hugged me. Gently.

"Cait Morgan, I love you, and I'm so very proud of you," he said, smiling, "but it's the hospital for you. Now. No more stalling. You're done. Go." He pointed to two paramedics who were waiting to put me into a chair to wheel me out.

"It's okay, I'll walk," I said.

"No, you won't. Sit."

You can be quite bossy, Bud.

Three hours later, Bud and I were still hanging about in the waiting area of the emergency room: a pile up on the Bill Bennett Bridge had produced several casualties, all of whom were, sadly, more serious than a broken wrist and a twisted ankle. Colin and Serendipity had already been assessed, treated, and released.

It was just Bud and me, and some horribly uncomfortable plastic chairs.

I sipped the Cup-a-Soup that Bud had managed to wrangle out of a vending machine. He said he'd pushed the button for "chicken", but I couldn't taste anything remotely chicken-like about it.

"Just a few more questions," said Bud, "if you're up to it?" I nodded.

"Am I right in thinking that if you hadn't got locked in the apple store and found that other photograph, you wouldn't have worked this all out?"

"I was leaning toward Ellen – her hoarding and the traits that it indicated; her 'connection' to Raj. The pregnancy was what made it all fall into place. I should have seen it in the photo you gave me last week. I told you that one photo is difficult to interpret…though, if I'm brutally honest about it, it wasn't the photo, it was me. I was judging what I saw, not questioning what it meant. Immediately I saw that original photo, I should have asked myself why a woman so obviously proud of her appearance would wear an ill-fitting bra. Instead, I simply dismissed her out of hand as just another woman who couldn't take the time to be fitted for the right size. Then there was talk about Annette buying baggy clothes at the thrift store. In the photo you showed me, Annette was well dressed, if casual, and that's probably why her shirt and bra were too tight on her. She was still wearing her own clothes, rather than the bigger sizes she knew she was going to need in the months to come. So I won't be so quick to judge like that again – especially after two glasses of champagne and in the company of the man I love. If people's lives are going to depend on it, I should be more thorough. More dispassionate. Less judgmental. Though you have to admit, my summation of Ellen based upon the way she wrote those notes was pretty accurate."

Bud smiled and squeezed my good arm. "True," he admitted. "I'll give you that. So why did Ellen lock you into the apple store? I guess that's what she did? I know she was alone while I was getting dressed to be able to give her a ride."

"You know, Bud, I believe she'd become wary of me, and didn't want me around tonight. With a killer's instincts, she knew it was better to split us apart. Keep us from working as a team. It was clear that her attempt on her 'rival' tonight was premeditated; I think that my reaction to her denial that there was anything going on between Raj and Serendipity might have made her think that I knew more than I did. When she locked me in the apple store, she didn't know I hadn't quite worked it all out. But – and here's the wonderful, fabulous, and quite worrying, irony of it all – you're right, Bud, if she hadn't locked me in, I wouldn't have stumbled on that second photo. Actually, if I hadn't gone back to pick up my cigarettes I wouldn't have found it – but I'm guessing you don't want me to mention that, right?"

Bud tutted, and I carried on regardless.

"So, yes, if I hadn't been locked in, or gone back for my smokes, I wouldn't have twigged to Annette's pregnancy, nor extrapolated how that played with Ellen's obsession with Raj. I wouldn't have warned you to stick close to Serendipity when I did, shortening Ellen's window of opportunity to a timeframe when Colin was there with his replacement, lifesaving epinephrine pen. We know now that Sheri had a spare one in her purse, but I'm not sure she'd have thought of it unless it were her own boy in need. I would have got there in the end… but it might have been too late to save Serendipity."

"Well, that's where I almost let everyone down – especially Serendipity," said Bud quietly.

"No," I held up my hand, "don't start that again. You told her to not leave your side, but she chose to do so, anyway. She is her parents' daughter, after all. It wasn't your fault. It was all Ellen's doing."

"Would-have. Could-have. Should-have?"

I nodded. "Did they have any other flavors?" I asked holding up the Cup-of-*sort-of*-Soup. Bud shook his head. "Probably just as well," I muttered. "It might taste even worse."

I sighed, and looked into the eyes of the man I loved, and knew I would always rely upon. "Bud, when they've seen to my wrist, can we please go back to Anen House, get some sleep, then drive until we get home? Please? I don't want to be here any longer. I want to be in my own little place, with a giant pizza – with pepperoni, and extra cheese…and mushrooms – and maybe a beer. I think I'll be off wine, for a bit."

"Okay, we'll get you sorted here, catch a few hours of sleep, then hit the road. We'll collect Marty on the way, and we can pick up a pizza, or two. Because you're not very good at sharing. Not pizza…and not information pertaining to a crime."

"Sorry about that," I said.

"A heads-up a bit earlier might have been useful. After all, I couldn't possibly have been expected to suspect Ellen, could I? Not when she was the only one crying 'murder', eh?"

"That's precisely what put me onto her in the first place," I replied, as patiently as I could.

"So you said."

"You're right. I did."

"Hey – here comes the Doc to fix you up." Bud rose to meet the short, dark-haired woman walking toward us. "She looks like she'll take good care of you."

"Yes, you're right, she does," I replied.

You're always right…except when you're wrong…and that's what you've got me for, Bud.

Acknowledgments: abridged from the First Edition (2013)

Whenever I've visited the Okanagan Valley, especially the area in and around Kelowna, I've met only wonderful people. Those who work at the wineries, in the bookstores, at the lake-front facilities, hotels, bars, and restaurants are fully aware that they're living in a beautiful part of the world that offers the chance to enjoy an amazing life. And they do. So I'd just like to emphasize that the characters in this book are total fictions, created by me to work within this book, and within this book alone. If you visit this area, you'll meet an eclectic mix of people; it's just one element in the complex recipe that gives this region its unique flavor.

My thanks to Pinki Gidda and the entire team at Mount Boucherie Family Estate Winery in Kelowna. Pinki was a great help during the writing of this book: she checked facts and gave me wonderful insights. I also want to thank everyone at the winery for allowing me to use elements of the descriptions of some of their wines: I only drink reds, and can attest that they are all just wonderful. (I'm sure their whites are just as good.)

My thanks to Andy Cave, coroner at the BC Interior Region Coroners' Office in Kelowna, BC, for sharing his professional insights in such a timely, pleasant, and professional manner.

My thanks to my mum and sister: if not for their support and encouragement, I might never write another sentence. They read what I've written and give me the most honest feedback it's possible to give someone you love. Because I write, my husband puts up with a lot. Only he knows just how much, and he never mentions it. Thank you all.

Thanks, too, to the TouchWood Team.

Acknowledgments: Second Edition (2024)

It sounds as though editing a book that's already been published would be a straightforward task, but…it turns out that it's not.

I've lost count of the hours I've struggled with this edition, and I've also lost sight of how frustrated I became with myself during the process. I suspect my husband hasn't, nor will he. He's been my rock during what people euphemistically call "a journey", when they mean "a nightmare". Without his patience and wise counsel, I might have thrown in the towel…but perseverance is easier when you have a cheerleader. Thank you.

Sue Vincent, my proofer, has also been a stalwart: she and I have done our best to ensure that not one single error gets passed us…but, if you spot anything we missed, please let me know. (My email address can be found at my website.) I hope that anything we didn't manage to catch didn't pull you out of the story too much. We're only human (no AI interference here) and, apparently, to err *is* human; please forgive us our humanity.

Thanks to the Four Tails Publishing team: you were patient with me, and that means a great deal.

Thanks, finally, to all the printers, distributors, booksellers, librarians, reviewers, and bloggers who played a part in getting this book into your hands and, of course, my thanks to you, for choosing to enter Cait's world: I hope you enjoy your time with her. I know I always do.

Cathy Ace, December 2024

About the Author

CATHY ACE was born and raised in Swansea, Wales, and migrated to British Columbia, Canada aged forty. She is the author of The Cait Morgan Mysteries, The WISE Enquiries Agency Mysteries, the standalone novel of psychological suspense, The Wrong Boy, and collections of short stories and novellas. As well as being passionate about writing crime fiction, she's also a keen gardener.

You can find out more about Cathy and all her works at her website: www.cathyace.com

www.ingramcontent.com/pod-product-compliance
Lightning Source LLC
Chambersburg PA
CBHW030339310726
48979CB00001B/103